D1535419

ONE

"You're the scrawniest, most ungrateful pig of a cat I've ever had the goddamn misfortune to come across, you know that?"

The cat in question stared at me with a look that could only be described as utter satisfaction. He was an orange tabby with a pale, fluffy mane that made him look like a miniature lion and a coat that had random tufts of fur sticking out at odd angles. He looked older than Methuselah, even though he was only a little over three. The spirit within the cat, however, was *not* young.

I shook the hand he had all but shredded, flicking droplets of blood across pristine white tiles. "I should let you starve, you ungrateful wretch of a thing."

The cat blinked, his mismatched eyes—one amber, one blue—glinting in the shadow-filled kitchen. It wasn't my kitchen, and it certainly wasn't my cat. I was just here to feed the thing. Monty—my cousin and the cat's 'owner'— had gone to Melbourne to have the external fixation devices on his leg removed and to begin full rehabilitation. Nearly two months had passed since the soucouyant had kidnapped and basically broken him—or at least his left tibia—and between the hospital stay and his inability to move about with any sort of ease, he'd been less than pleasant to be around. Much like his cat, really.

Thankfully, the run of foul spirits and demons invading the Faelan Reservation—the only werewolf reservation in Victoria, and one of seven in Australia—had gone from a tidal wave to a trickle. We'd only had a couple of minor demons wander in seeking prey during that time, and Ashworth—the Regional Witch Association representative who now lived here, and who'd once again stepped into the vacant reservation witch position until Monty regained mobility—had little trouble dealing with them.

I dumped the rest of the tin's contents into the cat's bowl, then rose and did a wide detour around him, moving across to the sink so I could run water over the wound. The cat bent, took a sniff of the fish, then raised a paw and pushed the bowl away, a look a disdain on his face.

"Listen here, buddy, you may have Belle wrapped around your dangerous little paw, but she's not here today. You eat what I give you, or you starve."

The cat studied me for a moment, then rose and, with a flick of his fluffy tail, stalked from the room.

"Felines," I muttered, and thanked God my familiar was not only human, but also my best friend. Generally, familiars came in the form of animals—mostly cats, like Monty's orange nightmare—or a spirit. No one really knew why Belle had become mine, and no one had ever really cared enough to find out. I'd certainly never questioned it—why would I, when her presence in my life was the only reason I stood here today?

I turned off the tap, dried the wound, and then dragged the first aid kit out of the pantry. After spraying the three deep slashes on the top of my hand with antiseptic, I tossed the first aid kit back, then filled up the ungrateful feline's water bowl. Thankfully, Belle was back tomorrow—she'd gone down to Melbourne to see the latest incarnation of *The Rocky Horror Picture Show* and had decided to stay overnight rather than do the late-night drive back to Castle Rock—so she could resume feeding duties. The wretched cat seemed to like her; or, at the very least, he didn't go into berserker mode the minute she walked through the door. But then, aside from being a witch, Belle was both a telepath *and* a strong spirit talker; if the cat *did* decide to flex his claws and cause some damage, she could certainly return the favor. Clever spirits did *not* mess with her.

I grabbed my handbag from the table and slung it over my shoulder as I headed for the front door, my footsteps echoing on the wooden floorboards. Other than his bed, a sofa, and the largest TV screen I'd ever seen, there was very little in the way of furniture in any of the rooms. It had all been destroyed—along with the house Monty had temporarily set up in—when the soucouyant had kidnapped him. The loss hadn't actually fazed him all that much, simply because anything he really cared about—including his classic 1967 V8 Mustang—had been secured off-site.

As I swung the front door open and unsnibbed the wire door, the cat began to wail. But this was no ordinary cater-waul. It was a deep, haunting sound, and it sent a chill up my spine.

Something was wrong.

I spun and ran back down the hall. The cat was in the laundry, staring at the back door. I slid to a halt and quickly looked around. There was nothing untoward visible, and certainly nothing that in any way suggested danger.

The cat looked at me, gave another long, deep yowl, and

then pointedly gazed at the door again. Frustration stirred. "There's a goddamn cat flap next to the freaking door —use it."

The cat gave me a disdainful look, then, with another flick of his fluffy tail, did so. I muttered obscenities under my breath and spun around. I didn't get far; the cat's howling began again and this time held a deep note of demand.

For whatever reason, I was meant to follow him.

"Hang on, hang on." I ran down the hall to lock the front door and then headed out the back. The cat was sitting on the rear fence, but disappeared down the other side when it saw me.

"If you're having fun at my expense, I'm *not* going to be pleased."

The cat yowled in response. Again, it was filled with urgency, and trepidation pulsed through me. My psychic senses might be attuned to evil, but cats in general were far more sensitive to the other side, and *this* was no ordinary cat. If evil hunted in the growing haze of dusk, he'd sense it far sooner than me.

I grabbed the top of the fence, hauled my butt over it, and jumped down. Thankfully, Monty's new townhouse backed onto bush, so I didn't have to worry about neighbors calling the rangers on me. Not that *that* would have been too much of a problem in a situation such as this. Aiden, the head ranger, happened to be my lover, and while that didn't give me a pass to commit any sort of crime, all I had to do was tell him Monty's familiar had sensed a problem and had wanted me to follow him. The last few months had provided a very steep learning curve for the rangers in general—and Aiden in particular—when it came to witches and magic, but they now trusted us in a way I'd never thought possible.

Of course, they'd also had little other choice. Our magic was all that stopped this place from being overrun by evil, thanks to the presence of a large wellspring that had been left unguarded for entirely *too* long. Wild magic was neither good nor bad, but it would *always* draw the darker forces of the world if left in a raw, unprotected state—and the big one in this reservation had.

The cat disappeared into the lengthening shadows crowding the trees, but a short, sharp yowl gave me direction. I followed the sound, the crunch of leaves and the snap of twigs audible under every footstep. Another cry, this time to my right. I ducked under a low-hanging tree branch and ran on, my gaze sweeping the area but seeing or sensing little that suggested there was anything to be worried about out here in the scrub.

Maybe the snotty little creature *was* giving me the runaround...

I continued following the yowls, but never actually got close enough to spot the damn cat. Sweat trickled down my back and dripped from tendrils of hair hanging over my eyes. Summer had finally slipped into autumn, but apparently no one had notified the appropriate weather gods, because the day had been hot and muggy, and neither had noticeably eased now that dusk was giving way to night. I swiped at a droplet hanging onto the end of my nose and slid down an incline to a creek—one that thankfully wasn't very deep. I picked my way across the trickle of water, using various rocks as stepping-stones and then scrambled up the bank on the other side and ran on.

The shadows were getting longer as darkness closed in. I paused to grab my phone out of my purse, flicked on the flashlight app, and continued. The caterwauling was at least closer now, but the light threw crazy shadows across the trees and trepidation stirred anew.

Not because of the shadows, but because my instincts were finally kicking in. Something *was* out here—something *other* than a cranky cat playing a prank on a witch he disliked.

I crashed through a strand of young wattle trees, gaining scratches across my bare arms, and ended up in a clearing. The cat sat in the middle, his tail swishing from side to side. Beyond him, in the distance through the scrub, came the twinkle of house lights and the soft roar of car engines. Civilization wasn't that far away—but neither was evil.

I shivered and resisted the instinctive urge to reach for Belle. I wasn't in any sort of danger, and *she* deserved a decent time-out both from me and from whatever new piece of darkness intent on destruction had decided to step into the reservation.

I took a deep breath and flexed my fingers, trying to ease the tension as I walked across to the cat. He looked up at me and then at the ground. Obviously, I was meant to find something.

I squatted next to the orange menace and studied the leaf-littered area through narrowed eyes. There was nothing immediately obvious to see, and the vague sense of evil drifting across my senses certainly wasn't emanating from this particular spot.

The cat raised a paw, sharp claws exposed. I leaned away instinctively, but this time, he didn't aim his weapon at me. Instead, he pawed at the leaf litter and then gave me a somewhat pointed look.

I couldn't help but grin. That look suggested if I didn't

quickly do his majesty's bidding, the claws would once again find a home in my flesh.

I held out a hand, fingers splayed, over the area he'd clawed. Prophetic dreams and the ability to sense evil weren't my only psychic talents—I was also gifted with psychometry. It not only allowed me to find misplaced items and sense emotions via touch, but also gave me the ability to trace—or even slip into the mind of—the person who owned whatever item I was holding. The latter was *not* something I did very often—I'd heard too many tales of psychics getting trapped within the minds and emotions of others to risk anything like that without a very good reason.

A distant wisp of energy ran across my skin; whatever I was meant to find wasn't close. I frowned and moved my hand around in an attempt to get a stronger signal, but the wisp faded the further I went from the point the cat had clawed. I moved my hand back and caught the vague tingle again; either the item had been dug into the ground or whatever connection it held to the wearer was fading.

Maybe even both.

I carefully dug into the leaf litter, making sure there was nothing hidden in amongst the rotting matter before tossing it aside. After several seconds, the tingling got stronger and I caught a glimpse of leather. It looked like a watch strap, although how it had ended up here, buried under so much debris, I had no idea. It couldn't have been here for that long, if only because any sort of resonance would have faded if it had—and *that* suggested it had been deliberately buried.

Either that, or something very strange was going on.

Which, knowing this reservation, was entirely possible.

I moved the remaining leaf matter away from the half-buried watch. The face was shattered, which suggested it had been stepped on. Whether deliberately or not, I couldn't say.

I grabbed a small tree branch and used it to carefully scrape away the soil—which was surprisingly soft considering the long, dry summer we'd had—from the rest of the watch, then carefully picked it up. And saw the dried, almost gossamer-fine brownish-cream tendrils hanging from the end of the catch. It wasn't cotton or any other sort of man-made material. It looked like flesh. Dried human flesh.

My stomach twisted, and I swallowed heavily. "That's not what I think it is... is it?"

The cat gave me a look. One that said, "You know the answer, so why ask?"

My phone chose that moment to ring, and the sharp sound made me jump. I looked at the screen, saw it was Monty, and hit the answer button.

"Aren't you supposed to be resting in hospital?"

"Yes, but I *am* still reservation witch." His voice was tart and filled with frustration. "I want to be kept informed when evil stirs."

"Given your familiar is sitting right here beside me, I hardly think you can claim to be uninformed. And I'm not entirely sure evil is respon—"

"Seriously? There's skin—*human* skin—on that watch-band. If that's not a sign of evil intent, I'm not sure what is."

"Yeah, but it could be an *old* evil rather than new. The skin isn't fresh, and the watch was buried. Besides, if there was a dark spirit or demon roaming around the immediate area, wouldn't your wretched cat have sensed it?"

"My cat *does* have a name."

"And it's one I refuse to utter until he stops attacking me."

"Accord *him* the same sort of respect as Belle, and he just might."

"Belle doesn't claw the hell out of my hand the minute she sees me." Although I daresay she'd been tempted to swat me over the head on more than a few occasions over the years.

Monty snorted. "Eamon says he *did* sense something in passing, but lost the trail in that clearing. Have you tried to track the owner of the watch yet?"

"No, because someone rang before I could. Hang on."

I brought the watch into the light. "There's an inscription on the back—*Congrats on graduating, love Mom and Dad.*"

"Which suggests the watch isn't something the owner would have lost willingly. Is the catch broken?"

"Yes."

He grunted. "So it's minutely possible that—despite the strips of skin—he didn't realize it had fallen off. Can you hustle and do that reading?"

"If you'd stop bloody talking, I might just be able to."

He grunted again. It was not a happy sound.

I half smiled and wrapped my fingers around the watch face, trying to avoid the bits of dried skin, but nevertheless catching a couple. I shivered at the papery feel of them, but concentrated on the faint caress of energy and unleashed the psychic part of me.

For several seconds, nothing happened. All I could feel, all I could sense, was shadows and darkness. I frowned and tried to go deeper—tried to get some sense of not only who owned the watch, but also what might be happening to him.

Nothing.

Frustrated, I tightened my grip and pressed it harder into my palm. A dark force rose to resist me—one that *didn't* belong to the watch's owner, or even to whoever he might have been with.

That barrier was death—one that had occurred *days* ago.

Which was rather odd, given how deeply the watch had been buried—or was that merely the result of someone covering their crime? Was there, perhaps, a whole lot more than just a watch to be found here?

"Anything?" Monty said.

I eased the fierceness of my grip. "No. Whoever owned the watch died a few days ago."

"No ghost?"

"Not that I can sense, but Belle's the spirit talker, not me."

"You can't contact her? Get her out there?"

"No, I can't, because she's in Melbourne rather than here."

"What's she doing in Melbourne?"

"That's none of your damn business, dear cousin."

He chuckled softly. "So I guess this is basically a false alarm."

"Not necessarily." I carefully placed the watch on the top of the leaf pile, then scooped up a bigger stick and began shoveling more dirt aside. "It strikes me as odd that it was buried so deeply."

"You think it was deliberate?"

"I do." And we'd find out soon enough if I was correct or not—*if* whatever else might be buried here wasn't too deep.

"It might be worth going to grab a shovel," Monty commented. "It'd be quicker and easier than a damn stick."

"Have you got a shovel at your place?"

"Well, no, but I'm sure Aiden or one of the other rangers can supply one."

"And I'm sure they'll be pleased about me calling them out over a broken watch unless it's attached to someone's arm."

"Other than those strips of skin, there's no sign of bones and, according to Eamon, no smell of decay or putrefaction to suggest a body," he commented. "So why do you think it was attached to an arm? Wouldn't you have seen some sign of said arm when you dug the watch out?"

I grimaced—something he'd see only if his link with his familiar was deep enough to be using the cat's eyes. "Once you've spent some time in this reservation, you'll discover 'would have' and 'should have' often don't—"

I stopped as my makeshift shovel hit something solid. I swallowed trepidation and then carefully scraped away more dirt.

And found the arm.

Or, at least, what looked to be the bones of one.

I pushed away from the gruesome find and landed heavily on my butt. Several breaths did little to ease the churning in my stomach or the growing certainty that *this* was the beginning of a new reign of terror from yet another dark spirit.

"A fucking arm that's been picked clean?" Monty's voice held a mix of disbelief and excitement. "How awesome is that?"

"I can think of many words to describe the find, Monty, but awesome isn't one of them."

"Well, no, the death isn't awesome, but the fact we'll be hunting down a creature capable of doing such a thing *is*."

"You're certifiable, you know that? And may I remind you that you're in Melbourne and won't be hunting down *anything* in the immediate future."

"And may *I* remind *you* that rehabilitation doesn't stop

me from participating in at least the research side of things." His tone remained decidedly upbeat. Obviously, being attacked by a soucouyant hadn't in any way dulled his initial excitement over finally getting some magical action. "Besides, I've already been cleared to continue rehabilitation in Castle Rock, so I can be the control center while you and Ashworth do all the legwork."

Amusement bubbled through me; Ashworth would be mighty pleased to hear he'd been reduced to legwork. "This is all presuming that the bones were buried recently. My senses might be wrong—"

"Since when has that happened?"

"Well, not in recent months, but still—"

"Exactly," he cut in. "So stop with all the doubt bullshit and get the rangers in so we—"

I tuned out the rest of his sentence as a faint and yet agonized scream ran across the night—the scream of a man rather than a woman. The sort of scream that only happened in those final few seconds between the realization of death and death actually hitting.

The sound died as abruptly as it had started, but an ominous pulse of power now ran through the darkness. Its origin was not of *this* world, but rather the supernatural.

Demon.

The word whispered through my brain, and fear chased after it. A sane person would have run in the opposite direction, but self-preservation was something that had become somewhat spotty since I'd stepped into this reservation. Perhaps it was the connection to the wild magic; perhaps it was simply the growing certainty that there was to be no more running for Belle and me. That this place was home, and unless we did our utmost to take care of it, it would become hell on earth for everyone within—

whether or not Monty or Ashworth or any other witch was here.

Which was a rather weird thought and not one I had time to examine.

I scrambled upright, grabbed my phone, and ran after Eamon.

"Monty, call the rangers for me. Tell them where we are and what's happening. Then call Ashworth, just in case."

"Will do. Be careful."

He hung up before I could reply. For a change, Eamon remained in sight, keeping close enough to guide me, although I didn't need it with the pull of evil.

I silently wove the threads of a containment spell around the fingers of my free hand, though I had no idea if it would be strong enough to stop whatever lay ahead. But it was better than running into an unknown situation unarmed. I did have a couple of small bottles of holy water tucked inside my purse, but I had to be far closer to evil for them to be of any use.

The pulse of demonic power began to fade. I swore and dredged up more speed, crashing through the underbrush, hoping against hope that we got there in time to save the man who'd screamed, even though the psychic part of me knew it was already too late.

I stumbled through a thick strand of shrubs, snagging my T-shirt and tearing more skin. I swore, but caught my balance and ran on, winding my way through the trees as the glow of lights from the houses ahead grew ever warmer.

Part of me hoped I was reading this wrong—that whatever fate had befallen the stranger *wasn't* supernatural in origin... but even as that thought hit, I dismissed it. As Monty had said, my senses hadn't been wrong much of late. It was time I truly started trusting them, rather than always second-guessing or doubting—a habit I'd fallen into long ago. One that came from a childhood of having my gifts and magic constantly derided.

I leaped over a log and stumbled over a couple of rocks, my fingers brushing the ground as I fought to maintain balance and keep moving. Up ahead, the cat paused and looked around, its eyes gleaming like jewels in the phone's light. Checking on me, seeing if I was still close.

Meaning it didn't want to face whatever lay ahead alone —and that only ratcheted up my tension a whole lot more.

I ran on desperately, well aware the caress of evil was growing ever fainter. If we didn't get there soon, we wouldn't be able to stop it. I flexed my fingers, and the threads of the containment spell stirred uneasily. I hoped it would be enough, but that fading force was damnably strong.

I powered up a steep incline and then through another strand of trees. Ahead, the cat made a sharp turn left, sending debris scattering. I followed, grabbing an overhead branch to steady myself as one foot slipped on rotting leaves. The trees were now thinning out, and the sounds of nearby civilization were growing stronger—the rumble of car engines mingling with the sweet sound of someone singing and the bellows of a frustrated mother yelling at her kids.

Had any of them heard the scream? Surely they should have, given how close they were. And yet, if they *had*, wouldn't the rangers already be on the way? Did the fact I couldn't hear any sirens mean there'd been some sort of magic involved in this death? There were certainly demons capable of hiding their presence from witches, so it wasn't beyond the realm of possibility that they could also restrict sight and sound.

We came out of the trees onto a rough stone road. It was barely wide enough for a car and wasn't used all that much if the weeds growing up through the stone were anything to go by.

The cat paused; I did the same, looking right and left. That thread of evil was now so faint it was little more than a tremor on the wind. But that was all we needed; we went right.

The broken road began a long curve around to the left. Up ahead, streetlights glowed, a beckoning promise of safety—and a lie. Whatever evil had stalked this area had centered on the crossroad ahead.

But nothing lurked in the warm puddles of light or the shadows that lay beyond them. Whatever had caused the man to utter such a bloodcurdling scream had left; the only question to be answered now was, where was that man? There was no sign of anyone up ahead. No indication of anyone lying on the ground, broken, bleeding, or even dead. Maybe he'd staggered down the road or sought help in one of the nearby houses—but again, surely there'd be a ranger or ambulance response by now if that had been the case.

The gentle singing ceased and, for a brief moment, the night was still. I slowed and scanned the area ahead, looking for something—anything—out of place. There was nothing.

I glanced down at the cat. "I'm not sensing anything—are you?"

The cat studied the street ahead for several seconds, his nose twitching. Then he yowled and stalked on. I followed, the threads of the spell still swirling around my fingers, despite the fact the demon who'd been here doing God knows what to that young screamer had now departed.

We were maybe a dozen feet away from the streetlight on the corner when I was hit by a wave of emotion so fierce my breath snagged in my throat and my heart went into overdrive. And then I saw the dark gleam of moisture on the ground...

There was too much blood for anyone to have survived such a loss. Far too much.

The cat skirted the pool and walked toward the light pole on the right-hand side of the road.

And that's when I saw them.

Bones.

Bones that had almost been picked clean.

Human bones.

And stacked neatly on top of them, with hair and eyes still attached, was the skull of a young man.

TWO

Horror twisted through me, and I briefly closed my eyes. There'd only been five or six minutes—if that—between the scream and our arrival here, but in that short amount of time, the young man had not only lost his life but also his skin, muscles, and organs.

That there was a demon capable of doing such a thing was bad enough, but to do it so damn quickly? I shuddered, and couldn't help but step back. In part because I didn't want to see if there were bits of flesh or tiny bone fragments in that vast pool of blood, and partly because everything the victim had felt—all his terror and pain—still blanketed the air. I may have seen far worse since we'd set up our café in this reservation, but *this* death was far too fresh. The thick waves of agony were bad enough here; they'd be nigh on suffocating if I stepped any closer.

I took a deep breath, then, as the wail of approaching sirens finally echoed across the night, switched off the flashlight app and called Monty.

"Tell me what your cat is seeing."

"Undoubtedly the exact same thing as you—"

"I can't get close to the remains. Too much of his agony still rides the air."

"That's a new development, isn't it?" An odd mix of curiosity and concern edged Monty's voice.

"Yeah, it is."

Normally my shields were strong enough to counter any sort of emotional output, even the ones that lingered after a violent death. They had to be, as my psychometry skills meant one unguarded touch could very easily overwhelm my mind.

It was only when I tried to read the mind of a fresh corpse—tried to capture whatever memories remained before the creeping darkness of death swept them away for good—that I risked this sort of emotional overload and a whole lot more besides. Which was why I rarely attempted doing that sort of thing, and certainly *never* without Belle— or, at least, another strong witch—close by to pull me out if necessary.

"Wonder if it's got anything to do with your connection and control of the wild magic?"

"You're asking me that question like you think I can answer it."

"Yeah, sorry. But you have to understand my fascination, given the connection shouldn't even exist in the first place."

I did understand. I also understood just how dangerous it could be. My mother—who was one of the strongest blue-blood witches alive today—had amply proven that, when she'd tried to contain some unfettered wild magic and had almost died in the process.

But I now suspected that might be the reason behind my ability to interact with wild magic so easily, as she'd been pregnant with me at the time. In drawing the wild magic to her body in an attempt to contain it, she'd somehow embedded it into my DNA—although until I'd stepped into this reservation, no one, including me, had been aware of that outcome.

I certainly had no idea how it yet might affect me.

"How about you put the fascination aside for a few seconds and tell me what Eamon is seeing."

Monty hesitated, no doubt conferring with his cat. "Nothing much."

"Has he any suggestions as to what we might be dealing with?"

"Not really." Monty hesitated again. "He said it smelled like a demon, but he can't say what type. There're a few who like to strip their victims of flesh like this."

"But how many of them like to stack the bones into a nice little pile on the corner of a crossroad?"

"Unknown, but it does at least give me a starting point for a search."

The sirens were now so close that Monty's reply was all but lost to their noise. I raised the phone to my ear and said, "If these bones are connected to the ones we found in the clearing, why would they bury that lot and not these?"

"Maybe the demon simply didn't have the time—maybe it sensed your presence and decided caution was the better bet."

I snorted. "It had enough time to neatly stack its victim's bones. That hardly suggests it was in any sort of hurry."

Besides, if there was a common factor amongst the supernatural nasties that had raided the reservation of late, it was their utter disdain for my natural magic. They only ever thought twice about attacking me when I used the wild magic, and even *that* wasn't any guarantee.

"Is Ashworth on his way here?" I added.

"Yes. He was under his truck fixing something or other when I rang, so it might take him a few minutes longer to get out there."

Ashworth's truck—like our station wagon—had been burned out by the soucouyant and written off by the insurance company. While Belle and I had gratefully accepted the council's offer of a brand-new replacement, Ashworth had bought his beloved truck back and was now in the process of restoring it. Until that point, however, he had the use of a ranger vehicle.

"The entity has well and truly gone," I commented, "so it's not like he really needs to hurry."

"True, but it'd still be better if he was there before they move the bones, just in case there's magic or a trap attached to them."

My gaze darted back to the bones. I couldn't see the shimmer of a spell hanging over them, but that didn't mean the spell's threads couldn't be hidden within the neat but bloody stack. "How possible do you think that is?"

"Unlikely, but I'm here and not there, and Eamon isn't as sensitive to the disguised spell stuff."

Few familiars were—which made me doubly lucky when it came to Belle being my familiar.

"Tell me," he added, "is Belle heading home tonight, or tomorrow morning?"

"Tomorrow—why?"

"I was wondering if she could pick me up from the hospital on the way through."

"I'm sure she'd be absolutely delighted to."

"There's evilness in your tone." *His* was dry.

"As long as you remember you're in a confined space with a witch who has a very short fuse when it comes to unwanted advances, I'm sure it'll be fine." I glanced around as three trucks pulled up on the main road; one was Aiden's blue truck, and the other two were the green-striped white SUVs that the other rangers used. "The cavalry just arrived, Monty. Talk later."

"We will."

I pocketed the phone, then released the spell from around my fingers and walked up to the main road, making a wide loop around the blood and bones and doing my best to ignore the waves of agony that still rode the air.

Aiden jumped out of his truck and walked toward me. Like most werewolves, he was tall and rangy, but his shoulders were a good width, his arms lean but muscular, and his sharp features easy on the eye.

His gaze swept me, no doubt taking note of the multitude of minor scratches, and then rose to meet mine. His eyes were a deep blue rather than the usual amber of a werewolf, and his hair a dark blond that ran with silver in the darkness. The O'Connors were gray wolves, a rare color amongst Australian packs, which tended to be mainly brown, red, or black.

"You okay?" He caught my hand and tugged me closer.

"For a change, yes."

I pressed my cheek against his chest and listened to the beat of his heart. It was a steady sound that had the tension within me slipping away. There might be another deadly demon on the loose, but when Aiden's arms were around me, holding me so tenderly, for a few really brief seconds it didn't matter.

He dropped a kiss on the top of my head and then pulled back. Though the caring remained in his eyes, his expression was all business. The ranger rather than the lover now faced me. "What have we got?"

I grimaced. "Bones. Two sets."

His gaze scanned the immediate area. "Where's the second set?"

"Buried in the forest. We found them first, and then heard this poor guy scream. He was like this by the time we arrived."

"We?" He looked past me, and his expression narrowed. "Ah. The cat."

"Yeah. He's been keeping Monty updated."

"Have either of them got any theories as to what did this?"

"Not as yet, but I daresay Monty will be searching Canberra's archives tonight to see if he can find anything."

"Good."

He glanced around at the sound of slamming doors. Tala—his second-in-command and a tall, dark-skinned woman with silver-shot black hair—and Ciara—who was both his sister and the coroner—walked over.

Ciara eyed the gruesome pile dubiously. "And here I was hoping we'd seen the last of the weird and overly horrific deaths."

"Unfortunately, that's not going to happen for a while yet," I said. "And we're dealing with two bodies rather than one."

"Oh, fabulous," she muttered. "Just as well I'm no longer flying solo in this job."

"And it might be wise to get Luke out here." Aiden glanced past her. "Tala, do you want to secure this scene? And call in Mac—he can start interviewing the neighbors. Liz, can you take me to where the other body is?"

"If I can remember—I wasn't really taking much notice of location in the race to get here." I glanced at the cat. It gave me a deadpan, narrow-eyed look. He knew what I wanted, but wasn't about to give any sort of help without a bit of groveling. He really *was* a bastard. "But I'm sure the lovely Eamon can help us out with that."

The cat blinked, satisfaction apparent, then led the way down the road. I breathed easier once we were well past the bones and the waves of agony had finally fallen behind me.

"I get a feeling you don't like that cat," Aiden said, clearly amused.

"That's because the cat is an irritable asshole."

"Maybe he's simply echoing his master's mood."

"No, he's naturally an asshole. But even if he *was* echoing his witch's mood, neither of them have to take their grumpiness out on me."

"True." He paused. "Was it your psychic senses that led you to the first set of bones?"

"No, it was Eamon. I was at Monty's feeding him when he caught the scent of whoever did this. Unfortunately, he lost the trail in the clearing where we found the first set of bones." I shrugged. "I tried to do a reading on the watch we found there, but the man had been dead too long to sense anything."

"And he's in a similar state as the second victim?"

"I only saw his arm, but yes, I think so."

Aiden grunted. "Hopefully, Ciara will be able to ID them both through dental records."

If the monster behind this wasn't collecting the teeth as some sort of macabre souvenir... The thought sent a shiver down my spine.

"You cold?" Aiden said instantly.

I smiled. "In this heat? Hardly. It was just another of those vague prophetic warnings that may or may not mean anything."

"Those warnings tend to have more truth behind them

than not." His warm tones held a grim edge. "I take it you think there won't be any teeth?"

I glanced up at him. "Considering you're not telepathic, it's rather scary just how well you can read me at times."

"I'm a ranger and a werewolf. We notice the little things." His smile flashed, bright in the darkness. "Besides, we have been going out for a few months now. It's not like we don't know each other's odd ways and intimate secrets."

"You may know mine," I replied mildly. "But you can hardly say I know all yours. You've been remarkably recalcitrant to talk about the wolf who broke your heart, for instance."

"And now is neither the time nor the—"

"That answer is getting monotonous."

He grimaced. "I know, but I really can't see why—"

"Aiden, remember that whole spiel you gave me about secrets and not wanting to go into another relationship where honesty wasn't a priority? Well, ditto."

He took a deep breath and blew it out softly. Reluctantly. "Fair enough. But not now."

"Agreed." If only because I'd probably need a gallon or two of whiskey to cope. Hearing about the wolf who'd broken his heart would be difficult in the extreme, if only because that woman had won what I so desperately wanted and had yet to find: a man who totally and utterly loved her, even after she'd long left his life.

That it was *this* man's heart made it even harder, simply because no matter how much I might wish otherwise, no matter how good we were together, we were also witch and werewolf. And in this world, it really was a case of 'never the twain shall meet'—at least not on a permanent basis.

I pushed away the heartache that rose whenever such a thought intruded and continued on in silence. Eamon found the clearing easily enough, and Aiden squatted beside the hole I'd dug into the soil. "There's no scent of decay, which suggests this death is more than a few weeks old."

"Unless, of course, the demon behind this picked the entire body clean this time, head included."

He glanced up at me. "Why would it do that here and not with the other victim?"

"Maybe, as Monty suggested, it sensed our presence and left the head as some sort of macabre message." Although, if that was the case, it was one I didn't yet understand.

"How many demons bother to strip their victims of all clothing and then remove them from the scene of their crime afterward, though?"

"Probably not that many, but maybe we're dealing with a demon with a weird fetish."

A smile tugged his lips. "And how likely is that?"

"Knowing as little as I do about demons, I couldn't honestly say. But fetishes exist in our world, so I can't see why they wouldn't in the supernatural one."

"I'm thinking it's more likely they've been removed simply to ensure no clues were left behind."

"That *is* the sensible possibility." And yet this reservation didn't often do sensible—at least when it came to bad guys.

He rose. "How likely is it that the demon will come back?"

"Not very." I glanced at my watch. "But Ashworth should be up top by now. Monty called him before he called you."

"Ah, good." He paused. "Are you going to hang around, or do you want a lift back home?"

"There's no real point in me hanging around—Ashworth can answer any questions you might have." And deal with any magical problems a whole lot more easily than me. "I'll walk back home—it's a nice night and it's not that far."

"Fine." He stepped around the disturbed patch of soil, then snaked an arm around my waist and pressed my body against the power of his. It felt nice. More than nice. "I know you said the immediate danger is over, but given you tend to be a trouble magnet, please be careful. I have plans in place for tomorrow night."

I wrapped my arms around his neck, a smile teasing my lips. "Not another dance lesson, I hope? Because I don't think your poor feet will cope."

"No, although dancing of the more intimate variety might be on the menu later in the evening, if you're feeling up to it."

"Always," I murmured, then claimed his lips with mine.

For several minutes, there was nothing more than the passion that rose with the kiss—one that was so raw, so powerful, and so very erotic that it rocked my very soul.

"And this," he murmured eventually, his breath little more than warm sharp pants against my kiss-swollen lips, "is why I avoid getting too close to you when I'm on duty."

I chuckled and pulled away. "Then perhaps I'd better go back to your place so I can be on hand to cure your... not so little... problem whenever you finish duty tonight."

"*That* only makes me ache harder." He brushed the damp hair from my eyes. "Do you remember the alarm's key code?"

I nodded. He'd added the alarm after a number of houses in the Argyle area had been broken into, and so far

I'd set the damn thing off three times. "If I'm asleep, feel free to wake me."

"If it's not too late, I will." He kissed me again, but as it threatened to turn into more, he pulled back and, with a soft curse, turned and walked away.

I grinned and watched until he'd disappeared. The cat had already gone back to the second murder scene—Monty had obviously gotten sick of waiting.

It didn't take me long to arrive back at Monty's. Instead of jumping over the fence, I simply followed it along to the end house in the row and then cut across the small park to the road. Nothing moved except the shadows playing across the footpath between each light pole, with little to be heard beyond the distant song of cicadas and the occasional growl of a car driving past on nearby Johnson Street. My psychic senses were mute, and yet... the odd feeling of being watched stirred. I casually glanced around, taking in the nearby houses. Nothing. Nor was there any sense of movement within the tree-lined verge that separated this street from Johnson.

Nevertheless, there *was* something in those shadows.

I had no immediate sense of evil and no idea if it was the demon or not. But whatever it was, it was old. *Very* old.

I shivered, but fought the desire to wrap a repelling spell around my fingers. Whatever—whoever—watched from those shadows presented no immediate threat, but that might well change if I did anything to spook it.

I flexed my fingers, but it did little to ease my growing tension. Why were my psychic senses all but mute when it came to whatever watched from those shadows? Was it simply a matter of them becoming so attuned to evil they'd lost the ability to sense beings who dwelled on the edges of that spectrum? Or was something else happening? Was it possible my watcher shielded its presence from me? Although, if it *did*, why was I getting any sense of it at all?

Did it, perhaps, simply wish me to know it was there and nothing else?

That certainly seemed to be the case.

I resisted the urge to increase my pace and kept my eyes on the lights ahead, even though every other sense was attuned to the shadows and whatever hid within them.

The distant thump of bass-heavy music soon replaced the cicadas, and it was accompanied by the happy rise and fall of conversation—all of it coming from the pub one street over. It was tempting to head over there, if for no other reason than to lose my unseen follower, but that might well end badly. Even if I had no immediate sense of threat, I also had no idea what it wanted. Until I did, I simply couldn't risk leading it to a heavily populated venue.

I continued on. My tail kept pace and, despite the well-lit street and fewer shadows, remained out of sight. There had to be some sort of magic involved, even if I wasn't sensing it.

I swung onto Mostyn Street and strode toward our café. I used the shop windows to study the street behind me, but there was no telltale shimmer to suggest magic was being employed, no acidic, demonic scent riding the drifting breeze, and no sound of footsteps even though I had a bad feeling my watcher was closer now than when I'd first sensed him or her. If not for the inner certainty that appeared to be emanating from the prophetic part of me, I might have thought it was nothing more than nerves.

Once at our café, I dug my keys out of my purse and casually looked around. Just for an instant, the air between two parked cars a few shops down shimmered, briefly forming a humanoid shape that jagged across the road and then retreated.

It wasn't nerves or imagination. Something *had* been following me.

I opened the door and stepped inside the café. After locking up again, I ran toward the rear, weaving my way through the multitude of bright tables and mismatched chairs until I reached the stairs that led up to our living quarters. Once there, I threw my purse toward my bed as I passed the doorway then ran through the kitchenette and into a living area that had little room for anything more than a TV, a sofa, and a coffee table. I threw open the glass sliding door at the end of the room and strode out onto the balcony.

The breeze stirred around me, bringing with it the distant sounds of music and laughter. This part of town might be all but dead at night, but there was plenty of life on the outskirts of this retail area.

I leaned against the railing and studied the street below. It wasn't empty—cars went past intermittently, and there were a number of people strolling toward nearby Hargraves Street. But once again, I wasn't picking up much in the way of the supernatural or magic; either the shimmer had disappeared or the person responsible was standing far enough away that even the prophetic part of me couldn't pick it up. Though why *that* part of my gifts had sensed it over my other abilities was puzzling—did it perhaps mean that whatever I was sensing wasn't actually here? That it was a threat yet to come?

Was Monty right? Was my growing connection with the wild magic also altering my psychic gifts?

I wished I'd delved more deeply into the history of psi abilities when I'd been younger, but it wasn't something my parents had ever encouraged; psychics were considered little more than charlatans by most bluebloods, and my parents certainly hadn't wanted everyone reminded they'd produced such a child. It was bad enough that I was on the weak end of the scale when it came to magic.

I flexed my fingers against the growing frustration of not knowing enough—either about my abilities or what was happening to me. Maybe it would have been better to stay with Aiden; at least then I wouldn't be worrying about an unseen follower who may or may not intend future harm.

As I pushed away from the railing, a number of glowing, silvery threads drifting on the breeze caught my attention. Wild magic, here in the middle of town, the one place where it really shouldn't have been—if, that was, you believed everything ever written about it. I was beginning to think that we definitely shouldn't—at least when it came to the magic in *this* reservation.

I raised a hand, and the threads curled around my fingers, as fragile as moonbeams and yet pulsing with power. Within that power was a sense of acknowledgment. Of kinship.

It no longer frightened me, although I daresay it should have, given what had happened to my mother. While my use of it had so far caused very little in the way of *bad* side effects, I couldn't help but think that might yet happen. All power had its drawbacks, and I'd be foolish to believe there wouldn't be some sort of fallout from this union. It had already changed my eyes from green to silver, although that only meant I now looked like the blueblood witch I'd been born rather than a mixed breed.

The threads continued to twine around my fingertips, and their force hummed through my body. The air became brighter, the night sharper, the light of the moon more intense.

Even as unease stirred, I glanced down at the street. There, at the far end of Mostyn, near the corner of Hargraves, was a pale, almost insubstantial woman. She was slender and small in stature, and her pale hair was long, flowing behind her like a veil. Her full-length dress was white, and she walked with a grace that was somehow regal. Threads of magic spun around her, their color a strange mix of grays and silver. It was a concealment spell but not one I'd ever come across.

As she reached the corner, the shimmering threads died, and the woman's body dissolved.

Meaning what I'd seen was either a ghost or a specter; the two were not the same, despite the fact many believed them to be. Ghosts could be souls trapped in this world because of an untimely death, an unwillingness to move on, or even the desire to complete unfinished business. Specters, on the other hand, were nearly always out for vengeance of one kind or another.

What category this one fell into, and why it had been following me, I had no idea. The wild magic might have strengthened my senses enough to see the entity, but to have any hope of understanding what she'd wanted or why she'd followed me, I had to uncover who she'd been in life. And to even *begin* that process, I first had to see what she actually looked like. While it *was* possible for Belle to summon a ghost or specter on description alone, to truly ensure success it'd be better if we had some form of identification.

Of course, she may have simply been curious. Not all ghosts were bound to the area in which they'd been killed. Some were free to roam, although most of these did so out of confusion or because they were still seeking something.

Either way, it was something Belle could tackle if or when the entity made another appearance.

The threads of wild magic unwound themselves from my fingers and drifted away again. It left me feeling oddly alone.

I moved back inside and, after locking the sliding door, grabbed an overnight bag and shoved in everything I'd need for tomorrow. While a lot of my toiletry stuff had migrated over to Aiden's, I'd yet to move any of my clothes or shoes, even though he'd suggested it a number of times and had even cleared out space in his wardrobe. My reluctance was due to nothing more than fear—a deep belief that the minute I took that step, the minute I committed to sharing his home on a semi-permanent basis, fate would present him with the wolf he was destined to be with.

Of course, it was ridiculous to think that *not* moving in would, in any way, stop that from happening, but I just couldn't take the risk. I needed to keep some distance between us, even if that distance was in reality more illusion than fact.

With my packing done, I made myself a coffee, then called a cab and headed outside to wait. It took just over thirty minutes to get to Argyle from Castle Rock, and I managed to get in without setting off the alarm—something the neighbors were no doubt thankful for. His home was situated at the far end of a six-unit complex that had been built close to the sandy shoreline of the vast Argyle Lake. It was a two-story, cedar-clad building, with the lower floor being one long room divided by a wooden staircase. In the front section of the room, there was an open fireplace, a huge TV, and a C-shaped leather sofa. On the other side of the staircase there was a modern kitchen diner, complete with a bench long enough for six people to sit around. The open stairs led up to two bedrooms, each with their own en suite. Aiden's was the front one, which had a balcony and lovely long view of the lake.

I helped myself to some leftover lasagna, poured a glass of whiskey, and then plopped down on the sofa to watch TV. He still wasn't home by the time I headed up to bed at ten-thirty.

Sleep came relatively quickly, but it was haunted by visions of a lady in white whose form gradually morphed into that of a blood-soaked hag holding a small but broken body close to her chest as she wailed in utter grief. I stirred restlessly, my heart rate climbing, but I couldn't escape the visions or even wake up. It was only when an arm snaked around my waist and warm lips brushed my bare shoulder that I was finally released.

I stirred and pressed my butt back against him, needing the contact to erase the unsettling remnants of the visions.

"What time is it?" I murmured.

"Just past midnight." His hand slipped upward, and his clever fingers began teasing my nipples. "It took longer than we expected to exhume the first body."

The last thing I wanted to think about—let alone talk about—was bones. I shifted to face him and gently ran my fingers from his chest to his washboard abs. "At least you finally did get here."

He stopped me just as my touch went past his belly button. "Going any further could be dangerous."

I raised an eyebrow, amusement twitching my lips. "Maybe I like to live a little dangerously."

"Oh, there's no doubt about that at *all*." His eyes were bright in the darkness, gleaming with amusement and desire. "But in this particular case, I'd rather ensure *both* parties are primed and ready."

"How do you know I'm not?"

"I'm a werewolf. We can smell these things." His hand slipped down my stomach and then cupped me. "Shall we get down to the business at hand?"

"I think we should."

From that moment on, there was little in the way of sound beyond those that spoke of exploration and rising pleasure. When satisfaction came, it was glorious.

He kissed me gently, then slipped to one side and gathered me close. When sleep claimed me for a second time, the visions of that wailing, grief-stricken woman were little more than a distant tremor.

One that whispered of trouble yet to come.

After cooking me breakfast the following morning, Aiden dropped me home and then continued on to the ranger station. The café was closed on Mondays, but that didn't always mean we got the day off—especially when the previous day's trade had all but wiped us out of cakes and salad prep. Once I'd dumped my stuff into my bedroom and shoved a load of washing into the machine, I headed into the kitchen to rectify all that. For the next five hours I made a variety of cakes, cheesecakes, and slices, and was finally on the last leg of veg cutting when Belle came home. She tossed her handbag onto the serving counter and then walked around to flick on the kettle. "You want a coffee?"

"Yes, thanks." I swept the sliced onions into the container, then shoved on the lid. "How was the show?"

"Brilliant. I might go down and see it again before its run ends."

She leaned against the doorframe and crossed her arms.

She was a typical Sarr witch in coloring, with ebony skin, long black hair, and eyes as bright as polished silver. She was also just over six feet tall with an Amazonian build, which made her almost the polar opposite of me. I was five inches shorter with a body that tended to curviness. I also had pale skin, freckles across my nose, and the crimson hair of a royal witch.

"I notice," she added, voice dry, "that you didn't ask how the trip home was."

I grinned. "I don't need to. I can feel the disgruntled vibes from here."

She snorted. "It wouldn't have been so bad if he'd just shut up for five minutes. But no, he felt the need to talk *all* the way home."

"Maybe it was nerves. You are a pretty impressive specimen of womanhood, after all, and he did fancy you even when you were a scrawny teenager."

"And still does." She shook her head, her smile somewhat wry. "No matter how many times I state he and I will *never* happen, it appears to have made absolutely no dent in his determination to take me out."

My eyebrows rose. "Implying he *did* actually ask you out?"

"Yeah." She pushed away from the wall as the kettle began to whistle. "He has some tickets for the opening night of *Evita* and was wondering if I wanted to go."

I couldn't help grinning. *That* was a very clever ploy on Monty's part, given Belle's love of the theatre and red-carpet events—not that she'd ever been to many of the latter.

"What did you tell him?"

"What do you think?" She reappeared, two coffees in hand. "How often am I able to go to a fancy opening night? There will, however, be ground rules."

My grin grew. "And do you seriously expect him to obey them? Especially when you're all made up and looking gorgeous on the red carpet?"

A reluctant smile touched her lips. "Well, no, but the threat of literally freezing him on the spot will at least curtail the most overt of his seduction attempts. The rest I can basically ignore."

I washed my hands and then accepted my coffee with a nod of thanks. "And what if he averts your threat by buying a stronger anti-telepathy band?"

The bands were something we'd been made aware of when two RWA witches had come into the reservation to help track down a vampire hell-bent on revenge. Monty had also been wearing one when he'd first arrived, but had subsequently learned that while it *did* stop casual intrusion, a determined effort by a strong enough telepath could still get through.

Belle had since released the restrictions she'd placed on his thoughts, but only because he now knew the truth of why we'd run and had sworn not to mention our presence to anyone up in Canberra—particularly anyone who knew either my parents or the bastard I'd been forced to marry. I wasn't entirely sure Monty believed my father—who was one of the government's most sought-after advisors—was capable of such treachery, but that didn't really bother me. The longer I could keep my presence here secret, the better —even if I knew in the end it wouldn't matter. My father and Clayton would eventually arrive here, forcing the confrontation I'd been running from since I was sixteen years old.

"I doubt he'll go to the trouble of buying another band," Belle said. "Especially after I broke through the first one relatively quickly. Besides, he may just surprise us and be the model of decorum."

I almost choked on a mouthful of coffee. "This *is* Monty we're talking about. You know, the man who paired a Kermit the Frog tie with an Armani suit at our Year Ten formal, and who then spent most of the evening trying to convince you to dance with him."

A smile tugged her lips. "I know, but hey, stranger things have happened, especially in this reservation."

Stranger things might have, but I doubted even this reservation could work that particular miracle. "How is he, besides chatty?"

"Good. He can certainly scoot around on his crutches easily enough, although he's not going to be able to drive the Mustang for a few weeks yet."

No surprise there given his pride and joy was a manual. The last thing he'd want was to scratch or—heaven forbid—dent the thing. "Did you dump him at home or at the ranger station?"

"Neither. He wanted to go straight to the morgue to examine the remains."

I grimaced. "Whatever's responsible for these murders didn't leave a whole lot behind to examine."

"I think he wanted to do some sort of magical examination. I don't think he trusted Ashworth's declaration there were no detectable spells or magic layered onto the remains."

"I'm gathering he had the good sense *not* to say that to Ashworth."

My voice was dry, and her lips twitched. "It appears the slap over the ear he received the last time he said something about our favorite witch's abilities did do the trick." She rested a hip against the bench. "I get the feeling those remains are not the reason for the vague uneasiness I was sporadically receiving before you went to sleep last night."

"No. Sorry, I thought I had everything locked down."

"You did—if it had been anything more substantial, I would have contacted you. So, give."

I quickly told her about the woman in white and the unsettling visions I'd had before Aiden had so delightfully woken me. "There was no threat in her presence, but those images suggest that might not remain the case."

Belle frowned. "A ghostly woman in white is a common occurrence throughout many cultures, but they're usually associated with some sort of tragic event—such as the loss of a husband or child. They're known for seeking vengeance."

"She carried the body of what I think was her child in the vision."

"But not when she was following you, which is odd. It suggests there's some other reason for her presence here."

"Could she be the mother of one of the victims?"

"The current victims? Unlikely, as her appearance happened too soon after the deaths."

"We haven't got a time of death for the first victim, though."

"It's still unlikely." She took a sip of coffee, her expression thoughtful. "But I guess it's possible there are more victims out there than the two we've found. Maybe you should mention it to Aiden and see if there've been any recent suicides."

"I actually don't think it was recent—she felt far older than that."

"It's still worth asking, especially if the suicide happened soon after a child had been killed."

I nodded. "In the meantime, we can hit your gran's

books and see if she has anything on white ladies or flesh-stripping, bone-stacking demons."

"She likely has—it's just finding which books they're in that'll be the problem."

Her grandmother's handwritten indexing system tended to be somewhat haphazard, which made it hard to find anything quickly. But recent events had made us realize we needed an easier means of quickly accessing the information within the vast number of books—most of which were secured off-site, as we simply didn't have the room here to store even a quarter of them.

To that end, Belle had asked a techie friend of hers to help catalog and then convert them over to an easily accessible electronic format. One that would not only provide a backup in case the High Witch Council ever discovered we had Nell's library—which should, for all intents and purposes, have been gifted to the National Library on her death—but also protect us against a natural disaster destroying part or all of the library. Castle Rock might not get much in the way of floods, but it *was* in an extremely high-risk fire zone. And while I'd recently added a fire protection spell to the multiple layers protecting them, there was no guarantee that what worked against unnatural flames would work against real.

"How much of the library have you and the lovely Kash managed to convert?"

"About a third, I think. It's slow going thanks to the age of some of the volumes."

"I'm thinking you're not overly worried about the length of time it takes."

My voice was again dry, and she grinned. "Indeed no. I am, in fact, due over there this afternoon for another session."

Amusement twitched my lips. "And will this 'session' actually include any scanning or text conversion?"

Her grin grew. "Once we've satisfied other hungers, quite possibly."

I chuckled softly. "Then you'd better go get ready. I'll go through your gran's index and see what I can find."

She raised an eyebrow. "You don't want me to help with the rest of the food prep?"

I shook my head. "I've only got to decorate a few remaining cakes and slices, then get the scalloped potatoes ready and I'm done."

Besides, Belle had covered for me often enough in the kitchen. It was about time I returned the favor.

"Awesome—thanks. But you will contact me if that specter makes a reappearance, won't you? The sooner we get to the bottom of *that*, the better."

"It's not likely to make an appearance during the daylight hours—is it?"

She hesitated. "Generally no, because most of them simply haven't the strength to project their form in sunlight. But this one is capable of magic, which means anything is possible."

"Have you ever heard of or seen a concealment spell whose threads are silver?"

She raised her eyebrows. "We went to the same school, remember? If you didn't recognize the spell, I sure as hell wouldn't."

"Yeah, but you did make a habit of reading through your gran's spell books before you went to sleep."

"Only to find innocuous old spells to fling at our class-mates when they annoyed us."

Like the 'shoelace constantly undone and tripping you up for a day' one she'd used. While the whole 'do unto others, because it will come back threefold' rule did generally apply to spells, it couldn't actually be enforced if you didn't wear laces. It also didn't apply to spells cast by dark or blood witches—maybe because such witches were already bound to hell or had their souls so stained by their evil that they were irretrievable and little else could be done to them.

"But you *do* know a whole lot about ghosts and specters," I said. "How usual is it for them to be able to perform magic after their death?"

"It's rare, but there are some who can interact with our world, so this may just be an extension of that."

If that were the case, then I could only hope that she didn't start aiming her magic at us. "Are you driving the SUV across to Kash's?"

She shook her head. "It isn't that far away, and it's not too hot to walk."

"For you long-limbed types who don't burn after ten minutes in the sun, maybe."

She grinned. "I burn. I just don't go flame-red and then peel afterward. You want me to bring something back for dinner?"

I raised an eyebrow. "You're not staying overnight at Kash's?"

She shook her head again. "His bed is too damn uncomfortable, and he refuses to get another, so he pays the price by not being able to sleep with this luscious bod."

"So, despite high intelligence, he's not actually that bright?"

"Indeed. But it doesn't matter, given neither of us are looking for anything serious." She pushed away from the bench. "I should be home by about eight."

I nodded and continued the prep. When that was done,

I grabbed another coffee, a thick slice of freshly made caramel shortbread, and then headed upstairs to go through the index and jot down the numbers of any books that might contain information about flesh-stripping demons or ghostly white ladies.

It was close to four when a sharp ringing startled me awake. I blinked for the second or two it took for true alertness to catch up, and then realized it was the café's phone rather than mine. I carefully shifted the book—which had obviously dropped onto my chest when I'd fallen asleep—then pushed upright and ran downstairs.

And knew, even as I reached for the handset, trouble was about to step my way again.

THREE

"Is this Elizabeth Grace?" a somewhat distraught voice said.

My stomach sank, even though intuition wasn't yet suggesting that whatever this woman wanted in any way involved the evil we'd discovered last night.

"Yes, it is, but I'm afraid we're closed until—"

"Yes, I know, and I'm sorry, but my son is missing, and I desperately need your help. I don't know where else to go."

I closed my eyes and briefly wished I had strength to ignore the desperation in her voice. But I didn't, and probably never would, simply because I understood it. I'd felt exactly the same way the day my sister had been snatched and subsequently killed by a serial killer—a tragic event that had no doubt given birth to this inner need to help others when and where I could. Still...

"Have you tried the rangers?"

"Yes, but they think I'm being paranoid, and I'm not. I know I'm not."

I seriously doubted they'd said or thought any such

thing, but there was little point in saying that. It was pretty obvious she wasn't in any state to listen.

"When did he go missing, Mrs...?"

"Hardwick. Marion Hardwick. And I haven't seen him since yesterday afternoon. He went to a party at a mate's, and hasn't come back."

"And you've talked to them? Asked when they saw him last?"

"Of course I did." Her voice was a mix of indignation and desperation. "They said he left them at midnight to walk home. But he never made it here, and he's not answering his phone."

"Have you tried to find his phone via a locator app?"

"Is something like that even possible?"

"Yes, but only if it's been previously set up." I sighed and rubbed my head. Maybe if I did this quickly enough, Aiden's plans for the evening would not be curtailed yet again. "I'll need something of his—something like a watch or a neck chain he wore on a regular basis—to find him. And you'll need to come here."

While instinct might be suggesting whatever had happened to her son wasn't related to the events of last night, I wasn't about to take a chance. Our reading room was probably one of the safest places in Australia when it came to dealing with any sort of magic or occult entities. Not only was the café surrounded by multiple layers of spells that guarded us against all manner of things—from preventing anyone intending us harm entering the café, to protecting us against a wide variety of supernatural nasties—there were also a whole range of additional measures *within* the reading room. No spirit or demon was getting in there, even if it somehow broke through the main spells.

"I'll be there in fifteen minutes," Mrs. Hardwick said. "Thank you for doing this."

"It's not a problem."

She hung up. I took a deep breath and rang Aiden. "Guess what?"

He groaned. "You're getting another bad feeling?"

"No. This time it was a rather desperate call from Marion Hardwick—"

"Whose son is missing," he finished.

"I take it she's been to the station already?"

"Yes, and this is not the first time the kid has disappeared. The last time he hitched a lift down to Melbourne to see some band with a girl he'd met the day before."

I frowned. "How old is he?"

"Sixteen going on thirty." Aiden's voice was dry. "He's basically a good kid; he's just a little headstrong."

"I take it you've had people out looking for him?"

"Yes, but there's no sign or scent of him on the usual tracks back to his mom's place." He paused. "You want me over there?"

"No, because I'm actually not getting any bad vibes about this disappearance at the moment. If that changes, I'll call you."

"Fine. But let me know if you're not going to be ready by seven, so I can cancel the dinner reservation."

"Where were we going?"

"It's a surprise, and will remain that way until we get there."

"And if we don't?"

"Then it'll wait for another day."

"You know you've just set me a challenge, don't you?"

"I welcome said challenge, but I will not break."

I grinned. "We'll see about *that*, Ranger."

He chuckled softly. "Call if there's a problem."

"Always do."

I hung up, then made myself a big mug of hot chocolate and shoved a ton of marshmallows into it. I had a feeling I'd need the sugar hit to cope with the onslaught of Mrs. Hardwick's emotions.

As it turned out, I should have shoved a whole lot *more* marshmallows into the drink.

Marion Hardwick was a tall, thin woman with short black hair and brilliant green eyes that were currently puffy and red. She was also surrounded by a fierce halo of fear and panic, and her aura was a writhing mess of dark blue—a sign that she either didn't trust the future or couldn't face the possible truth of it.

I plastered a smile onto my face and kept my hands well clear of her. "Please, continue on down to the reading room."

She swallowed heavily and wound through the tables, her fear and worry trailing behind her like a long, dark cloud. I drew in another breath that did little to ease the desire *not* to follow her into that room, and then shut the front door and did exactly that.

"Right," I said, once we were both seated. "Before we proceed, I need you to be aware there's no guarantee I'll be able to find your son. Psychometry can be a fickle talent at the best of times, and if your son's vibes don't linger on whatever item you've brought here, then there's not much I can do."

She nodded, opened her purse, and placed what looked to be a couple of hundred dollars on the table. "I'm told that's how much something like this costs."

"There's actually too much there, but we can worry about that later—"

"No." Her voice was surprisingly firm. "If this doesn't work, I'll be in no fit state to deal with such matters afterward. Besides, I know I'm taking up your time on your day off. The money on the table is fair payment for what you're attempting."

I didn't bother arguing. "Can you place whatever item you've brought onto the table?"

She nodded and immediately produced a paint-speckled silver watch. "He wears it when he's working—he's an apprentice painter."

"What's his name?"

"Joseph, though he prefers Joe."

I waited until she'd removed her hand and then carefully picked up the watch. Almost instantly, my psychic senses came to life. Joe was very definitely alive, but there was a thick haze of pain emanating from the watch that suggested he was in some sort of trouble.

I opened the psychic gates a little wider to deepen the connection and uncover what might be happening to him. The sensation of pain became a deep throbbing whose epicenter seemed centered on the lower part of my leg.

I frowned, but made no attempt to go any further. It was too damn risky without Belle here to pull me out if something happened. Besides, the connection between the watch and its owner was deep enough that I didn't need to.

I returned my gaze to Mrs. Hardwick. "The good news is, he's alive."

Tears flooded over her eyelashes. "Oh, thank God. Where is he? What's happened to him?"

I hesitated. Although I was pretty sure he'd shattered his leg, I couldn't tell her that, especially given I had no true idea if that was *all* he'd done. "I'm not sure of either yet, but if you'll lend me his watch, I can use it to find him."

She immediately thrust to her feet. "Can we go now, then?"

I took another of those deep breaths and said, as gently as I could, "I'll go, but it's better if you return home—"

"I can't. I *won't*. Not until he's been found and I know—"

"Mrs. Hardwick," I cut in, "as I've already said, psychometry is a fickle beast. I'm afraid fierce emotions can block my receptors, and your presence will make it very difficult to follow the connective trail to your son."

"Oh." She wiped away her tears with the heel of her hand, then dug into her purse and handed me a business card. She was the manager of The Red Door, a very posh restaurant two streets over. "You'll ring me the minute you find him?"

"Of course I will."

She nodded, gave me a fleeting smile, and then left. I got my phone out and rang Aiden back.

"Dead or alive?" he said without preamble.

"Alive, but injured, if what I'm getting from the watch is anything to go by."

"Do you need a driver?"

"I do indeed."

"Be there in five."

He hung up. I carefully placed the watch in a small silk bag to dull some of the sensations rolling from its surface, then—after grabbing my phone, purse, and keys—headed out to the street to wait for Aiden. He pulled up two minutes later and leaned across the front seat to open the door.

"I canceled dinner," he said as I climbed in. "Better to be safe than sorry. Where to?"

"Swing left onto Hargraves." I put on my seat belt and

then twisted to face him. "Why all the secrecy about the dinner location?"

"It's a surprise." His voice was mild. "There's nothing wrong with that, is there?"

"Nothing beyond the fact that curiosity will now kill me."

He grinned. "Curiosity only ever kills cats, so I think you're pretty safe. Ciara finished her prelim examination on the two sets of bones, by the way."

"A not-so-subtle redirect, but I'll let you get away with it this time. Did she manage to identify either victim?"

"No, not at the moment." He glanced at me, the amusement leaving his expression. "It appears your intuition was right—the teeth were missing."

I shuddered. "I'm guessing that means identifying them will now be difficult."

"Maybe not. They're going to use a forensic facial reconstruction program to get a workable image of both victims. Thankfully, the current list of missing persons isn't a large one."

"That's presuming both victims are from the reservation. They may not be."

"True, but once we have an image to work with, we can access the database used by the state cops if they're not listed in ours."

"Was she able to get an idea of approximate age from the bones of either victim?"

"The length of their tibias suggests they'd both reached maturity and stopped growing, which means they were at least eighteen or nineteen. But there was also little in the way of the degenerative changes that start happening in the late twenties, and that means they were probably in their early twenties." He swung the truck left and then sped up. "How far away do you think Joe is?"

I briefly tightened my grip on the silk-covered watch and then screwed up my nose. "Hard to say, but not far. Where does Mrs. Hardwick live?"

"Over near Campbell's Creek."

"And the mate who had the party?"

"Preshaw Street."

I frowned. "Why does that sound familiar?"

"Because it leads onto Stephenson's Track."

An area that was riddled with disused mineshafts, including the one we'd fallen into. What was the betting that Joe's trail would lead us into that area again? "How likely is it that he walked home that way?"

"Very. And before you ask, we did search the immediate area either side of the track, but couldn't find his scent."

"Given they were partying, maybe he took a shortcut through the scrub rather than remaining on the track."

"It's possible, although most of the kids who live in that area are well aware how dangerous it can be."

"We're talking about a teenage boy here; they believe they're invincible at the best of times, let alone when they've been drinking." I motioned to the upcoming street. "Left here."

The truck's tires squealed as he obeyed and then accelerated toward the end of the street. Which was, I noted as I motioned him right, Preshaw Street. The houses soon gave way to wilderness, and the track narrowed and became gravel, forcing Aiden to slow down. As the scrubby trees became more numerous, the pulse from the watch got stronger and stronger—and then, abruptly, started to fade again. We'd passed him.

"Stop," I said, and then scrambled out when he had. I

walked around to the rear of his truck and held the watch out in my hand. The pulse was strongest to my left. I motioned toward it with my free hand. "He's in there."

Aiden's gaze swept the area, then returned to mine. He didn't look happy. "There's a lot of old shafts in there—I really hope he hasn't fallen down one."

"It might explain why he wasn't scented." It might also explain why his mom couldn't get him on the phone—maybe he'd broken or lost it in the fall. But if his phone and his leg were all that he'd broken, then he was one lucky kid.

Aiden opened the rear of his truck and pulled out a couple of ropes and some climbing gear. He must have seen my surprise, because he said, "I added this lot after our fall. I wasn't about to rely on chance or someone passing by next time."

A smile twisted my lips. "First off, let's hope there's *not* a next time, and secondly, unless you're intending to carry that gear around with you whenever we head into the bush, it won't do us any good."

His smile flashed. "Maybe, but it will at least be in the truck for others to retrieve if we ever do get caught again. You give directions, but I'll lead the way."

I nodded and followed him off the road. Almost instantly, the scent of eucalyptus became more noticeable, and the soft crunch of stones underfoot echoed across the silence. This area wasn't overly hilly, but there were plenty of old tailing mounds visible through the trees, all indicators of just how heavily the area had once been mined.

We continued on, guided by the strengthening pulse of the watch. Eventually, the beats within it drew so close they were almost indistinguishable from each other.

"Aiden, stop. He's close." I swung the watch around and

detected a slightly stronger signal from the left. "I think he's somewhere between those two piles of stone."

Aiden raised his head, his nostrils flaring as he dragged in a deeper breath. After a moment, he shouted Joe's name. I couldn't hear a response, but Aiden grunted, satisfaction evident. "He's alert enough to answer, so that's one good thing."

He pulled the ropes over his shoulder and handed them to me while he put on one of the harnesses. Then he attached one end of a rope to a sturdy tree and hooked himself up. "You stay here and call Tala. Tell her we'll need an ambulance and the rescue boys with their gear."

I did so as he disappeared behind the two rubble piles, then crossed my arms and tried to ignore the desire to follow him in; that would be nothing short of stupid, given I didn't have the keen sight of a werewolf and had no idea how to spot the difference between solid ground and ground that had simply been thrown over a hastily boarded-up mine shaft.

The minutes ticked by; I shifted from one foot to the other, tension growing.

Then the rope went taut—an indication, perhaps, that he'd found the right mine shaft and was now climbing down.

A few more minutes went by. The sharp wail of approaching sirens shattered the silence, growing closer fast. Then Aiden reappeared, still wearing the harness but no longer attached to the rope.

"How is he?"

"Damn lucky." His voice was grim. "He landed on some boarding about twenty feet down. Had he fallen one foot either side, he'd be dead."

Relief swam through me. "And his injuries?"

"Aside from the shattered leg and a few deep scrapes and bruises, he's okay." He unbuckled the harness. "I put the spare harness on him and made sure he's roped on, but with the state of his leg, we can't risk moving him. Not until it's braced and he's got a truckload of painkillers on board."

"Is the shaft wide enough to get a backboard down there?"

He grimaced. "Maybe. It'll be a slow process, no matter how we decide to extricate him."

Because most of these old mines were decidedly unstable—something we'd learned the hard way. Just thinking about our close call had my pulse rate rising. "Do you want me to ring Mrs. Hardwick?"

He shook his head. "We'll do that once we've got him free of the shaft. She'll want to come out here, and it's far better for him *and* the rescue if she simply meets us at the hospital."

I nodded. "Then I might head back to the café. Do you want to come back for coffee and cake once you're finished here?"

"When have I ever refused the offer of cake?" He glanced past me. Tala and Jaz—another ranger—appeared, accompanied by a couple of men from the reservation's search and rescue team. "Jaz, can you take Liz home?"

"There's no need—it's not that far. I can walk back." After being cooped up in the café all day, it would be nice to get some fresh air.

He gave me the look—the one that said 'don't be daft'. "The last thing I need is you falling down another mine shaft, so humor me and at least let her guide you through the scrub."

"That I can agree to." My gaze dropped to his mouth. I desperately wanted to kiss him but he'd already stated his preference for keeping work and private life separate, and it wouldn't be fair of me to keep blurring that—especially when we weren't alone. "Call me later."

He nodded, a hint of a smile touching his lips. He'd known what I'd been thinking, damn him. I spun around and walked over to Jaz. Aside from Aiden, she was the only other ranger I'd call a friend. We caught up on a fairly regular basis—sometimes for dinner, sometimes for a movie, and sometimes simply for a coffee and a chat. I suspected part of the reason for her ease with me was the fact that she'd only recently married into the Marin pack, and therefore didn't have the same level of distrust when it came to witches that the reservation's three packs initially had.

"How's that hubby of yours doing?" I said as I followed her through the scrub.

She flashed a grin over her shoulder. "He opens his café next week, so he's something of a stress head at the moment."

A statement I could totally understand, given we'd gone through the exact same thing the first time we'd ever set up our own place. But then, we'd also been a whole lot younger and had had little in the way of training other than the few years we'd worked as kitchen hands and short-order cooks in various venues. At least Levi was a barista who'd worked at some of the top cafés in Melbourne before moving back to Castle Rock.

"Tell him it does get better. Eventually."

"I hope so, because I'm getting very little action at the moment, and that's a sad state of affairs when we've only been married a few months."

I laughed. "I'm sure things will improve once the café is open and running smoothly."

"I damn well hope so." She skirted a large pile of rubble

and then continued on. "Have you any idea who or what was behind the deaths last night?"

"I'm afraid it takes a little longer than *that* to track down these things."

Her grin flashed again. "Maybe I'm just used to you having all the answers."

I snorted. "And maybe you're just forgetting how often I *don't*." I paused. "Have there been any recent missing person reports that match the suspected age of the bones?"

"No recent ones, but Maggie's going through the records to see what she can find."

"What about juvenile disappearances? Have there been any that resulted in the mother's suicide?"

She swung around. "That's a very specific question— did your psychic mojo show you something we need to know about?"

I hesitated. "I saw a ghost in my dreams last night, and she was carrying the body of her child."

"And you think it's connected to the current case?"

"Honestly? I have no idea—but the body was whole rather than stripped of flesh, so there's the chance it isn't."

"Which doesn't omit the possibility that it is." She walked on. "I'll do a search through the database and see if there's anything like that listed."

"She felt old, so it may not be a recent event."

She glanced at me again, curiosity stirring across her sharp but pretty features. "How does a ghost feel old?"

I hesitated. "It's their metaphysical output—the older they are, the stronger they tend to be."

"Huh. You learn something every day." She stepped out onto the road and then stopped. "Are you sure you don't want a lift home?"

"No, I'm fine. And if I don't see you before, we'll see you next week for dinner. About sixish?"

Her cheeks dimpled. "*If* the man hasn't had some sort of coronary by then, most definitely."

I grinned. "He'll be fine—and so will the café. He's got a great location and his hot chocolates *are* the best."

"Yes, but as he keeps saying to me, there's more to a café's survival than good hot chocolate." She gave me a lopsided smile. "But nothing ventured, nothing gained, as the old saying goes."

"That's a good motto to live by, I think." Even though it was one I hadn't really followed until recently. And even then, I still tended toward caution rather than adventurousness.

Except when it comes to Aiden, Belle commented, amusement in her mental tone. *Your inner adventurer has definitely blossomed in his presence.*

I wasn't referring to the whole sex thing.

Jaz handed me a flashlight, then headed back into the forest. I spun around and strode back toward Castle Rock, the crunch of the stones under my feet lost to the rowdy song of the cicadas.

Tell that to someone who can't read your mind. Where are you?

On Stephenson's Track, walking home.

What the hell are you doing out there?

I gave her a quick update and then added, *Did you get much cataloging done?*

Surprisingly, yes. I think he's rather fascinated by all the old legends and spells.

Did you find anything related to flesh strippers or White Lady ghosts?

Only a couple of minor mentions, but I grabbed some

books on the way home. Do you want me to come pick you up? Or shall I just shove the Chinese food in the warmer for you?

I hesitated but the call of Chinese was just too strong. *A pickup would be good. I'm starving.*

That's probably because you had nothing more than a huge chunk of caramel shortbread for lunch.

I grinned. *And I don't regret a single calorie of it.*

She snorted. *Be there in five.*

Thanks.

Her mind left mine, and I trudged on. The trees on either side of the road began to thin out, allowing the moonlight to filter through, but the noise of cicadas didn't abate. There had to be hundreds of them in the trees, if not thousands—which made me glad I was following the road rather than walking through the scrub. The horrid insects had a habit of peeing on passersby.

As the lights of civilization grew stronger, a faint wisp of energy stirred around me—the same sort of energy that I'd felt last night when the specter had appeared.

I glanced around, but couldn't immediately see her. But then, why would I if she was concealing her form again?

I took a deep breath and then said loudly, "I know you're out there—what do you want? Why do you keep following me?"

There was no response. I frowned and kept on walking, but the awareness of her presence grew. She was in the trees to my right, pacing me. Watching me.

"If you need help, I can get it for you. But I need some sort of indication that's what you're after."

Again, nothing.

Maybe the fault was mine rather than hers. I might be able to sense the presence of ghosts and specters, but I wasn't capable of communicating with them. Not unless Belle joined her mind to mine on a deeper level, and even then, it wasn't me doing the ghost talking, but rather Belle through me.

The caress of the specter's energy drew closer, stinging my skin with its proximity. I scanned the trees, trying to spot that telltale shimmer without success. If she did want something, then she either wasn't sure I could be trusted or wasn't yet ready to tell me.

Belle? How far away are you?

Only a minute or so—why?

The witchy White Lady is pacing me again.

And are you wearing your charm, on the off chance she decides to attack this time?

I doubt she will, but yes, I am. I don't ever take the damn thing off. Not even when I was showering. Though the charms looked innocuous—they were little more than multiple strands of intertwined leather and copper, with each strand representing a different type of protection spell —they were probably the most powerful things we'd ever created. Only silver would have made them any stronger, but that wasn't really practical in a werewolf reservation. Or when I was dating a werewolf.

I'd made duplicate ones for both Belle and Aiden, and while Aiden had initially been a tiny bit skeptical—something he hadn't said out loud—he'd been won over after witnessing the charm's protection capabilities the day we'd rescued Monty and the soucouyant had tried to crisp me.

I frowned and studied the shadowed scrub. Our specter might be close but she remained out of sight. "I can't help you if you don't reveal yourself."

Still no response. It made me wonder what she was waiting for.

Maybe she's aware you're not capable of hearing or speaking to her.

Maybe. My gaze was drawn away from the trees to the street ahead as twin lights appeared in the distance and sped toward me. "A friend who's a spirit talker will be here in a few seconds, so if you do need help—"

The specter immediately fled. I swore and darted into the forest after her—which wasn't a very bright move if there were mineshafts in this area, but I couldn't let her escape. I had a growing suspicion she might play a vital part in our quest to stop whatever might be responsible for the flesh-stripped destruction last night.

I plunged on, raising my free hand to protect my face from whip-like tree branches and scrubby shrubs that were lined with needle-like foliage. The flashlight's beam did a mad dance across the forest, and the song of the cicadas fell silent as I neared them, only to rise again as I left them behind, creating a wave of sound that would pinpoint my location to anyone who was listening. And I rather suspected the specter was. I also suspected she wanted me to follow her—why else would her energy be maintaining a steady distance rather than pulling away or even completely disappearing, as it had last night?

I'm coming in, Belle said.

No, don't, in case this is a trap.

Then let me see what you're seeing.

I'm not seeing a goddamn thing at the moment. Nothing other than the thorny bushes briefly highlighted in the flashlight's beam.

Even so, I immediately reached for her and deepened the connection. Her being flowed through mine, fusing us as one, though not so deeply that I lost physical control or that her soul left her body and became a part of mine. But she could now see through my eyes and also use her talents *through* me if necessary. The ability to achieve this sort of remote connection was only a recent discovery; but then, until we'd arrived in this reservation, we'd really had no need for it.

You're right, came Belle's thought. *She is old. And while the magic wrapped around her is making it difficult to read her, I'm getting the impression she wants to show you something.*

I really hope it isn't another body.

I leaped over a moss-covered log, landed awkwardly on the other side, then caught my balance and ran on.

I don't think it is. She paused. *But I do think it'll be connected.*

Which suggests she's here to help. And, quite possibly, that she didn't trust us enough to fully reveal her presence or talk to us yet.

And she may never—remember, she fled when you mentioned I was a spirit talker.

Which only made her behavior even odder. *If she wanted to help us, why would she avoid talking to us?*

Why is she even following you at all? Monty's the stronger witch, and Ashworth was there last night. Either of them would be a more logical choice.

I wrinkled my nose and ducked under a low-hanging branch. *Maybe it's nothing more than the fact that I was there first last night. She couldn't have known Eamon was Monty's familiar rather than mine.*

True. She shrugged mentally. *Whatever the reason, until I either see her face or we uncover her past, I'm not going to be able to summon or question her.*

Presuming you can get past her magic.

The spell's a concealment one—it can't and won't stop me from summoning her.

Except she now knows you're a spirit talker and may well add a thread or two to counter that.

Also true.

The ground dropped away suddenly, and I slid to a stop, sending stones bouncing down the steep, scree-filled slope. At its base was a wide creek that wound its way through what looked to be more a man-made ravine rather than a natural one. On a large rock in the middle of the water was something white. The slight shimmer of air that was our specter hovered above it. I narrowed my gaze, and after a moment saw the faint silver and gray threads that was the concealment spell.

Belle sucked in a breath, a sound that echoed loudly through my brain. *Damn, the magic behind that spell is powerful.*

Yes. She must have been a strong witch in life.

Which begs the question, why would a witch give over her afterlife like this? There are plenty of other ways to seek revenge, if indeed that's what she wants.

Seeking such revenge in life could be what landed her in this position.

If she had gone after whoever was responsible for the death of her child, why would she be here—in this state—now? It makes no sense at all.

That's another question to be added to the list if you do manage to summon and talk to her.

I carefully started down the slope. An ever-increasing wave of stones rolled ahead of me, and a thick cloud of dust rose, tickling my throat and making me cough. The noise of the cicadas faded away and the night became still—hushed.

Trepidation stirred, even though I had no immediate sense of threat.

I was halfway down the slope when the specter rose and fled. I swore softly but kept my concentration on the unstable ground under my feet; the last thing I needed was to fall. By the time I made it to the ravine's base, sweat trickled down my back and my legs were on fire. I made another of those somewhat useless mental notes to do something about getting fitter and walked along the creek bank until I was opposite the rock that held the small white pile.

In the flashlight's bright light, it looked a whole lot like feathers.

Feathers that were covered in blood.

FOUR

Why on earth would she be showing us a pile of bloody feathers? Belle asked.

It could be she's not involved with last night's murders. Maybe she's just a ghost intent on a little mischief. I stepped onto the nearest rock and threw my hands out for balance as the thing wobbled under my weight.

If that were the case, you wouldn't have seen her as a lady in white.

Unless that's part of her game.

Ghosts generally can't alter their forms. If she presented as a lady in white, it's because she is one.

I stepped onto the next rock and then hesitated. The rest were half-submerged and moss covered, and while there were others scattered about that sat above the water-line, none of them would get me closer to the big rock holding the feathers. I grimaced and carefully stepped forward, only to slip on the moss and go sliding into the water. One wet shoe might as well be two, I thought, and splashed on. The feathers, I soon discovered, weren't the only things covered in blood. The top of the rock was, too. And there were bones. Tiny birdlike bones.

She's obviously trying to give us a message by showing us this, Belle said. *But it's certainly one I don't understand.*

Me neither. It obviously wasn't a new kill—while the blood on the feathers still held a gleam of red, the stuff on the rock was black and flaking. If a specter hadn't led me here, I would have presumed it was a favorite eating spot for whatever hawk or eagle hunted in the area.

And yet...

I narrowed my gaze and studied the feathers. They were obviously from a largish bird, and had dark brown stripes alternating with lighter gray. There were no signs of spell threads and certainly no indication that this was anything other than the remains of a hunter's snack.

But doubt persisted.

I carefully reached out, but as my fingers neared the feathers, I felt the faint caress of magic. And, underneath that, evil.

I quickly withdrew my hand. *Belle, I'm going to need my spell stones.*

I'll have to go back for them.

Do so. I'll wait. The magic might not have had the feel or look of a spell, but that didn't mean a whole lot given my lack of knowledge and training when it came to spell craft. I wasn't about to risk triggering something that could reverberate through the rest of reservation, doing God only knows what damage.

The water seeping into my runners was damn icy, so I splashed back to the bank then sat on a nearby rock. After taking off my shoes and socks and squeezing out as much water as I could, I laid them out on the rock, hoping the day's heat still emanating from it would go some way to drying them. Then, with little else to do but wait, I hugged my knees close to my chest and kept the flashlight's beam pointed at the feathers, trying to figure out what lay within them.

It was nearly half an hour before lights began to dance through the trees above me. Several minutes later, Belle appeared at the top of the scree slope, and she wasn't alone. Ashworth was with her.

Thought it prudent, she said. *If there is some sort of magic attached to the feathers, he can deal with it.*

Good thinking, 99.

I'm not just a pretty face and fabulous bod, you know. Besides, if anything is going to blow up, I'd rather it do so all over Ashworth than you.

I snorted. *You're forgetting the fact that I'll be standing right beside him. But I don't think anything will blow up.*

You can't be certain of that.

Well, no, but I've spent the last twenty-eight or so minutes studying those feathers, and the magic within them simply doesn't feel active.

If there's one thing this reservation has taught me, it's that things aren't always what they seem.

A statement I couldn't disagree with.

Ashworth helped Belle down the slope—although she didn't really need it given she was probably stronger and steadier than either him or me—and then strode toward me, looking more like an aging biker than an RWA witch of some power. Tonight's outfit—a moth-eaten Metallica T-shirt and faded, grimy jeans that were frayed at the pockets and knees—didn't help that impression. Though I doubted any biker worth his salt would wear red sneakers so old that his right toe stuck out. Obviously Eli—who was Ashworth's partner—hadn't yet followed through with his threat to burn the damn things.

"I can always rely on you to break the evening's boredom," he said, his wrinkled features creased into a wide smile.

I raised an eyebrow. "I thought you were entertaining relatives tonight?"

"Eli's relatives, not mine. I love the man, but his sisters drive me insane." He stopped beside me and studied the feathers. "I'm not feeling a spell, but there's definitely something there."

I nodded. "The stone's surface is covered in blood, but I suspect most of it is old. The blood on the feathers is fresher."

Belle handed me the backpack. "Our White Lady hasn't completely disappeared, either. She's watching from a distance."

My gaze snapped to hers. "Can you contact her?"

She shook her head. "She's right on the edge of my range, and without a name or a specific image to lock on to, I risk summoning every other ghost who haunts the area."

"Not something I'd recommend, given mass summonings often end disastrously." Ashworth handed Belle his flashlight, then took off his shoes and socks and dumped them onto the rock next to mine. "Shall we go investigate?"

I slung the pack over my shoulder and followed him into the water. And quickly discovered the pebbles that lined the riverbed were *not* as smooth as they looked. "I take it you've witnessed such a summoning?"

"I was once assigned a case where a couple of teenagers had gotten hold of a Ouija board and decided it might be fun to raise a soul." He strode toward the larger rock, not seeming to care about the roughness underfoot. "Unfortunately, they did so in the middle of a graveyard and one of them was an untrained talent. Not only did they end up with more than a dozen souls answering, there were multiple generations of the same family who did *not* get on."

We reached the rock and stopped. Ashworth raised a hand and skimmed it above the blood and the feathers. "It's definitely not a spell."

"Then what is it?"

He hesitated, his eyes narrowing. "I think the magic— and the evil—we can feel is an intrinsic part of whatever bird these feathers came from."

"That suggests their origin is shape shifter rather than a bird." While some birds—like magpies in breeding season— could be evil, attacking bastards, it wasn't an intrinsic part of their nature.

"Yes," Ashworth said, "although whether the blood and bones belong to said shifter or their victim is another matter entirely."

"It's doubtful the White Lady would have led us here if whoever those feathers belonged to was dead," Belle commented.

"Agreed. But the truly important question here is, are these feathers related to last night's murders? Or is it a completely separate case?"

"Yet another question we currently can't answer," I said.

His grin flashed again. "Not true. A little magical divination should do the trick, I think."

"But there's little more than old blood and feathers here —how are you going to divine anything from them?"

He glanced at me, eyes gleaming in the light. "Your witchy knowledge—or lack thereof—is sometimes very shocking, you know that?"

I grinned. "My witchy knowledge—or lack thereof—saved your ass, old man, so don't be preaching at me."

He chuckled softly. "We're not going to be able to use our spell stones to set a protective circle, thanks to the water, so we'll have to create an incorporeal one."

"You'll have to step me through it, as I've never done something like that."

He nodded and glanced around. "Belle, keep an eye on the specter, just in case this is some sort of trap. White ladies often have a vengeful bent, and we have no idea what this one wants as yet."

"I will, but given she ran the minute Liz mentioned I was a spirit talker, I don't think she presents any immediate danger."

Ashworth grunted and glanced at me. "Ready?"

"I guess. What do you want me to do?"

"Stand on the opposite side of the rock. Once we join hands, I'll start the spell. You repeat my words, and the result should be a protection circle that's anchored by our presence rather than spell stones."

I raised an eyebrow. "Why do I have to go into the deeper water?"

"Because I'm older and frailer."

I snorted and moved into position. Once I'd positioned the flashlight securely on the rock, I reached out and clasped his hands. His power crawled over my fingers, probing my energy, testing its depths—an automatic reaction rather than a deliberate one. Even so, he sucked in a breath. "Damn, the wild magic is strong in you these days."

I met his gaze warily. Ashworth might be aware of my connection with the wild magic, but I hadn't yet mentioned the reason I believed it was happening. The fewer people who knew about *that*, the less chance there was of the information getting back to my parents or husband.

And yet it *would* happen. Eventually. No matter how discreet Monty and Ashworth were in their requests for information on either the wild magic or human interaction with it, sooner or later, one of the higher-ups would get curious and come investigating.

I'd always had my mom's features, but with my eyes now silver rather than green, there could be no mistaking whose daughter I was. The only reason it hadn't happened before now was the fact that all the witches—Monty aside—who'd come into the reservation so far, generally had little physical contact with either Canberra or the High Council.

I tried to ignore the almost instinctive wave of trepidation and fear that rose whenever I thought of the place I'd once called home, and said, "Did you ever get an answer to that request you put in for more information about it?"

"She's still searching—it takes a while to do these things when you're trying to be careful."

I hoped she was doing more than being careful. I hoped she was using every trick in the book—magical or not—to cover her search tracks. "Will the presence of the wild magic affect your spell?"

"Given its tendency to weave itself through your spells these days, I daresay it will—but it'll probably only strengthen it and that's never a bad thing. Ready?"

I took a deep breath to center my energy and then nodded. He began the spell, and faint threads of gold pulsed into existence. I waited until he'd finished the first layer, and then repeated his words, weaving my spell through his, keeping my threads close without the two actually touching. We continued on, layering in multiple levels of protection until the air shimmered and a mix of gold and silver threads formed a wide dome over the two of us.

Once we'd both tied off the spell and then activated it, he released my fingers and said, "Right, let's see what's going on with these damn feathers."

He swung his backpack around, pulled out a silver knife, and then carefully touched the nearest feather. When nothing happened, he pushed the tip of the knife deeper into the pile and then spread them out. The wind stirred, catching several of the smaller feathers and tossing them into the air. I half raised a hand to grab them, then immediately clenched my fingers against the action. Ashworth hadn't yet cleared them of any spell, so caution was the best option. Besides, he didn't seem too worried about them drifting away; his concentration was on the larger ones currently pinned under his knife. His magic surged anew, a force so strong that in this confined space it made the hairs on my arms stand on end. He spent several minutes probing the feathers, then grunted and put his knife away.

"There's definitely no spell. It's residue we're feeling, nothing more." His gaze met mine. "Do you want to try your psychometry?"

I hesitated and then slowly reached out. The caress of darkness was definitely fainter now than it had been only half an hour ago, which suggested the residue was rapidly fading. If I didn't try this now—if I waited until we got the feathers back to the café—we might well lose any chance of uncovering just who or what these feathers belonged to.

I'm here, Belle said. *I'll pull you out if anything nasty happens.*

I know. But it didn't do a lot to ease the trepidation stirring inside.

I picked up one of the larger feathers, being careful not

to touch any of the blood staining the striped quills. For several seconds I simply stared at it; then I opened the psychic gates and reached.

Images came. *Clouds above me, trees below, juveniles on either side, wing tip to wing tip. Hunger stirring, sharp eyes scanning. Movement. Prey. We swoop lower, skimming past leaves and branches, silently approaching. The prey senses us, starts to run. Too late. Far too late... then energy hits us from the side and flings us off course. We tumble, tail over beak. My sisters hit tree trunks. I roll on, tearing feather and flesh as I drop into a ravine and crash onto a rock. Lie there, stunned, unable to move, blood and feathers and pain rolling all around me...*

The vision faded, and I blinked.

"Anything?" Ashworth asked.

I twirled the feather lightly between my fingers, watching the paler stripes glimmer in the light as I gathered my thoughts. "We're definitely dealing with a shape shifter, but there was something odd about the flow of her memories."

"Define odd."

I frowned. "There were fragmented and yet not. It's almost as if she wasn't entirely human—"

"Well, she's not—she's a shape shifter in bird form."

"Shifters are still human," I replied tartly. "They're just from a different evolutionary branch of the tree."

"I think you've been spending too much time around Ashworth," Belle said, her voice dry. "You sounded just like him then."

I snorted and dropped the feather. "From what Aiden has said, shifting from human to animal form doesn't alter your being or your thought process. The owner of these feathers just didn't feel right."

Which, considering the fading caress of evil still emanating from them, wasn't really surprising.

"What was she doing in the area?" Ashworth asked.

"Hunting—although I never saw the prey—and she wasn't alone. There were three of them." I paused. "Something blindsided them as they neared their prey and sent them tumbling. The chief shifter was the one who landed here."

"I'm guessing you didn't see who or what hit them?"

"I didn't see the who, but the what was magic."

"Suggesting we have another witch on the reservation."

"Our specter is capable of magic, remember," Belle said. "And she's the one who led us here."

Ashworth frowned. "I think I'm going to have to contact Canberra about this—it's not a situation I've ever come across before. Which, I might add, seems to happen a lot in this place."

"Monty will be miffed if you don't consult with him first," I said.

"To which I can only say, good."

I grinned. "He *is* the reservation witch—"

"Not at the moment he's not. Let me gather the feathers and then we can dismantle the protection circle."

He pulled several small plastic bags out of his pack, putting the feathers in one and then chipping off some of the blood from the stone with his knife before putting it in the other. Once the spell had been dealt with, we made our way back to the shoreline.

"What are you going to do with the samples?" Belle reached out to grab my hand and helped me out.

"Thought we might go back to your place and try a little location spell."

"Not without eating first, we're not," I said.

"With that, I agree. What's on the menu tonight?"

"Nothing—not for you, anyway." Belle's voice was dry. "You need to go back to your guests. We can meet up once you've finished playing host and we've consumed the takeout waiting in the warmer."

He shook his head sadly, but the expression was somewhat spoiled by the glimmer of amusement in his eyes. "You're cruel women, the pair of you."

Belle snorted. "And now you're dilly-dallying. Move, old man."

"You know, if Monty had called me that, he would have gotten a clip over the ears."

"He *has* called you that," I said, amused. "Multiple times."

"True, but I've only got so much patience."

I snorted and started up the hill. From what I'd seen, patience and Ira Ashworth weren't often bosom buddies.

By the time we'd scrambled up the loose slope, even Belle was breathing heavily. We made our way through the scrub, following the clear trail I'd made when I crashed after the specter. Our new SUV—a deep red Subaru Outback that was totally awesome to drive—sat this side of the track, while Ashworth's borrowed vehicle sat on the other.

"See you in a couple of hours," he said, then climbed into his SUV and disappeared down the road.

We followed at a more sedate pace. Once home, Belle grabbed the containers out of the warmer, while I got plates and cutlery.

"Might want to get another set," Belle said as I placed them on the table. "Aiden's about to knock on the door."

I all but bounced across the room, unlocking the door and then throwing my arms around his neck, kissing him with all the passion I'd somehow contained in the forest.

"That's one hell of a nice welcome," he said, when he finally could.

I laughed. "When it comes to things I desire, you're a smidge above food, so consider yourself lucky."

His gaze went past me, and his nostrils flared. "Is that black bean beef I'm smelling?"

"Yes." I stepped back and waved him in. "There's also lemon chicken, sweet and sour pork, roast duck, and special fried rice."

"Are you expecting an army or something?"

Belle came out of the kitchen with the last of the containers. "No, just a werewolf who times his arrival to perfection."

He laughed and sat down. I continued on, grabbing an additional plate and some cutlery before sitting beside him.

"How's Joe? Did you manage to get him out?"

"It took a bit of effort, but we did eventually extract him. Aside from a shattered leg, he seems to have come out of it all relatively unscathed." He began filling up his plate. "What were you two and Ashworth doing near the Poverty Valley Track?"

I raised my eyebrows. "How did you know we were all there?"

"It's my job to notice things." A smile teased the corners of his lips. "And that red SUV of yours doesn't exactly fade into the background."

"Which is why that color was picked." Belle claimed the lemon chicken. "Given your overprotective tendencies when it comes to our girl, you will at least be able to see the car easily enough if we get lost or get into trouble in some forgotten back forest."

"While that may or may not be true, I haven't dared

bring out the overprotectiveness since that last flash of temper."

"Neither of us believes you were, in any way, intimidated by that very minor display of annoyance, Ranger." My voice was dry and his smile widened.

"So, to repeat, what were the three of you doing there?"

"Following a ghost."

His eyebrows rose. "Why?"

"Because she's been following me, and I thought I'd return the favor and see what she wanted."

"Did you get an answer?"

"Do we ever?" Belle said, amused.

"Well, yes, even if it does sometimes take a while."

"I suspect this is going to be one of those times." I piled up my plate. "Although she did lead us to a blood-covered, bone-strewn rock and some random feathers. We collected samples of each, and Ashworth's coming over once his dinner guests leave. We're going to attempt a locator spell."

"On the samples or the ghost?"

"On the feathers. They belonged to a shifter who felt evil."

"Then I'll definitely stick around, just in case."

"Which is just another excuse to consume more brownies after you've finished the Chinese," Belle said.

"A fact I cannot deny."

I shook my head and got down to the business of eating. Conversation flowed easily, and we were halfway through cake and coffee when Ashworth finally appeared.

"The bloody rellies wouldn't leave," he grumbled as he stomped through the door. "I was just about to give them a magical prod when they finally made tracks."

"I'm sure Eli would have loved that," Belle commented.

"The oldest of his sisters was at that drunk enough to be

argumentative stage, so he was seriously considering doing it himself."

"Wouldn't they have sensed it?" I asked curiously. "They're all witches, aren't they?"

"Growing up with three younger sisters made him very adept at concealing spells. For a start, it was the only way he could keep them from snooping in his room and stealing his things." He tugged the plastic bags out of his pocket. "Shall we do this here, or in your reading room?"

I hesitated. "While a locator spell is rarely dangerous, we've no true idea what we're dealing with, so caution is the better option."

He nodded and continued on into the room. I picked up my coffee and followed, but Belle and Aiden remained at the table. Aside from the reading room being on the smallish side, Belle could follow events through our connection.

If there's an event to follow, she commented. *It's been hours since we found those feathers, and the resonance was fading fairly fast.*

Ashworth is a more knowledgeable spell caster than us, so he should succeed where we can't. I closed the door, then moved around to the table and sat opposite Ashworth.

I'm glad you didn't say he's stronger magically. Her voice was dry. *Because he's not, you know. Not these days.*

The wild magic hasn't altered my magic capabilities that much, Belle.

I wouldn't bet on that.

Neither would I, if I was being at all honest. I took a sip of coffee. "What's the plan?"

He placed the plastic bags on the table. "Given how quickly the echoes were fading, we'll use your psychometry skills to pick the feather with the strongest resonance, and then weave a locator around it."

"The only locator spells I know are fairly basic—"

Liar, liar, came Belle's comment,

Enough comments from the peanut gallery, if you please.

As her chuckle ran through my mind, Ashworth said, "Which is why I'll be doing it rather than you."

I nodded. "What happens if the shape shifter is also magic capable?"

"They're very rare beasts—"

"Then how do you account for the magic clinging to the feathers?"

"It could be nothing more than the innate magic every shifter or werewolf possess that allows them to shift—"

"Except it isn't magic that gives them that ability, but rather DNA adaptions."

"Yes, but it's *magic* that covers the change and saves the rest of us from being grossed out." He motioned toward the feathers. "The sooner we start, the better chance we'll have."

I somewhat reluctantly unzipped the top of the plastic bag and then upended it, letting the feathers float to the table. Only one held any resonance, and even that was barely detectable. I picked it up and opened the psychic gates. No images swarmed my mind, and there was no sense of where the shifter was or what she might be doing. Going deeper didn't help; too much time had elapsed, and the connection between this feather and the shifter was all but severed.

"Anything?" Ashworth asked, a touch impatiently.

"Yes, but it's too vague for my psi abilities. It might even be too vague for a spell."

He grunted and plucked the feather from me. After a

moment, his power rose; the protections within the room stirred briefly in response and then died down when no threat eventuated. I narrowed my gaze and watched him weave the various threads around the feather. While I couldn't always remember the exact wording of a spell, I could generally visualize the patterns and then repeat it. It certainly *wasn't* the approved way of doing things, but it had always worked for Belle and me.

When he tied off and then activated the spell, the threads sparkled lightly, an indication that the spell was not only working but also feeding him information.

"Unfortunately, the link to our shifter remains tenuous," he said, "so we'll need to get a move on if we're to have hope of tracking her down."

"Any luck?" Aiden asked as we both came out.

"Yes, but I have no idea how long the spell will remain viable," Ashworth replied. "Do you want to drive, Ranger?"

Aiden immediately gulped down the rest of his coffee and then led the way out. Belle handed me the backpack as I walked past and then followed to lock the door.

"I'll do some research while you're out," she said. "Although if shifters capable of magic *are* a rarity, then Gran might not have much information on them."

"There's always Google if we draw a blank with her books."

Belle snorted. "Because Google isn't at all full of all sorts of misinformation when it comes to magic and the supernatural."

I grinned. "There's plenty of wheat amongst Google's chaff."

"Yeah, but who wants to sort through chaff all the time?"

I laughed and ran after the two men. Once we were

seated in Aiden's truck, Ashworth said, "Do a U-turn and head toward Moonlight Flat."

Aiden did so and then flattened the accelerator. "Is there any indication this shifter is up to no good?"

Ashworth hesitated. "Other than the fact that evil seemed part of its essence, no."

"Meaning she could just have stopped in the reservation to hunt down some food."

"Yes," I said. "But it's highly unlikely, given she was attacked by magic from an unknown practitioner *before* she got to her prey."

Aiden grunted. "If that's the case, why haven't either of you sensed the presence of another witch in the reservation?"

Ashworth directed him left onto Murphy Street and then growled, "We're witches, not radars. We don't have magi-sensitive antenna that lets us know the minute another witch moves into the same area."

"Besides which," I added, "the reservation is huge. We'd sense them if they were on the same street, but anything beyond that can be haphazard."

"And yet you can sense the use of magic from a fairly decent distance, so why one and not the other?"

"Because most witches generally mute their output," Ashworth growled. "Makes it easier to be around each other —no power friction, if you like."

Aiden glanced at me through the rear-view mirror. "Do you and Belle do this?"

"Yes, but not entirely successfully."

"Which was the reason I suspected there was more to the pair of them than what they were admitting, remember," Ashworth said.

Because he'd seen how deeply my magic meshed with

Belle's—something that shouldn't have been possible even if she was my familiar. Not so completely, at any rate. It was certainly something I didn't want other witches seeing, although none of the other witches who'd been called into the reservation to date appeared to have noticed.

Or maybe they noticed and just didn't comment on it, Belle said. *Maybe they simply made a side note on their reports to the RWA and Canberra. It would certainly go some way to explain your conviction that your parents will come calling.*

Could be. To Ashworth, I added, "Which means you need to teach us the proper method of concealment, because I certainly don't want any other witches spotting what you did."

"Few other witches have my experience, lass," he said. "But yes, I'll teach you both my highly modified and very dependable muting spell. Another left at the next street, Ranger."

Aiden briefly slowed to get around the corner. "Do you still have the bones and blood samples you took?"

"Yes," Ashworth said. "Why?"

"I'll get Ciara to analyze them. We'll at least know whether they belonged to a human or animal."

Ashworth grunted and then leaned forward to put a plastic bag into the center console. "Just in case I get side-tracked and forget later."

"Thanks."

The deeper we moved into Moonlight Flats area, the narrower and rougher the roads got. Acreage properties soon gave way to scrubland, and the road began to climb. It was the perfect area for hawks and eagles to hunt, which made me wonder why—if our shifter had decided to bunk down in this area—she was seeking prey in more distant forests. Not that the diggings area was very far away, especially by wing.

"Here—stop here," Ashworth said, and scrambled out the minute Aiden did.

I grabbed my gear and followed him out. Once I'd pulled out the flashlight, I hooked my arms through the backpack's shoulder straps and scanned the area. The cicadas weren't as noisy here, which meant the haunting note of an owl was clearly audible. The wind stirred restlessly through the trees, and the moon silvered the wattles. Nothing moved through the immediate darkness, not even the little bats that were plentiful in this area. Though Castle Rock was little more than ten minutes away, it seemed like we were in the middle of nowhere.

Ashworth walked around the truck and then into the trees lining the road, raising his free arm to brush away the lower-hanging branches. Aiden caught them as they whipped back, only releasing them once I'd moved past.

We wound through the trees, moving deeper into the forest. There was some movement to be heard now—possums or sugar gliders scrambling away from us, no doubt—but overall, the forest remained quiet. It was almost as if the trees were holding their collective breath.

Tension stirred through me, even though the gentle breeze held no hint of evil and there was no whisper of a threat.

"Ashworth," I asked eventually, "are we getting any closer?"

I couldn't help the uneasiness in my voice, and Aiden glanced sharply over his shoulder. "You're sensing something?"

I hesitated. "Not exactly."

"Which is generally a precursor to 'yes, I am' and then hell breaking loose." His voice was grim. "Ashworth?"

"As I said earlier, the resonance is so faint, there's no guarantee the spell will actually lead us to our shifter."

"But you're still picking up a signal?"

"I wouldn't be trudging through this goddamn forest if I wasn't, laddie."

Aiden snorted and glanced at me. "I don't suppose you can define the direction of whatever—"

The rest of his words were cut off by a scream.

A horrendous, high-pitched scream.

The same sort of scream last night's victim had uttered before death had swept in and ripped his flesh from his bones.

FIVE

Aiden leaped forward, his form swiftly changing from human to wolf.

"Wait for us!" I yelled.

He didn't. I swore and hastily cast a spell after him. It hit just as he leaped over a log and disappeared from sight. For one horrible second, I thought I'd missed. Then the spell came to life and a sparkling thread appeared in the air, spooling out between Aiden and me, providing a visible trail to follow.

Ashworth immediately did so, leaping the log with surprising dexterity. "I hope he's wearing the charm you made him, because he could be in a whole world of trouble if the flesh stripper is the cause of that scream."

"The only time he takes it off is when I need to add another spell layer." And while the 'repel demons' spell I'd attached to the charm was fairly general, it should still protect him from *thi*s demon long enough for us to catch up with him. "What about the directional beacon on the feather? Has it changed at all?"

"Yes—it's now ahead of us."

"Suggesting she heard the scream and decided to investigate."

"Possibly, although you'd think anyone with any sort of sense would be running in the opposite direction."

"We're not."

"Yes, but I'm paid to run after bad guys, and you're the reservation's chosen guardian."

I opened my mouth to argue, then snapped it shut again. While Aiden's sister—who, via a spell cast by her witch husband, was now forever a part of the wild magic—was the true guardian here, few knew that. And because she was something more than spirit, I was basically the only one she could communicate with. Thanks, no doubt, to my own growing connection with this place.

The screaming stopped abruptly, and silence returned. It was eerie. Unnerving.

Ashworth swore and picked up his pace. For an old man, he moved damn fast. I did my best to keep up with him, batting branches away from my face but tearing clothes and skin. It didn't matter. Nothing did, except getting to the attack point not too far behind Aiden.

A thick sense of evil now stained the drifting breeze. I swallowed heavily and wove a repelling spell around my fingers. A spell to cage whatever evil lay ahead would have been far better, but I had no idea if the cages I could construct were strong enough to contain a demon so powerful it could strip flesh from bones in a matter of minutes.

The trees abruptly gave way to a small, rock-strewn track. Ashworth skidded to a halt, brown dust pluming around his legs as he looked around and then turned left, following the faint glimmer down the road.

I followed, my gaze on the uneven ground rather than

the scrub on either side. Even so, I was aware that the locator thread no longer spooled; Aiden had stopped.

I hoped he was okay. Hoped the silence meant the demon had fled, even if it also meant we were once again too late to save whoever had been attacked.

The track widened and the pulse of my spell grew stronger. I found speed from who knew where and all but flew over the ground, catching up to Ashworth and then pulling slightly ahead. Had Aiden in any way been in danger, Katie would have no doubt come to get me, but I still needed to see him with my own eyes.

Which said a whole lot more about the depths of my feelings for the man than I really wanted to think about.

The trees thinned out and the road flattened. A figure appeared up ahead, his hair silvered by the moonlight. Relief surged but just as swiftly died.

Aiden might be okay, but death now rode in the air, and it was accompanied by such a fierce wave of confusion and agony that it sent me stumbling.

Ashworth grabbed me before I hit the ground. "You okay, lassie?"

I dismissed the tendrils of the repel spell from around my fingers and then nodded. "It's the backwash of the victim's emotion. You go on; I'll try to strengthen my shields."

He hesitated long enough to ensure I wasn't about to fall over again and then continued toward Aiden. I retreated just beyond the reach of the emotional wave then took a deep breath and concentrated on my shields. I needed to double down on what already existed, rebuilding the unseen walls just as I'd been taught so long ago, before adding the tweaks I'd learned since. Only this time, those tweaks involved the wild magic. It was in me, a part of me, and even in something as simple as this—something that didn't involve magic, but rather mental strength—it would not be denied.

Which is a bit of a worry, really, came Belle's comment.

I think that qualifies for the understatement of the year.

She chuckled softly. *I can help with additional shielding, if you want. It'll only be temporary, but that's all you need right now.*

Hang on, and I'll test the psychic waters.

I finished shoring things up then drew in a deep breath and took several steps forward. The wave of emotion washed around me, but it held none of the fierceness of before. I moved closer, ready to jump back the second it became too much. The dark wave grew stronger, a turbulence that would wash me away the second my shields wavered. They didn't.

Excellent, Belle said. *But I'll remain in contact and jump in the second they do.*

Thanks.

Aiden glanced up as I approached. "You okay? You look a little pale."

I nodded and stopped beside him. The bones once again sat on the edge of a crossroad, although this one was little more than the intersection of two walking tracks. They were also somewhat scattered rather than either buried or neatly piled, and I couldn't help but wonder why. It almost looked as if there'd been some sort of feeding frenzy... I swallowed heavily, then switched off the flashlight and shoved it in my pocket. I really didn't need to see anything more.

Ashworth stood several feet away from the bulk of the remains, probing them magically. After a few more seconds, he grunted and stepped back. "There's nothing dangerous here."

Aiden walked closer. I remained where I was. My shields might be holding but I didn't want to push them.

"And the demon?" Aiden asked.

"Long gone." Ashworth pulled the feather from his pocket. The spell had faded to the point where it was little more than a faint spark. "And the shifter has also left the area."

"Could the shifter and this demon be connected?" Aiden asked.

Ashworth hesitated. "It's always possible, but the shifter's trail was heading in the opposite direction until the victim screamed."

"Maybe she raced here in order to join in on the fun." I rubbed my arms and did my best to ignore the blood slowly dripping from the leaves above the main pile of bones.

Aiden glanced at me. "Shifters don't eat humans."

"Evil shifters might. I don't think we dare discount the possibility."

"Agreed," Ashworth said heavily. "How long until Ciara gets here, Ranger?"

Aiden glanced at his watch. "It'll be Luke rather than Ciara, and he lives near Maldoon. It'll probably be another ten or fifteen minutes before he arrives."

I wasn't sure I could stand here that long. The dark wave might not be sweeping me away, but it continued to press against my newer shields and might eventually break them down.

"I think I'll head back to the truck—there's not much I can do here anyway." I met Aiden's gaze. "And yes, I can find the way back without you having to escort me."

A smile twitched his lips. "I wasn't about to suggest you couldn't, but—"

"You've a crime scene to process," I cut in, perhaps a little more curtly than necessary. "And there's nothing I can do here that Ashworth can't."

He raised his eyebrows. "As I was about to say, it'd be quicker if you followed the path behind you. It heads out onto the main track we drove up here on. If you turn left and follow the road around the sweeping bend, you'll find the truck."

"Oh. Thanks."

His smile got stronger. "If you do happen to get lost, shout. I'll hear."

"I will."

I spun around and quickly retreated. The moonlight provided enough light to see by, so I didn't bother using the flashlight. Thankfully, the emotional wave fell away quickly and the normal sounds of the night returned, free of any sort of death or danger. I drew in a deep breath and released it slowly. Hopefully, that would be—

Don't, Belle cut in. *You're only tempting fate if you finish that sentence.*

I couldn't help smiling. *I think even fate would agree she's thrown enough shit our way tonight.*

Belle groaned. *Seriously, you had to do it—had to tempt her.*

I chuckled softly. *Did you manage to find anything in the books?*

There was a vague mention about Empusa, who are demons that feed on the flesh of men, particularly those who are sleeping and/or virgins.

None of our victims were sleeping. Whether or not

they'd been virgins would be impossible to discover unless Belle contacted their souls.

Which we might have to do if we don't quickly get a handle on what we're dealing with.

Technically, we shouldn't be dealing with anything.

Her mental snort echoed loudly. *You no more believe that we'll ever be allowed to step away from these investigations than I do. Not now.*

Which was another of those statements I couldn't disagree with. *Did you find much else about them?*

Not in this book, although she did mention a fun fact— Empusa were once thought to be demigoddesses who had a leg of bronze and the foot of a horse.

Something that wouldn't go unnoticed in the general population, I'm thinking.

Which is why they're more likely to be hiding out in a remote area. It could also explain why their victims are being found in such places.

The scrub behind Monty's isn't exactly remote, and the first two victims were found there. An owl hooted softly, a haunting sound in the silence. Uneasiness stirred, even though there was nothing in the air or the night to suggest danger. I frowned and picked up the pace. *Was there any suggestion on how to track or kill an Empusa if that is what we are dealing with?*

No. As I said, the mention was vague, but it at least gives us a possible starting point. She paused. *Damn it, Monty's just arrived at the café.*

Why the hell is he there at this hour? He should be home resting.

She didn't immediately answer, no doubt scanning Monty's thoughts to see what he was up to. *He rang Eli to see what was happening, because Ashworth wasn't answering his phone. He's coming here because I wouldn't answer mine.*

I snorted. *So you basically brought this visit on yourself. No sympathy.*

I'll remember that comment the next time I have to make you a revive potion.

You couldn't possibly make them taste any worse than they already do.

I wouldn't bet on that.

Neither would I, actually. *If you don't want to entertain him until I return, throw him in the Outback and come pick me up. He can wait next to Aiden's truck and get a direct update.*

That means putting up with his chatter for the fifteen minutes it'll take to get there.

Better than entertaining him for the hour or so he'll wait until I get back.

Point. See you soon.

As her thoughts left mine, the owl hooted again, and that surely meant there wasn't much around to disturb it. So why was I suddenly so spooked?

I rubbed my arms and continued on. Up ahead, the trees arched over the path, blocking the moon's light and creating a tunnel of deeper darkness. Though I could see moonlight at the far end, my steps nevertheless slowed. No sense of wrongness or evil rode the breeze, and yet...

I shivered and got the flashlight out, but the bright light only made the shadows seem that much more threatening. It was possible—more than possible—I was reacting to things that didn't exist. That after the discovery of an evil shifter and another flesh-stripped victim, the psychic part of me simply expected something else to happen. Death didn't always travel in threes, but I *had* chanced fate with my comment to Belle. It'd be just my luck that this was the one time fate was listening.

I flexed my fingers and wove another repelling spell around them. As protection spells went, it was pretty much a good all-rounder that would counter most things intent on evil, be they supernatural *or* human. And the charm around my neck could protect me from the rest.

I hoped.

I marched on, my gaze on the inky shadows beyond the light's beam. Nothing moved... but even as that thought crossed my mind, something did.

My heart leaped into my throat, but almost immediately dropped again. Wild magic. It was nothing more than wild magic.

I swallowed heavily and continued. The threads drifted toward me, pulsing brightly in the shadows, a song of power I could both see and hear. Its source was the main wellspring, which was positioned within the O'Connor compound, and it really shouldn't have been out in such force here. Or, for that matter, anywhere else. Not now that it had been contained and protected.

It's not like either of us knows much about the stuff, came Belle's comment. *For all we know, this behavior is very normal for wellsprings, protected or not.*

Possibly. Where are you and Monty?

Just reached the Moonlight Flats Road, so about eight minutes away.

I'm farther up the track than Aiden's truck.

We'll find you.

Of that I had no doubt. I just hoped she did so before the odd feeling of unease crystalized into a reality.

More wild magic emerged from the trees; it chased away the shadows and shone off the overarching branches, silvering the leaves. A couple of threads twined themselves around my right wrist, making it look as if I were wearing a bracelet of glowing moonlight. While the sheer closeness of its power made the hairs on my arms stand on end, I nevertheless felt safer. And that, I suspected, was its intention. Whether it also meant there *was* something out there to fear, I couldn't say.

I flexed my fingers and kept walking. The majority of the wild magic floated beside me, the gentle hum of its energy rolling across the night. As I drew closer to the end of the tunnel, all but a couple of those threads faded away. The remainder continued to pace me, and I had a distinct feeling there was a purpose behind its actions. Which shouldn't be possible, because the wild magic wasn't sentient—unless, of course, my connection to it worked both ways, and it was drawing as much from me as I was from it.

It was yet another scary thought, and one that made me wonder where it would all end.

I came out into the moonlight and took a deep breath. It didn't ease the tension within; the wild magic still paced me, still encircled my wrist, and that only amplified the belief that it was here for a reason.

After a few minutes, with the main road finally in sight, the threads pacing me darted sideways and disappeared into the scrub on the left-hand side of the trail. When I didn't follow, they returned and tugged lightly at my hand. It was then I heard a soft voice say, *Follow.*

Katie.

Her energy—her soul—had somehow infused the magic of the main wellspring.

Only when you are connected, came the response. *Follow.*

I glanced down at the bracelet of wild magic. It was

obviously the connection, but the fact it had obeyed Katie suggested the spell that had been cast to make her part of the younger wellspring's magic was now affecting the main one—something else that shouldn't have been possible given spells normally died when the caster did.

Except this spell was cast in the presence of wild magic, came Belle's thought. *It's also possible Gabe always intended her to be able to command both wellsprings. He did foresee she was meant to be this reservation's guardian, remember.*

It would have taken one hell of a spell to do something like that.

The spell did blow him apart, she said. *And very few are capable of that.*

The wisp of Katie's energy released me and spun back toward the trees. I flexed my fingers and then followed as bid. Leaves crunched under every step, and nearby shrubs rustled as small animals skittered away. I hoped like hell none of them were snakes; they weren't generally active at night, but the weather had been warm enough lately to stir them. I kept half an eye on the ground, just in case.

After several more minutes, we came into a small clearing. A semicircular mound of rocks and dirt taller than me dominated the area to my left; on the top of this a number of large tree branches had fallen, and in such a way that they formed a roof over the rocks to create a cave.

I had no sense of anything untoward, so why on earth had I been led here?

A little confused, I walked across to the cave—and almost immediately gagged. The emanating stench was one of dead meat combined with the sickly sweetness that sometimes came with cheap perfume. I shoved a hand over my nose and stuck to breathing through my mouth. Then, fearing what I was about to find, I squatted down and shone the flashlight's beam in.

The cave was deeper than it looked and would have fit at least several kneeling people inside. The dry grass had been flattened, suggesting something—or someone—had been using it as a den, but the ground was too dry to hold any prints. There were a few bones scattered about, but the puffs of gray fur and dried bits of leathery-looking tail ends suggested they belonged to either rabbits or bush rats. A fox must have set up home here; it certainly wouldn't have been a werewolf, as they didn't hunt within the reservation—not in wolf form anyway. According to Aiden, it simply wasn't worth the risk, given the reservation depended on tourism to survive. Rumors of wolves on hunting sprees would be the quickest way known to kill that. They might have become an accepted part of the world's fabric a very long time ago, but old fears still ran deep in many sections of society.

And yet, despite all that, I did have to wonder if his statement was the absolute truth, given how fiercely the three packs here guarded their compound boundaries. No humans were allowed within them—not without permission from the pack's alphas, anyway—and even then, there had to be a *major* crisis for ingress to be allowed.

Despite the fact I was going out with Aiden, I'd only gone inside the O'Connor compound twice—once to help Ashworth protect the wellspring, and once to save him from the dark witch who'd been determined to claim the wellspring for his own. We had crossed the boundary edges over the course of other investigations, but that was it. I'd never met Aiden's parents or—Ciara aside—any of his siblings. I wasn't ever likely to, either; I was a fun time, not a long time, as far as Aiden and his kin were concerned.

I ignored the ache that rose and studied the cave for a

few seconds longer, looking for but not finding the source of the putrid scent.

In the end, I gave up and instead walked around the rocks to see what else was here. There had to be something —I doubted Katie would have led me so far off the track just to show me rabbit and rat remains.

And I was right; the rock on the opposite side of the mound was not only stained with blood, but had feathers lying at its base. Those feathers looked exactly like the ones we'd found earlier this evening.

A fox wasn't the only one who'd been using these rocks for a lair.

My gaze jerked toward the trees—a ridiculous reaction, given that even if the shifter was watching me, I wasn't likely to spot her. But the evil I'd felt earlier no longer stained the air, and while that was no guarantee I was alone, it nevertheless released some of the tension.

I returned my gaze to the rock. The blood had to belong to the shifter, because surely there would have been at least some scraps of skin and bone if it had come from her prey. But if she'd been seriously injured when the magical blow had thrown her so badly off course, why hadn't she shifted to human form and healed herself? Why had she moved from there to here in order to bleed and shed more feathers? That made no sense.

Unless the magic that blew her off course also somehow restricted her ability to shift out of bird form, came Belle's thought.

My gaze rose to the trees I'd come out of. *You feel close.*

That's because we are. I told Monty the wild magic had come to fetch you, and he immediately wanted to see what you'd found.

He's on crutches.

He is indeed, and tripping over every tree root and rock there is to find. A mix of amusement and annoyance ran through her mental tone.

If he's not careful, he'll break his other leg.

I did mention that. He scoffed at my lack of faith in his balance.

I snorted. *I'm surprised he hasn't used some sort of transport spell to make things easier.*

He said they're physically draining and aren't good over long distances. He didn't want to risk exerting himself too much when he might need all his strength later.

He's not exactly conserving strength crutching his way through scrub.

I also mentioned that. He gave me a disapproving look and told me to get a move on.

I chuckled softly and held a hand above the pile of feathers. The magic emanating from them didn't quite have the same feel as the other feathers we'd found, suggesting my initial guess was wrong and that these feathers actually belonged to one of the other shifters. The caress of magic was also much stronger, but only, I suspected, because it was fresher. That meant we might have better luck using them to track the shifter down.

The sound of twigs snapping had me looking up again. A violent curse and then a laugh that was only half swallowed followed.

Monty appeared a few seconds later. He had a multitude of twigs in his hair and scratches on his arms. Belle followed him, her grin unrestrained.

"What have we got, Liz?" He hobbled over surprisingly fast.

"Well hello to you, too," I said, voice dry.

He had the grace to look chastened, if only momentarily. "Sorry, just eager to get back into the action. Been going a bit stir-crazy after all the inactivity and hospital stays."

"You worked in spell cataloguing for most of your working life. You should be used to inaction."

He stopped beside me. His face was flushed with heat, and sweat dribbled down his cheeks and stained the underarms of his shirt. "It seems I've gained a taste for action, despite being in the reservation for only a short time. What do we have?"

"Feathers."

He gave me the look. "I can see that much."

I grinned. "Did Belle tell you about the ones we found earlier?"

"Yes, and Ashworth should have waited for me. I *am* the stronger witch."

"Dare you to say that to Ashworth," Belle commented.

He grinned. "I'm not actually that silly. I take it these are from the same shifter?"

I hesitated. "There's some very minor differences, so I don't think so. But the output is stronger."

"Yeah, I can feel it from here." He hesitated. "There're two threads of magic running through the wave though."

I glanced up sharply. "There are?"

His smile was smug. "More powerful witch, remember?"

I snorted. "I wonder if the second thread is the residue of whatever magic flung the shifter off course."

"More than likely," he said. "But that begs the question, why attack them and not follow up?"

"Maybe he or she simply intended to stop the shifters taking their prey," Belle said.

"At least two of them were fairly badly hurt," I said.

"That suggests the attacker's intent was deeper than just interfering with their hunt."

"I agree." Monty glanced at me. "Have you got any containers in that backpack?"

"I have Ziploc bags." And disposable gloves. Aiden might have a seemingly endless supply in his pockets, but I figured it wouldn't hurt to have additional ones on hand. "Why?"

"To scrape some of the dried blood into. Might be worth seeing if it's the same blood on both rocks."

I got out one of the bags and my blessed silver knife and began scraping. Light rippled down the edge that touched the blood, an indication that it still held the taint of either darkness or magic. "What about the feathers? Do you want to try tracking their owner tonight?"

He hesitated and then motioned toward them. "Let me feel one of them."

I picked out the one with the strongest vibe and handed it up. He studied it for several moments, testing and probing it magically, then grimaced. "We won't get very far—the magic we're feeling is actually some sort of tracking barrier."

"Why would she magically protect the feathers rather than simply picking them up and taking them away?" Belle said.

He shrugged. "She might have been dazed, either from blood loss or the remnants of whatever spell sent her flying."

"If she was lucid enough to spell," I said, "she was lucid enough to simply pick them up. Why leave a magic marker like that?"

"Maybe she doesn't think we can trace her via her magic."

"Can you?" Belle asked.

Monty gave her the 'of course I can' look. "But those sorts of spells have a very limited range."

"Then what good is it?" she said. "We can't exactly drive around the entire reservation in the vague hope the spell will activate."

"No, but if I unpick her spell and study its structure, I might be able to cast a spell that will have a greater range." He shrugged. "There's no guarantee it'll work—especially if she continues to hide out in uninhabited areas—but it's worth a shot."

And it was better than what we currently had—nothing. I carefully gathered the feathers, placed them in the plastic bag, and then handed it up to him.

He briefly caught my wrist. "What in the hell is that?"

"Wild magic—"

"Obviously, but why is it around your wrist like that?"

I hesitated. "Remember how I mentioned Aiden's sister was now part of the wild magic? Well, apparently this makes it easier for her to communicate with me."

Which was only a slight variation of the truth. Monty hadn't yet discovered the second wellspring, and I damn well intended to keep it that way for as long as I could. Neither Gabe nor Katie deserved to have their clearing disturbed by another witch, even a well-meaning one.

Given the strength of the shielding around that clearing, Belle commented silently, *it's doubtful if he'd ever find it. There's probably a redirect spell entwined through the layers somewhere.*

If there is, it didn't work on me.

No, but you were meant to find it. He's not.

Monty shook his head. "This shouldn't be happening. Nothing I've read about the wild magic has ever mentioned the connection you seem to be forming with it. I really, really think we need—"

"No," I cut in curtly. "Don't even bother finishing that sentence, Monty."

He hesitated, his expression troubled. "I understand why, but I really think this could be dangerous."

"Maybe, but I fear Clayton a whole lot more than I fear the wild magic. You know him, Monty. You know how strong he is. Do you honestly think that if he did come here, you'd be able to keep me safe? That you could counter any spell he placed on me."

"No, but the risk—"

"Is worth it, at least for me. I'm not being dragged back to Canberra, Monty. Not to be prodded and probed, and certainly not to take up the position of that bastard's wife."

He took a deep breath and released it slowly. "It makes it damn difficult to find journals relating to human interaction with wild magic without explaining why, you know."

I gripped his arm. "I know, and I'm sorry, but I just can't risk him ever finding me."

Monty grunted. It wasn't a happy sound. "Then at least tell me why you've formed the connection. I think you know that, at the very least."

I hesitated, and then did so. "It's only a theory, but it's also the only thing that makes sense."

He scraped a hand through his unruly hair, sending broken bits of leaves and twigs flying. "I agree. But, holy fuck—your mother almost died, so by all accounts you certainly should have."

I shrugged. "The wellspring was brand-new. So was I. Maybe that's why I survived what would kill most."

"History is littered with tales of strong witches trying—

and failing—to embrace the wild magic. You were little more than an embryo; it should have simply fried you."

"Perhaps that's the very reason she *did* survive," Belle said. "Her cells were so new they were able to adapt."

"Maybe." He shook his head and smiled. "I guess if nothing else, it's going to be interesting to see where all this ends. But if it does happen to kill you, can I submit my observations to the council?"

I rolled my eyes. "Yes, but I hope you understand my fervent wish that never happens."

His grin flashed. "Well, of course, but hey, one has to ask these things, just in case."

"One really doesn't," Belle said dryly. "What's the plan, then? Are we dropping you off at Aiden's car, or are you going home?"

"I notice you didn't give the option of going back to the café." His hurt expression was somewhat spoiled by the glimmer of amusement in his eyes. "One would think you didn't want me around or something."

"One could also remember that it's damn late. I need my beauty sleep."

"Anyone who says that is a liar. You're perfect, eye bags or not."

Belle rolled her eyes. "Seriously, Monty?"

He simply grinned. "You can drop me back at my place. It's too early for me to sleep, so I'll fiddle with the feathers and see if I can create a tracker."

"Done. Let's go, Hopalong."

He snorted, but nevertheless followed. I hesitated, then quickly created a simple alert spell—adding an exception for small animals—and wove it around the perimeter of the rocks.

"If the shifter is at all sensitive to magic, that's not going to work," Monty commented.

"I know, but it's still worth trying." I wove a couple of strands of wild magic through the spell to ensure it fed off that rather than me, and then tied it off and followed Monty and Belle out of the clearing.

As we neared the main road, the wild magic encircling my wrist released and drifted away. It once again left me feeling oddly bereft.

We drove Monty to his place and watched until he was safely inside, before driving off. Once we were home, I made us both a cup of hot chocolate and then headed upstairs to do some more reading. Aiden hadn't rung by the time I'd finished my drink, so I went to bed. While no dreams hit, I remained restless, unable to escape the feeling that trouble was coming our way—fast.

I woke up earlier than usual and went downstairs to make myself a revitalization potion and do the few final bits of prep for the café. We were busy all day, and Aiden, Ashworth, and Monty were all conspicuous by their absence. Which was frustrating, because I really wanted to know what—if anything—had been uncovered last night.

My phone finally rang just as we were finishing for the day, the ringtone telling me it was Aiden.

"Busy day, I'm gathering," I said by way of hello.

"Yeah." Tiredness was etched into his voice. "Do you mind if I call it a night and go home?"

Disappointment slithered through me, but I kept my voice light. "No sex for two nights in a row—are you sure you'll survive, Ranger?"

He laughed softly. "Even a werewolf has to sleep sometimes."

"I've seen little enough evidence of that so far."

"Says the witch who wakes me at all hours."

"I told you, I have many years of abstinence to catch up on."

"And I'm more than happy to meet that demand. Just not tonight."

I chuckled softly. "Come over for breakfast tomorrow, then, if you want."

"I will, thanks. Oh, and while I think about it, you up for dinner tomorrow night?"

"Is this a regular dinner date or the mysterious one?"

"The latter."

"Sure. We going anywhere fancy?"

"Yes."

"And you won't tell me where?"

"No. It's a surprise."

"I hate surprises."

"So I'm discovering. Night, gorgeous. Don't let the bedbugs bite."

I harrumphed. "I only ever let certain werewolves bite me."

He chuckled and hung up. Almost immediately, the phone rang again. It was Monty.

"What's up?"

"I need transport."

"Then call a cab. Or an Uber."

"Not that sort of transport." His tone was annoyed. "I think I can track our shifter, but I can't drive and follow the directional spell at the same time."

He wasn't supposed to drive at all, but I restrained the urge to point that out. "I'll be around in ten."

"Good." He paused. "Is Belle coming along as well?"

"No, she is not," came Belle's response from the kitchen.

"I heard that," Monty said. "Anyone would think she's avoiding me."

"She has a date," I said.

"Really? Who?"

"That's none of your damn business, cuz."

"How am I supposed to beat the competition when I have no idea who the competition is?" he grumbled.

"You're not. That's the whole point."

"You're a mean woman, Lizzie, but you won't stop the course of true love."

I grinned. "Give it up, Monty."

He laughed. "Why? It gives me something to do."

"I'm never going to be your something to do, Monty," Belle yelled. "So please *do* give it up."

"Have you told her it's not polite to be listening in on your conversations?"

"She's my familiar. It's her job to listen in. Now hang up so I can get ready."

Once he had, I went into the reading room to grab my gear. We might find absolutely nothing, but I wasn't about to bet my life on that—a thought that had me wondering just what my prophetic soul sensed.

Belle came out of the kitchen, wiping her hands on the tea towel slung over her shoulder. "Do you want a coffee to take with you?"

"Yeah, and you'd better make one for Monty too, or he'll get all grumpy on us."

"Grumpy might be an improvement over lustlorn."

"He's definitely persistent."

"Always was." She shook her head, a smile teasing her lips. "I was never sure why, given who he was and who I was. I mean, his parents would have had conniptions if he'd ever dipped the precious Ashworth pen in my well."

I laughed. "Maybe, but he did have an eye for good-looking women, and you are quite stunning."

"That may be true now, but it didn't stop him chasing me when we were teenagers."

"Maybe he just recognized the potential for gorgeousness within that scrawny bod of yours."

"Possibly." She grinned. "You know, if he wasn't your cousin and wasn't so damn annoying, I might have considered it. He was never bad-looking, and he's certainly filled out nicely since then."

I raised an eyebrow. "I'm sure he'll be pleased to hear you noticed."

She gave me a deadpan look and slid two coffees across the counter to me. "Tell him, and he'll be around here every free second. We both know you want that no more than I do."

"Very true." I slung the pack over my back, then picked up the coffees. "Have fun with Kash tonight."

"Planning on it. But I'm only a mind-shout away if you need anything."

I nodded and headed out. Monty was already waiting at the front of his place, so I undid my seat belt and leaned across to open the door for him. He threw in his backpack and crutches, then climbed in.

"That additional coffee for me?" he said as he retrieved the spell-wrapped feathers from his pack. It was quite intricate, and I wished I had the time to study it more closely.

Wished—probably for the very first time since that fateful day we'd fled Canberra—that I'd been given the chance to finish my studies. Teaching ourselves via Belle's gran's books was all well and good, but there was so much we didn't know. So much that I wanted to know.

"Yes, it is. Where to?"

"Go back up to Duke Street." He picked up his coffee and then grinned. "How can you say Belle doesn't care when she made me a coffee?"

I raised an eyebrow. "How do you know I didn't make it?"

"Magical fingerprint on the top of the cup—yours are only on the sides, indicating you carried but she made it. You'd left Canberra by the time we got to all those lessons."

Which was just another reminder of how little I knew when it came to magic. "I knew every witch has a distinct magical 'signature,' but I wasn't aware it was evident in our fingerprints."

He nodded. "Most supernatural beings have specific print characteristics, but they're harder to record."

"Does that mean you can catalogue them like regular fingerprints?"

"Yes, but only with a specific spell, and only then if they're caught early enough. There is, in fact, a database in Canberra containing both finger and magical imprints of some of history's nastiest witches."

"Huh." I did a right-hand turn into Duke Street and then sped up again. "I take it you've searched said database to see if there's a match for our shifter?"

"Indeedy. There isn't."

"Did unpicking her magic—or what remained of it on those feathers—give you any idea as to who she is? Or where she might have come from?"

"Not exactly."

I glanced at him. "Meaning?"

He hesitated. "Her magic feels very old."

"Some shifters do live for a very long time."

"Yes, but her imprint just feels... off."

Like the thoughts of the first one had been. "If she's a

witch as well as a shifter, isn't that to be expected? The two usually don't go together."

"It's not that. Her energy is almost otherworldly."

"Could she have done a deal with a dark witch? Or even a demon? *Our* demon?"

"At this stage, I'm not discounting any possibility." He glanced at me. "But you did say there were three shifters who were attacked, and it's very unusual for a demon to bind itself to more than one entity at a time."

"Unusual but not unknown. I've read plenty of texts about dark witches enslaving their children, siblings, or even lovers to gain greater power."

"True. Turn right into Fryers Road—it's just after the swimming pool."

I did so. The road narrowed alarmingly, forcing me to slow down. We drove under an old brick rail bridge, and the houses gave way to rolling, tree-covered hills.

"Perfect area for a shifter to hide out in," I commented. "Lots of roosting areas."

"Bird shifters no more spend the majority of their time in their alternate form than werewolves do," Monty commented. "I thought you'd know that, given you're dating one of the locals."

I rolled my eyes. "Yes, but maintaining an alternate form is the easiest way to hide in plain sight. Non-witches wouldn't know the difference, and werewolves probably wouldn't either, unless they were close enough to scent them."

"Also true." He paused and glanced down at the pulsing spell. "Slow down—it's that house on the left."

I pulled onto the side of the road and stopped the Outback. The house was more a cottage, with a door in the middle and single-pane windows on either side. Its tin roof was rusted, but the small front garden was well-tended and the grass cut short.

"What do you think?" he asked.

I leaned my arms on the steering wheel and studied the place. Curtains had been drawn across the windows and I couldn't see a car, though there was no driveway entrance at the front, either. The cottage was obviously accessed from the side road up ahead.

"I'm thinking this looks too easy."

He glanced at me. "She couldn't know I'd be able to unpick her magic and use it to track her."

"I know. I just—" I grimaced. "Maybe it's my inner pessimist coming to the fore, because I'm certainly not getting any bad vibes from the place."

"Would you, from this distance?"

"Possibly."

He grunted and returned his gaze to the cottage. "We need to go in there and look."

"Yes. But it's too open here to do that."

I shoved the SUV back into gear and continued on to the small road. As I'd guessed, the cottage's driveway came off this. I parked on the grass under a large gum tree and then twisted around to look back at the property. There were a number of old sheds in the main yard, and a couple more in the paddocks beyond—most of which seemed to be shelters for a small assortment of sheep and cattle. There was also a large metal water tank sitting next to the house, though it looked as rusted as the roofing. The cottage had to be connected to the town's main water supply, because no one in their right mind would be drinking from a tank that degraded.

"The back of the house looks as locked down as the front," Monty commented. "And I can't see a car."

"It could be in one of the sheds." Two were certainly large enough to hold a vehicle. "What do you want to do?"

"Go in, of course. It's the only way we'll know if she's in there or not."

"And if she is?"

"Then maybe we can speak to her."

I snorted. "Yeah, a shifter who's possibly done a deal with the devil—or, at least, one of his demons—is really going to calmly sit down and have a nice little chat with the reservation witch."

His grin flashed. "Hey, you never know until you try."

"Things are never that easy in this place. Trust me on that."

I jumped out and hurried around to hold the door open while he maneuvered out of the SUV. Once he was balanced on his crutches, I grabbed both packs and slung them over my shoulder.

"You want to check the sheds?" he said. "I'll see if the doors are locked."

I nodded and, once he was safely on the driveway's smoother ground, headed across to the first of the old sheds. As I reached out to open the old wooden door, the vague sensation of being watched stirred.

My heart rate instantly leaped several notches and I glanced around sharply. Monty was making his way down the left side of the house, and there was nothing or no one else moving about. Nor was there any hint of evil to suggest my watcher was either the shifter or the flesh-stripping demon.

But something was out there.

My grip tightened on the door handle and the faint threads of a repelling spell began to stir across my fingers—

the instinctiveness of the reaction was almost as scary as whatever watched me.

Then my 'other' senses caught a wisp of energy and my gut tightened as recognition stirred. That energy belonged to the White Lady.

She was here.

And watching.

Waiting.

SIX

I took a deep breath and released it slowly. It didn't do a whole lot to ease the rapid pounding of my pulse. While I doubted the White Lady intended me immediate harm, the fact she continued to haunt my steps was rather unnerving.

"If you want something," I whispered, certain she'd hear it, "you really should let my friend speak to you."

She didn't move and—naturally—didn't reply.

"I can't help you if I don't know what you want."

Again, silence.

I hesitated, and then opened the shed's door. It creaked loudly, and wings fluttered in response. I looked up and saw a couple of sparrows staring balefully at me from cobwebbed metal rafters—they'd obviously flown in here through the cracked side window to escape the afternoon's heat.

I stepped further inside and looked around; the old wooden workbenches and various gardening tools were covered in dust and yet more cobwebs, an indication they hadn't been used in a while. The ride-on lawnmower parked to my right was free of both, though, suggesting it had at least been used in the last couple of days. There was little else here beyond the usual assortment of garden tools, hoses, and buckets.

I left the sparrows to their shadows and headed across to the next shed. My watcher drifted with me, her distance neither increasing nor decreasing. I flexed my fingers, a move that sent tiny sparks spiraling. Unease stirred anew, and I quickly drew the energy pressing against my fingertips back into my soul. The means of controlling innate power was something every blueblood witch learned almost as soon as they could walk, but with the wild magic becoming a stronger force within me, it was pretty obvious I'd have to revisit those earlier lessons. Otherwise—as teachers and parents constantly hammered into every young witch—the results could be calamitous for those I cared about.

There was a rusted old Ford wagon with flat tires parked on one side of the next shed, and a newer-looking sedan on the other. I walked over to the latter. The doors were unlocked, so I opened the passenger side and leaned in, checking the middle console. It contained little more than a packet of Minties and a half-consumed block of chocolate. I moved on to the glove compartment. Aside from more snacks, it held the vehicle's service book and a couple of old bills. A quick sort through the latter revealed the car's owner was a Mrs. T. Vaughn; at least we had a name to work with if she had become a victim of the shifter. If nothing else, Belle might be able to recall her spirit and see what had happened.

I checked the rest of the vehicle, but couldn't find anything that made my psychic radar tingle. Once I'd checked the station wagon, I headed back out. The White Lady continued to drift along with me; there was no sense of urgency in her movements, no indication that she wanted me to find something... and yet I had a growing suspicion that there *was* something here to find.

Monty appeared around the other end of the house and hobbled toward me.

"Anything?" he said.

"The house belongs to a Mrs. Vaughn, and we're being watched by a White Lady. Other than that, no. You?"

He did something of a double take. "The White Lady is here?"

I nodded. "Watching from a safe distance over to my left."

His gaze narrowed, and after a moment, he grunted. "I'm not sensing anything."

"That's because you're using magical radar, not psychic. Trust me, she's there."

"Oh, I'm not doubting it, but it's damn unusual for a White Lady to be proficient enough at magic to hide her form like that. Even if we *are* dealing with a former witch, I've never read anything that says your power can cross over when your soul does."

"Which means there's no indication that it can't, either."

"True." He glanced toward the house. "All the windows are curtained, the doors are locked, and there's no indication of magic around the exterior. But given the presence of our specter, I'm inclined to think we should go inside and investigate."

I raised my eyebrows. "What happened to obeying the law and all that?"

He grinned. "You're the one who told me the rangers won't say anything if it's case connected. Don't blame me if I use it to my full advantage."

I smiled. "Do you want to do the honors, or shall I?"

He motioned toward the crutches. "It'd be easier if you did it."

I walked over to the door and pressed a palm against it, just above the handle. The 'unlock' spell—like many others I knew—was self-taught, though I'd honed my technique somewhat after witnessing Monty doing it. The quicksilver spell threads glittered briefly before slipping into the wood. A heartbeat later, the bolt unlocked.

"Impressive," Monty said. "Another variation, but a very efficient one."

I pushed the door open with my fingers, revealing a small laundry room and a second door—this one half-closed. The still air was thick and warm and held a vague hint of rotten egg.

"That," Monty commented, "is not a good sign."

"If you're implying it's demon scent, doesn't that basically confirm at least one of our shifters is working for—or with—the flesh stripper?" I cautiously stepped inside. Other than the soft ticking of a clock, there was little in the way of sound.

"Well, I doubt it's a coincidence the shifter and the demon were hunting in the same area last night."

"Except she was headed in the opposite direction until the victim screamed."

"There's three of them, remember. One might have been acting as a decoy."

"I guess." I carefully opened the next door, my heart rate once again jumping several notches even though there was no indication of danger. The room beyond was shadowed and compact, with the main room being a combined kitchen and living area. To my immediate left was a small bathroom, and on the right, a bedroom. The place looked and felt empty. Or, at least, empty of life. The jury was still out on anything else.

"You want to check the living area?" I said. "I'll head into the bedroom."

I walked across the room without waiting for an answer. The bedroom ran the full width of the small cottage and held a double bed and a large wardrobe. In a corner near the front window, a new-looking iMac sat on an antique desk. Tucked against the wall close by was a plush executive chair. On the opposite side was a small dressing table. I walked over and skimmed a hand across various items on the dresser, but none of the jewelry—or anything else in the room, for that matter—drew a response.

I wrinkled my nose and headed back out. "Anything?"

Monty shook his head. "The locator is still saying this is the spot, though."

"Are you sure it's working properly?"

He gave me a 'don't be stupid' sort of look. I grinned and added, "Then why is the damn thing insisting she's here, when she's obviously not?"

"Maybe this is her roost, and that's what the spell is picking up." He shrugged. "We'll have to place a watch on the place, just in case she returns."

"It's not exactly a thriving metropolis around here—a vehicle that's stationary for any length of time will be noticed." Especially when we were dealing with a winged shifter—even if she didn't suspect we were following her, she'd be damn wary after being attacked magically. "And as you said in the clearing last night, she'll more than likely sense any sort of alarm spell."

"Which is why we'll use something more mundane." He motioned for his pack and then pulled out a small camera. "It has got a range of around nine meters, so if we attach it somewhere to the side of the house, it'll cover a good portion of the yard as well as the back door."

"How is that going to help us? We still can't park nearby."

"It'll push alerts to my phone, so we can wait at a safe distance."

"Monty, I have no intention of sitting in an SUV all night waiting for a shifter that may or may not appear. I have to work tomorrow."

"Then we'll call Ashworth. He can take over watch duty after ten or so."

"Oh, I'm sure he'll be thrilled."

"Given he's still technically the acting reservation witch, it *is* his task to do." His voice was dry. "Let's go set things up."

I locked the door while Monty briefly studied the yard and then headed across to the water tank. The White Lady remained at a distance, and once again I couldn't escape the notion there was something here she wanted us to find. I frowned and followed Monty across the yard, only to have to do a quick side step as he stopped abruptly.

"Oh, that's not good."

"What?" I frowned at the tank but couldn't immediately see anything untoward.

"There's magic lingering along the top of the tank."

My gaze jumped up. After a second, a vague, almost otherworldly energy caressed my skin—one that didn't feel foul. Then the shimmering threads of a fading spell came into view. I couldn't immediately guess what type of spell it was, as the threads continued to move, weaving in and out of the tank's metal roof.

"Whatever it is, I don't think it's connected to our shifter. It hasn't got the same feel."

"No." His gaze narrowed. "It's recent, though, and quite intricate."

"Any guess as to what its purpose is?"

"Not a one." He hesitated. "There *are* some thread similarities to a demon containment spell."

I swallowed heavily. "You don't think—?"

"If the demon's in there—dead *or* alive—we'd surely know." Monty's voice was grim. "I think you'd better climb up and have a look."

"Not without checking out the rest of the area first," I snapped, and then took a deep breath to calm my nerves. "If anything jumps out of that thing, make sure you're ready to knock it into the next time zone."

"That's hardly going to get us any answers."

"When we're dealing with a flesh stripper, I don't care."

He laughed. "If a flesh stripper jumps out of that thing, I'll swear off chasing Belle for the next month."

A smile tugged my lips. "A statement that would have placed Belle in quite a quandary if she'd been here."

He laughed again and motioned toward the tank. "Go check. If anything moves, I'll hit it first and ask questions later."

"Good."

Fortunately for me, the tank's perimeter held nothing more dangerous than several pretty but thorny roses. I stopped beside Monty again and studied the still-moving spell threads. "Are you able to disengage them? We need to look inside, but I'm not about to risk triggering that spell."

The words were barely out of my mouth when the threads stopped moving and the spell simply disappeared. A cold prickle ran up my spine, and my gaze went to the distant energy that was our watcher.

It had been her spell.

"Oh, fuck," Monty said, in an exact echo of my thoughts. "Our White Lady is not only capable of magic, but able to use it to affect things within *this* world."

"How is that even possible?"

He shrugged. "There are ghosts capable of interacting with physical objects within this world, so it's more than possible that a strong enough witch could not only interact, but also spell."

My gaze returned to the tank, and goose bumps prickled my skin. "Which begs the question, what exactly was her magic interacting with in that tank?"

"I guess there's only one way we're going to find out—and, given I can't climb a ladder, that delightful task falls to you."

"Fabulous." Not.

I spun around and went in search of a ladder. I found one in the first shed and set it up next to the tank's inlet strainer, which was caked with dirt and old grass. It took a few minutes to clear it before I could pry it off. Nothing jumped out. No sense of evil stirred through the air. Relief swept through me, though my pulse rate remained high. There'd obviously been something here; why else would our specter have bothered spelling the tank?

"Anything?" Monty said.

I peered in. The water was dark and very close to the top, making it difficult to see anything beyond the first few feet of the opening. "Lean up against the tank and hand me one of your crutches."

"I'm not sure I'm enthused about you using it to stir up whatever evil lies inside."

"I could throw you bodily in instead, if you'd prefer."

He snorted and handed me the crutch. "I'd like to see you try. An Amazonian you are not."

"No, but I do know a levitation spell that might do the trick." I actually didn't, but he wasn't to know that.

I flipped the crutch around and then shoved the wider end into the water and swished it around in a vague attempt to move whatever might lie beyond my line of sight. The water became choppier, and the prickly energy that was the specter drew nearer. Then something pale drifted briefly toward the surface. For one heart-stopping moment, I thought we'd discovered another body, but quickly realized there was nothing human about it. I stirred the water some more, trying to get a clearer glimpse.

What appeared was a largish bird.

A bird whose feathers were alternating stripes of dark brown and lighter gray.

"You found something?" Monty said.

"Yeah—the body of our shifter."

He immediately straightened. "What?"

"You heard." I shoved the end of the crutch under the bird's body to pull it closer. It was then I noticed the thin strip of metal around its body and legs. It had been closely bound and tossed into the tank with no means of keeping itself afloat.

I looked across to the watching specter. Felt a vague sense of her rage and satisfaction. Whatever our White Lady was up to, it hadn't ended with the death of this shifter.

This was only the beginning.

Trepidation stirred—not because her vengeance was aimed at me, but rather the fact she appeared to want me to witness it.

I pulled the bird free of the tank and then carefully climbed down and placed the body on the ground near Monty.

"It's an owl." Monty accepted the wet crutch with a nod. "And bound with silver, from the look of it."

"Yes." I squatted next to the bird and held out a hand. Energy caressed my skin. "There's a spell attached to it."

"It's not one I've seen before, though it once again has some similarities to demon snare."

I glanced up sharply. "Why would our specter bother using something like that on a shifter? It's overkill, isn't it?"

"Yes—unless, of course, our earlier guess was right, and the shifters are working with our demon."

"I guess there's only one way to find out." I glanced over to the White Lady. "Can you remove the final spell?"

Energy immediately stirred, brief but potent. The vague thread lines wrapped around the silver wire faded, but nothing immediately happened.

"The silver could be constraining its form," Monty muttered. "You'll need to remove it first."

"Not without a protective circle and a spell ready to send its spirit back to the depths of hell if we *are* dealing with a demon."

"Excellent point. I'll do the circle, you go find some wire cutters."

By the time I returned with the wire cutter, Monty had not only laid his spell stones around the bird's body but also activated them. I silently watched while he created a spell that would shoot the demon back to whatever hell it had come from, once again taking mental notes on the process even as I hoped I'd never have to use such a spell.

With the force of his spell humming around us, he said, "I layered exceptions for your hands, arms, and the cutters into the protection spell, so you should have no problems removing the wire. If the bird so much as twitches, I'll unleash the second spell."

I nodded and squatted down. The threads tracking around the stones shimmered as my hands went through them, their power caressing my skin but holding no threat.

I shifted the owl to get better access then carefully positioned the cutter between the wire and her body and snipped. Or tried to. Either the blades weren't that sharp or our specter had somehow boosted the metal's strength, because it took two hands and a fair bit of effort to cut through it. I flipped the owl over, tried to ignore the cold emptiness of her body, and cut the wire on the other side. Then I pulled the bits free, dropping them on the ground next to her rather than taking any of them outside the protective circle.

As I removed the final bit of metal, feathers stirred. I squeaked in fright and pushed back, landing on my butt well clear of the shifter and the circle.

Monty raised his hand but didn't unleash his weapon. There was no need to. This shifter presented no danger—the movement had simply been her body disintegrating. Her soul was long gone.

If she'd had a soul, that was. Its loss was quite often the price paid for working with a demon.

We silently watched feathers, flesh, and bone become foul yellow air that then faded away. Soon there was nothing left except the bits of wire I'd cut and a thin, long needle. And if it was made of pure silver, it would explain why the shifter hadn't tried reverting form—it simply couldn't while the needle was embedded in its flesh.

I reached in to pick it up, but energy skittered across my fingertips. Like the shifter herself, the magic was fading, but I had no intention of touching something that had been spelled when I had no idea what that spell did.

I raised my gaze toward the White Lady. The fact she

was still here meant she'd obviously wanted us to find the shifter's remains. But why? What was she trying to tell us? I suspected it was something more than the fact the shifters were working with a demon—if not *the* demon—but it was damn frustrating that she seemed determined to avoid direct contact.

That frustration only increased when the sense of her energy faded away.

Monty dismissed both of his spells and then moved the end of one crutch, placing it next to the needle. "That has the remnants of a boomerang spell on it."

"A what?"

He screwed up his nose. "Seriously, your knowledge—or lack thereof—is astounding sometimes."

"Something that can be easily fixed if you start teaching me," I snapped back. "It's a far better option than constantly bemoaning my lack."

"A good point." His grin flashed. "And it has the benefit of placing me in Belle's general vicinity more often."

I rolled my eyes. "Proximity will not endear you to her."

"That's where you're wrong, dear Lizzie. It's written in the stars—we're meant to be." He grinned as I snorted loudly. "A boomerang is the slang term for a spell that can shoot the life force of the demon back to wherever they came from. It's the spell I was holding in reserve."

"Except the spell on that needle didn't feel anything like the one you conjured."

"Because there are variations, though I have no idea what the ones on the needle did." He motioned toward the needle. "It's safe enough to pick up now."

I handed it to him. "How common are pure silver sewing needles?"

"Not very, I'd imagine, but I'll contact Canberra and see if there's a record of suppliers."

I pushed upright again. "Are we still going to place the camera?"

He hesitated. "The other shifters would have felt her death, so it's unlikely they'll return. But I still think it's worth a shot."

"And what about Ms. Vaughn?"

He frowned. "What about her? I doubt she's involved, if that's what you're implying."

"I meant the fact she's not currently here so she's either away or dead. If the former, we'll have to contact her. We can't risk her coming back here in case the shifters do return."

"Oh, good point. I'll get Aiden onto that."

Aiden would no doubt *love* taking orders from Monty. "I also hope they don't decide to come after us. I've really had enough of being attacked by supernatural beasties for the moment."

"It wasn't our magic that destroyed the shifter, so I think we're relatively safe."

"I like the confident way in which you proclaim these things, even though we both know you're talking through your butt."

He smiled. "That doesn't mean I'm wrong."

I guess it didn't. I returned the ladder and wire cutter to the shed, then held open the SUV's door so Monty could climb in. Once I'd dropped him back at his place, I headed home. Belle had already left for Kash's, so I finished the prep for the next day, then headed upstairs to do some reading. I found several more references to the Empusa, and jotted down the reference numbers so Belle could grab them when she went to get the next lot of books for Kash to transcribe. I was yawning by the time ten o'clock came around, so I called it quits and got an early night for a change. If I dreamed, I didn't remember it.

My phone rang just as I was cooking breakfast the next morning, the ringtone telling me it was Aiden.

"I take it there's a problem and you're not coming for breakfast," I said by way of answering.

"Yes, because the council wants an immediate update."

He sounded grumpy, and I couldn't help smiling. "That's rather inconvenient timing on their part."

"I thought about mentioning that, but under the current circumstances, they wouldn't have been amused. We still on for our date tonight?"

"Barring intervention by flesh-stripping demons or White Ladies, definitely."

"I'll pick you up at six, then."

He hung up. I shoved the phone back into my pocket, then finished making breakfast for Belle and me. Business was brisk all morning, but it slowed down in the afternoon, which allowed us to do some more baking. Aiden had obviously spread the news about the goodness of our brownies, because we could barely keep up with demand.

I dithered over what to wear for our date for a good half hour before deciding on a formfitting dark green sheath dress whose only embellishment was a chunky golden zip that ran the full length of the dress's back, and paired it with gold shoes and handbag to provide a bit of extra bling.

Aiden—who now had his own key—appeared just as I was clattering down the stairs. His gaze traveled slowly down my length, and desire burned in his eyes. "Well, don't you look good enough to eat?"

I smiled and sashayed toward him. He wore black dress pants that hugged his hips, then skimmed the long, lean length of his legs, and a soft blue-gray shirt that emphasized his shoulders and sharpened the blue of his eyes. "So do you."

I wrapped my arms around his neck and claimed his lips. He tasted of coffee, passion, and desire, and all I wanted to do was remain in his arms for as long as I could, while I could.

A thought I *didn't* want to examine. Not right now.

"You have no idea just how badly I want you at the moment," he murmured, his breath a hot caress against my lips.

I laughed softly and pressed a little closer. "Oh, I think I do."

"Vixen." He kissed my nose and then pulled back. "I can also state that I'm going to take great delight in unzipping that dress of yours all the way down your spine and then slowly tasting every single naked inch of you."

Desire shimmered. "We could always skip dinner and go back to your place."

"Unfortunately, we can't." He held out his hand. "And we'd better get going, otherwise we'll be late."

"Why are you being so cagey about this date? What's going on?"

He opened the door and ushered me out, then caught my hand again and led me down the street. "You'll find out soon enough."

"And now you're making me worried."

"There's no reason to be."

"I'm not convinced." Especially when his aura was a riot of color that betrayed his outward sense of calm.

He opened the door of his truck and helped me onto the seat. "I'm under orders to keep things secret, so secret they will be."

"That's not helping, you know."

"I know, but it is what it is." He slammed the door once I was seated, then climbed in on the other side and started the engine. "It'll take us about half an hour to get there."

"Define 'there.'"

"Bendigo."

"We're going out of the reservation?"

"Indeed."

Curiouser and curiouser, as Alice was wont to say. But it was pointless questioning him any further; it was pretty obvious he wasn't going to give anything away. "How did the council take the news that we've a flesh-stripping demon on the reservation?"

"About as well as you'd expect. They're seriously worried tourism is going to be affected if this run of murders continues. And yes, they're well aware that the fault is their own."

"There hasn't been much in the local newspapers about them yet."

"No, but that's never stopped the news from spreading."

Thanks in part to the gossip brigade. Nothing seemed to escape their notice. Maybe I should have asked *them* what the hell Aiden was up to.

"Were you able to glean anything from last night's murder?"

He grimaced. "Not really. Ashworth is of the opinion that something must have gone wrong, as it lacked the finesse evident in the previous two."

Which was putting it mildly. "What about the victims? Any progress on identifying them?"

"The buried victim was Joseph Banker, who went missing four days ago. His parents confirmed the watch was his today."

"I take it they didn't view the remains?"

"Gerard did, against our advice." Aiden grimaced again. "That went as well as might be expected, too."

"What about the others?"

"No progress as yet, although last night's victim did at least have teeth, which should help. Ciara's completed the facial reconstruction image of the victim found at the cross-road, and Maggie's going through our missing persons files to see if we can find a match."

"That sounds like you have quite a number of people who go missing."

"We get two or three a week, on average. Most of them have simply gotten lost, but there's always one or two a month we never find. I suspect most of those have deliberately disappeared."

"One or two a month is a scarily high number over a year—I'm surprised it hasn't made the news."

"It's not that high—not when you consider that, on average, over ten thousand people in Victoria go missing each year." He glanced at me. "Did you and Monty manage to track down that shifter?"

I raised an eyebrow. "Monty didn't update you?"

"He said that he and Ashworth were staking out a possible hideout, but other than that, no."

I quickly told him what we'd discovered and then added, "He probably didn't mention the shifter because we have no body and no immediate way of tracking the other two."

"And the specter? Have you any idea why she killed that shifter or why she's haunting your movements?"

"No, and no. But given she's a White Lady, she's obviously out for revenge."

"On the shifters, or the demon?"

"Possibly both, given they appear to be connected."

He grunted. "What about Belle? Could she attempt to talk to the specter?"

"Not without her cooperation."

He frowned. "She can't summon her as she does other spirits?"

"She could, but without the name or something personal of hers, she also risks summoning every other spirit in the immediate area." And even if she did have one or both of those things, our specter was capable of magic. It was quite possible she'd already warded herself against a summoning.

"What are the chances of the remaining shifters returning to that house?" he asked.

"About as likely as Ashworth surviving an entire night in Monty's company."

Aiden laughed. "That I can believe."

Conversation moved on, and twenty-five minutes later we were driving into Bendigo. He found a parking spot just opposite Officeworks, then hurried around to help me out of the truck. Nerves rose, but I tamped the ridiculous things down. No matter what was going on, Aiden absolutely wouldn't do anything to break my trust.

He placed a warm hand against my spine and lightly guided me toward a small but stylish-looking restaurant. As soon as we stepped inside, a waiter approached, his outfit as understated and elegant as the room itself.

"Good evening," he said in a low but warm tone. "How can I help you?"

"We have a booking—Aiden O'Connor."

"Ah, yes," the waiter immediately said. "The third member of your party has already arrived. If you'd please follow me, we'll get you both seated."

He turned and moved toward the rear stairs. Aiden pressed me forward, leaving me little option but to follow.

"And just who are we meeting?" I whispered urgently. "What the hell are you up to?"

"Nothing serious," he returned evenly. "Someone just wanted to meet you, that's all."

"Who? And why all the secrecy?"

He hesitated. "The latter is at her request. I can't gainsay her, no matter how much I might want to."

Her. Not him, not my father or husband. I took a deep breath and tried to control irrational fears. Aiden would never contact either of those men. In fact, he was far more likely to go after them.

"Aiden—"

"Just wait," he said softly. "It'll all become clear in another few seconds."

Frustration stirred yet again, but I held my tongue and clattered lightly up the steps after the waiter. This area was smaller—and more intimate—than the downstairs room, and contained booths and half-walled rooms. We were led into one of the latter.

Seated at a small round table that dominated the area was a woman. She was rangy in build, with silver-gray hair and eyes that were a deep, almost sapphire blue.

I knew in an instant who she was, even though I'd never seen her before.

Karleen Jayne O'Connor.

Aiden's mother.

SEVEN

For a moment, I could only stare. In any other relationship, it would have been a natural progression for me to meet his parents, but this wasn't any other relationship. He was a werewolf, and I was a witch, and never the twain shall meet—at least not in terms of a serious relationship, anyway. His parents had only given way to Katie's desire to marry Gabe because she was dying.

His mother was the last person I'd expected to be here—the last person I thought would *want* to be here.

But it explained the secrecy. Explained why he couldn't say anything. She wasn't only his mother, but his alpha—one of his pack's leaders—and he certainly wouldn't gainsay her orders for someone like me. If I'd been a wolf, things might have been different... but I wasn't, and never could be, so it was stupid to even start thinking along those lines.

It also explained why we were meeting in a restaurant well beyond the reservation's boundaries, in a room shielded from prying eyes. It wouldn't do for her to give our relationship any sort of credence by being seen with me.

Aiden pressed his hand harder against my spine, all but

forcing me into the room. His mother stood, her gaze cool as it met mine.

"Elizabeth Grace." Her mellow tones belied the ice in her blue eyes. "I'm pleased to finally meet you."

"And I you."

I took her offered hand warily, but my psychic senses thankfully remained mute. Her aura wasn't giving a whole lot away, either—it was almost totally red, an indicator of someone who was powerful, passionate, and competitive. Everything you'd expect an alpha wolf to be, in other words. But there were also faint wisps of black moving through the red, and that was often an indicator of either grief or an unforgiving nature.

In her case, I suspected it meant the latter.

I forced a smile and added, "I hope you don't mind me saying this, but I'm utterly surprised to see you here, Mrs. O'Connor."

"Please, call me Karleen. There's no reason to be formal in a place such as this." Her gaze flicked to Aiden. "You did say she was straightforward."

"She's also astute enough to realize this is a rather unusual situation, so I wouldn't beat about the bush too much."

His voice, like his mother's, was pleasant but his aura continued its run of riotous color, suggesting that while he'd agreed to this meeting, he wasn't exactly happy about it. And that only increased my tension.

He pulled out a chair to seat me, then claimed the one between us. The waiter handed us each a menu and, once we'd ordered drinks, quietly left.

Karleen took a sip of water, her gaze once again on mine. Assessing me. Judging me. It was the why that worried me.

"My son tells me you're able to communicate with my daughter, Kate."

Now *that* was a statement I hadn't been expecting. "Yes, I can, although she mostly initiates the contact."

Grief flickered through her aura, even though her expression remained unmoved. "Then her ghost does indeed roam this reservation? She hasn't moved on?"

"It was her choice—something she wanted to do. But she isn't a ghost—she's far more than that."

"According to Aiden, she's become the reservation's guardian."

I nodded. "She's helped us on numerous occasions."

"So he's said." Her tone remained even but her disbelief was a thick wave that washed over me. "I'm afraid it's a situation I'm struggling to accept. You and your friend are both strong psychics, and we both know it's a field with a well-earned reputation for fooling the unwary."

"If I earned the moniker of fool, it was at the beginning of our relationship rather than now." Though his voice remained mild, anger sparked brighter in Aiden's eyes. "I let my hatred for witches override common sense, and I didn't trust Liz early enough. The end result could have been you having two dead children rather than just one, Mother."

"Be that as it may, you will have to forgive my skepticism without proof."

"If you wanted that, why all the secrecy?" I asked. "Why not simply come to our café and ask us to do a full séance?"

Another insincere smile touched her lips. "Because the gossips would have had a field day, and there's already enough talk about your relationship with my son."

"My relationships are neither their business nor yours,"

Aiden said sharply. "And again, that is not what you came here for."

She glanced at him, one eyebrow raised. If she'd been in wolf form, hackles would have been raised. "Indeed."

The waiter came back with our drinks. I nodded my thanks and resisted the urge to toss back my whiskey and ask for the bottle. Getting drunk would neither help the situation nor impress the woman sitting opposite. She was expecting the worst from me—thanks to the fact I was both a witch and psychic—and while it was tempting to give her exactly that, I wouldn't do it to Aiden.

Once our meals had been ordered, I leaned back in my chair and said, "The only way I can give you proof is to let her talk through me."

Aiden glanced at me. "That's dangerous, isn't it?"

"It'll take a lot of energy, yes, but Katie won't drain me—she wouldn't risk it, given our relationship."

The wisps of black in Karleen's aura thickened, though I wasn't sure whether it was annoyance at my mentioning the R-word, or grief over losing her daughter. "I still find it difficult to believe Kate would sacrifice herself in such a way."

"Katie was always more concerned about family than other people's expectations." This time, the edge in Aiden's voice was deeper and hinted at old hurt—one that went far deeper than Katie's death. "She did this for us—to keep *us* safe—as much as for the reservation itself."

"And yet it was her husband's actions that ultimately placed this reservation in danger."

Annoyance surged, but I tamped it down. Hard. This situation was tense enough without me unleashing emotionally. "That was *not* Gabe's intention, but strong magic always comes at some cost to its initiator. He simply didn't expect his death would be the price he paid."

She studied me for a moment. "You use the magic of this land—what's the price you pay?"

"That is yet to be fully revealed."

"Interesting." She took a sip of her red wine. "How would I know that I'm actually talking to Kate rather than simply you using information gleaned from Aiden over the last few months?"

"Mother—"

I touched his thigh, felt the taut muscles there jump in response. He glanced at me, anger briefly flaring in his eyes before he contained it. I suspected this time it *was* aimed at me; he was, after all, an alpha in waiting, and given I *wasn't*, my interrupting could be seen as overstepping boundaries.

"That is a question we get quite often from skeptics." My voice remained surprisingly calm, despite the inner turmoil. "And the easiest to answer. Ask her a question about something only you and she would know."

"Then when are you free to do this? Tomorrow perhaps, after the café closes? I wouldn't expect you to drop everything, of course."

There was something in her tone that suggested the wise would do exactly that, but I was nothing if not obstinate.

"No. If you want to talk to her, we do it tonight, after dinner." I couldn't quite help the edge in my voice. "It has the benefit of reducing any chance of you being spotted with me. Can't feed the gossip mill, can we now?"

The black in her aura abruptly sharpened. I had a vision of teeth being bared, even though she hadn't moved a muscle. As a pack leader, she was well used to controlling herself.

"Neither of us are dressed for walking around in the bush at night, my dear."

"We don't have to. We can stop on the road that circuits a good part of the O'Connor compound near the wellspring, and I can call her to me."

I crossed mental fingers as I said it, because in fact I had no real idea if it was at all possible for me to initiate contact via the threads of wild magic. It wasn't something I'd had to do—and until last night, something I hadn't even thought was possible.

"You don't usually carry your spell stones with you when we go out," Aiden said. "How safe is it to attempt such a connection without initiating an active protection circle?"

I hesitated. "Ashworth created a non-pinned circle around the first lot of feathers we found. I'll try and repeat that."

"And if that fails?"

"Then hope nothing attacks us while we're doing this." Or, if it did, that I could use the wild magic to protect us all.

Karleen frowned. "Why would something attack? And why would you need a protective circle when talking to my daughter?"

"Because, as I informed the full council yesterday, we have a flesh-stripping demon stalking the reservation." Aiden's tone was full of bite. "Allowing Katie to speak through her basically leaves Liz defenseless."

Karleen's frown increased. "But you have a gun—"

"Bullets are rarely a viable option against demons, unless they're made of silver and blessed by a priest, and we all know just how unwelcome any weapon made of silver is in the reservation." I was damn lucky to have gotten my silver knife back, and that had only happened because

Aiden had seen firsthand just how necessary items of silver were in the fight against supernatural beasties. "If you don't mind me asking, why the sudden desire to speak to her now?"

The black smoke flared again, but this time it was definitely grief, though it disappeared almost as quickly as it had appeared. Maybe the only reason her aura wasn't as dark and as turbulent as Aiden's had been when I'd first met him was thanks to sheer force of will.

She picked up her glass and took a drink and then studied me several seconds before replying softly, "Perhaps I simply wish to know that she is indeed happy in her choice."

It was a statement filled with so much unintended heartache that I couldn't help but feel for her. She was a mother who'd lost her child in what was initially thought to be a murder suicide, and no matter how strong a person you normally were, that would have been a hellish situation to cope with.

"Fine," I said. "We'll attempt it tonight, then."

"Thank you."

I nodded but didn't bother replying as the waiter came in with our meals. The conversation turned to more mundane things and, while an underlying tension remained, it was at least pleasant enough.

Once we'd had coffee and dessert, Aiden called for the bill, but Karleen insisted on paying for it. The night was filled with a misty rain by the time we left and, though it wasn't cold, Karleen nevertheless pulled on a light sweater.

"I'd don't suppose you'd be a dear and go get my car for me?" she said, looking at Aiden. "It's one block over, on King Street."

"We'll drive you over—"

"My dear boy, Elizabeth may be limber enough to climb into your truck with a tight dress on, but I, however, am not." She took her keys out of her purse. "It won't take you long, and I promise I won't scare her away."

The hint of acerbity behind that comment had me wondering just who she *had* scared away—Aiden's loved and lost wolf, perhaps?

He gave me a questioning glance, but when I nodded mutely, he took the keys and left. The tension that had eased over our meal immediately ratcheted up. Mrs. O'Connor, I suspected, was about to go all alpha wolf on my ass. She might truly want to speak to Katie, but it certainly *wasn't* the real reason behind her sudden desire to meet me.

I'd always known that if Aiden and I lasted more than a few weeks there'd be some form of push back from his parents. Aiden was destined to be a pack alpha once his parents stepped down, so him getting seriously involved or even marrying anyone other than an equally strong female alpha werewolf was totally out of the question. Aiden himself had warned me multiple times that we could never be anything more than lovers and friends, but his mother was about to emphasize that point, and in no uncertain terms.

"I hope you realize that there will be no repeat of Kate's situation." Her voice was so cold it sent a chill up my spine. "He will never marry you. Ever."

"And why would you think he'd even want to?" My voice was calm despite the mix of anger and anguish boiling through me. "I've never been under any illusion as to how this relationship would end, Mrs. O'Connor."

"Perhaps so, but the fact that he cares for you—"

"Caring is not love. We have a strong relationship, yes,

but I'm not a wolf, and neither of us have ever forgotten that."

Her eyes were chips of blue ice, and the spine chills got stronger. "His sister said such a thing, once."

"Yes, and had the situation been different, would she have been given permission to marry Gabe?"

"Of course not." Her gaze remained hard. Ungiving. "And for one very good reason—the offspring of any such union rarely survives. Those who are not stillborn often have such serious defects they die before their first birthday. Few are those who live to claim their wolf heritage, let alone make it to adulthood."

A few still meant some *had* survived. A few meant there was still hope.

And yet, there was no such hope. Not for me.

"I've seen the anguish of such a situation," she continued relentlessly, "I've seen what it does not only to the couple involved, but to everyone around them. I don't want that for my son."

"Your son is a grown man and he has the right—"

"I will *not* stand idly by and see him hurt," she cut in curtly. "Not when he was younger, and certainly not now. Perhaps one day, when you have your own children, you will understand. In the meantime, take a bit of advice and end this relationship. Soon."

I stared at her, feeling like I was standing on the edge of a precipice; one step either way would lead to my doom. My heart pounded and my throat was dry, but the fear she stirred to life was met by something else—obstinacy, and perhaps even a bit of stupidity.

If my growing suspicion that this was my home—that there was no going back for me, no leaving—was true, then I had to be respected by *all* the members of the governing council. And right now, one of the most outspoken members of that council had me in her sights.

"I've already foreseen the end of our relationship, Mrs. O'Connor, and it ends with *my* heart broken, not his." I stepped closer. We were, surprisingly, the same height, despite the fact her rangy form and the way she held herself made her appear taller. "Until that moment, however, I will continue to see your son and enjoy every moment I can with him. And you can't—and won't —stop me."

Her eyes were now so narrow I could barely even see the chips of blue, and her aura dark with anger. "I could have you thrown out of this reservation—"

"Oh, you can try," I cut in. "But I think you'll find neither Katie nor the wild magic itself would like that situation."

"Is that a threat?"

My answering smile held no humor. "No. Simply a statement of fact."

"Then at least we now know where we both stand on this matter."

"Yes."

She would be doing everything in her power to end my relationship with Aiden, and I would be doing everything in my power to thwart her.

Lights swept around the corner and sped toward us. I stepped back. The slight uptick of her mouth suggested she knew it *wasn't* a retreat.

Aiden pulled up and climbed out of her BMW. As he helped her into the car, I walked over to the truck and waited. Now that the confrontation was over, my gut churned and the shakes had begun. It took several breaths to calm them—or, at least, outwardly enough to hopefully fool

Aiden. The inward shakiness would take nothing less than several large glasses of whiskey to calm.

"Is everything all right?" He clicked the truck's remote and then opened the door.

"Yes."

He snorted and helped me into the cab. "I got the same monosyllabic response from my mother. I believe neither."

"Honestly, there's nothing for you to worry about."

"Meaning there's absolutely *everything* to worry about." He slammed the door shut and ran around to the driver side. Once he'd pulled out and was heading out of town, he added, "What exactly did she say to you?"

"Nothing I wasn't expecting." I shifted slightly to view him better. "I got the impression in the restaurant that she ran someone off—was that someone the wolf you loved and lost? The one you're reluctant to talk about?"

"No. I ran Mia off, not my mother." He hesitated and then grimaced. "I gave her a choice. She chose the second option."

Which wasn't him, obviously. "What did she do?"

"She lied. Everything she'd told me about herself—every single thing—wasn't true." He glanced at me, his eyes filled with shadows and hurt. He loved her still, despite everything, and that damn near shattered my already aching heart. "My mother never liked her, but she also never did anything physical to disrupt or otherwise end my relationship with her."

Which no doubt meant she'd done everything in her power to verbally run her off—something I suspected she intended with me. Thank God a good percentage of our customers at the café were tourists or human locals—even if she ordered the wolves to avoid our venue, we could still survive.

"But she *has* run one of your lovers off?"

"Yes. When I was eighteen and head over heels for a wolf who turned out to be a rather close relation." He glanced at me. "What did she say to you?"

A smile touched my lips. "That I would never be allowed to marry you. To which I replied, 'never fear, because that prospect has never been part of our equation.'"

"It looked a whole lot more serious than that when I came around the corner."

"That's the condensed version. Was Mia a local wolf?"

"I don't really want to talk about her—"

"And I don't really want to talk about your mother. Besides, you can't keep putting this discussion off forever. Not when you're the one who demanded utter honesty."

"I knew those words would come back to bite me," he muttered. He took a somewhat shuddering breath and released it slowly. "No, she wasn't local. She was a nurse who came here as part of the exchange program."

The exchange program being a means of ensuring reservations didn't get too inbred. "Where from?"

"The Raines, who hail from the Northern Territory."

And who were the only pack in that state, if I remembered correctly. "How long were you together before you discovered her lies?"

"Just over a year. We were set to marry." His expression was distant, and his aura swirled with pain that had neither been forgotten nor healed. "It was a simple text that alerted me something was wrong. It was from a man named Jude, demanding to know when the hell she was coming back home, because he was missing her something fierce."

"You read her texts?"

"Not intentionally. She was in the shower and the text

flashed up on the screen." He grimaced. "It did at least explain why she'd been so protective of her damn phone."

"And Jude was?"

"Her husband."

My gut dropped. No wonder he'd been so determined to uncover my secrets—he'd feared he was facing a similar situation. And, in many respects, he had been. "Oh fuck, Aiden—"

"Yeah." He shook his head. "She went back home five or six times while we were together, and I never thought anything about it. I just figured she was missing her pack. As it turns out, she was going back to see her husband rather than her family."

"Surely *he* must have suspected something was wrong?"

"Why would he? I didn't, not until that text. But even if he did, the Raine pack was going through hard times thanks to the long drought and a fall in tourist numbers. His entire family are omegas, and way down on the pack's food chain. It was her money that kept them going."

"Why go interstate to work, though? Surely she could have gotten at least some work in Darwin?"

"It's hard to run a cash grab scheme if you're well known in the territory."

"But she was married—surely that would have come up during a records search?"

"No, because it was common law."

I frowned. "But how would marrying you ease her pack's woes?"

His smile was bitter. "The O'Connors are a wealthy pack, thanks to our situation here. Any divorce settlement would have seen her well looked after."

And unless there'd been some sort of prenuptial agreement, she wouldn't have had to stay with him for long to gain a benefit.

"It's still hard to believe a wolf would let his mate—"

"Fuck another man?" he finished for me. "As an omega, he mightn't have had the choice."

"That suggests you think the pack gave its approval to the whole mess."

"Not so much approval, but forced a blind eye? Yeah, I suspect they did. Mia wasn't the only wolf who'd been placed in interstate packs to hook the unwary."

"But how—" I hesitated. "You used your ranger connections to find information out about her and the others?"

"I did indeed."

"So the ultimatum you gave her was either divorce him or break it off with you?"

"Yes. She obviously chose him, because she never came back."

I reached across and touched his thigh. He briefly wrapped his fingers around mine and squeezed them gently, but the thick sense of hurt and anger in him didn't ease. No surprise there—aside from the fact he'd loved her deeply, he was an alpha, and they never liked losing.

"I know it doesn't help much, but she's an utter fool." One who had no idea just what she'd thrown away, despite the fact she'd been with him for over a year.

"Thanks, Liz."

I gently extracted my hand and returned my gaze to the road. And tried not to think about the hurt that lay in my future.

Silence fell. We eventually stopped at the side of the road that ran along one of the compound's boundaries and climbed out of the truck. Mrs. O'Connor pulled up behind us and then wound down her window and said, "What happens now?"

"It might be best if you wait in the car, out of the drizzle," I said. "I'll attempt to create a protection circle and then connect to the wild magic."

Karleen nodded and wound the window back up. Aiden went to the back of his truck and hauled out a bright yellow raincoat. He held it up so I could slip my arms into it and then turned me around to zip it up.

"I know it's not exactly a fashion statement, but it will at least keep part of you dry."

"Thanks." I kissed him, well aware his mother watched and not really caring. "You'd better go join your mom."

"I'd rather stay right where I am. I'm not feeling overly happy with my mother right now."

I frowned. "I can't produce a protection circle large enough to encase us and her vehicle."

"Then don't. Just make it large enough for the three of us to stand within it. She and I are werewolves—a little rain isn't going to hurt us."

I had a feeling his mother wouldn't agree with that statement—at least not when she wore her Sunday best. But I kept my mouth closed and stepped into the gap between the two vehicles. While there was no protection from the rain, it did at least offer a little respite from the cool breeze.

I didn't immediately start spelling, though. Instead, I studied the trees opposite, looking for luminous, gossamer wisps. There were none evident, but I could nevertheless feel the distant pulse of power that was the main wellspring.

I just had to hope I could connect to either its threads or Katie's. To do anything else would not improve Karleen's opinion of me—though I personally doubted it could get much lower.

After a deep breath to center my energy, I began raising Ashworth's incorporeal protection circle, watching the spell strings closely, trying to keep them exactly as he'd structured them. But as the spell rose in the air around me, so too did the wild magic that was now a part of me. Or rather, had *always* been a part of me, but had simply lain dormant until I'd come into contact with the unrestrained magic here.

I ignored the fear-based shiver and continued with the spell. While the end result wasn't exactly the same as Ashworth's, it was close enough.

I tied off the ends but didn't immediately activate the spell, and glanced at Aiden. "Right, let's do this."

I might have said it softly, but his mother immediately left her car. There was certainly nothing wrong with her damn hearing.

I told them both where to stand and then activated the circle. "Don't move around too much, because if you hit the spell wall you'll tear it open."

Karleen's gaze swept the immediate area, no doubt seeking the threads she had no power to see. "How are we supposed to know where the boundaries are? And what use is a protection spell that's so easily shattered?"

"There's three feet of wiggle room around us," I said. "The circle's strength lies on the outside; had I made it similarly strong inside, it'd cause serious harm if you accidently stepped into it."

"Then let's proceed before the rain gets too much heavier."

Annoyance flared yet again, but I pushed it back and silently called to the wild magic. At first, nothing happened. The distant pulse of power continued unabated, and the night remained free of those luminous, fragile wisps of energy.

Then, gradually, a few responded, moving through the trees like slivers of moonbeams. I held out my hand; after a few heartbeats, the fragile strings slipped through the protection circle and twined themselves around my fingers. There was no sense of Katie within them, so I clenched my fingers and used them to amplify my call for her.

More moonbeam slivers responded. They curled around me, caressed me, amplifying the power of my call. After a few more minutes, a different sort of energy touched my skin. Katie had answered.

Your wish?

Her voice, I noted, was clearer and stronger than before. Either our connection was growing, or my tie to this place was. *Your mother wants to talk to you.*

I cannot speak directly to her. You know this.

You can if you inhabit me.

She was silent for a second. *That could drain you significantly, despite the wild magic's presence in your soul.*

A statement that basically confirmed my theory. *Then don't be long.*

Her amusement ran through me, as warm as a silvery sun shower. *I won't. Warn them.*

My gaze rose to Karleen's. "She's here, but you can't speak to her for long. As Aiden said, it'll take a lot of strength out of me."

She nodded, her expression a mix of hope and disbelief.

I took a deep breath and then closed my eyes. *Katie, the stage is yours.*

She stepped into me. Her soul sang with the energy of the forest around us, a force so fierce and bright that my skin burned and my heart raced. The air was sharper, thick with scents that stirred my soul and made my blood race with the need to hunt and chase. The night was brighter, too, and the moon a power I could feel deep in my heart, deep in my very soul.

Katie's soul, I reminded myself, not my own.

"What do you want, Mother?" Though the voice was mine, it held a cold power that was all Katie.

Karleen's eyes widened. Perhaps she recognized the tone if not the voice. "If this is truly Kate speaking, tell me what I said the night you told me of your intention to marry Gabe."

Katie forced a smile, though it was all teeth and little humor. "Over your dead body."

"And your response?"

"That no, actually, it was *my* dead body. Why are you here, Mother? What do you want?"

Karleen took a deep breath. Silver glistened in her eyes, but she quickly blinked the tears away. "I just want to know why you did this. Why did you sacrifice yourself in this manner?"

"It's no sacrifice to forever be a part of this land—"

"But none of us will live forever, and our deaths will leave you alone."

Katie smiled again, though this time it held none of the fierceness. "I will never be alone in this place. Gabe is with me in spirit, and I will always have kin—all my siblings will have children, and their children will have children, and so on."

"I still can't—"

"Mom, it was my destiny. It's always been my destiny. I suspected it when I was a child, and I foresaw it as a teenager."

"Then Gabe did not—"

"He was nothing more than the key that unlocked what

was meant to be. I convinced him, Mom, not the other way around."

The silver sheen made another brief appearance. "Then you *are* happy?"

"Yes. I have everything I've ever wanted."

"Then I can only be happy for you."

"Thanks, Mom." Katie hesitated. "But I do have a warning for you—be careful what you wish for, because you may just get it."

Karleen frowned. "And what is that supposed to mean?"

"You know well enough." Katie looked at Aiden. "Don't seek happiness in your past, big brother, even if it haunts you."

He frowned, his expression so similar to his mother's that I wanted to smile. I couldn't, because I wasn't yet in control.

"I don't—"

"You will, soon enough. I must go." To me, she silently added, *Contact the White Lady. The information she holds will help you track the flesh eater—but you must let her vengeance fly, otherwise her spirit will blight this reservation forever.*

And with that ominous warning ringing through my mind, she left my body.

EIGHT

The minute Katie left me, my knees collapsed and I hit the ground hard. My pulse pounded in my ears, and I couldn't seem to get enough air. The world spun around me, and for several seconds, unconsciousness loomed.

I clenched my hands and fought it. The wisps of wild magic were still wrapped around my fingers, and their energy surged in response, chasing away the darkness and lending me strength. It might only be borrowed strength, but right then, it didn't matter. Not if it kept me going long enough to get home.

There was a slight thump on the ground in front of me and then Aiden's hands on my shoulders, my face, concern evident in his touch. "Liz? Are you okay? Can I get you anything?"

I took a deep, shuddering breath and then opened my eyes. The night wasn't bright and the moon wasn't visible, and yet my eyes nevertheless stung.

I blinked rapidly, suddenly aware of the rain, the cold, and just how wet I now was despite the presence of the yellow raincoat. I shivered, and he instantly pulled me closer. The fierce, warm heat of him wrapped around me, and it made me feel as safe as I'd ever felt in my entire life.

And yet I couldn't help but be aware of a different kind of fierceness emanating from his mother.

"We need to get you out of these wet clothes and back home," Aiden said. "Before you catch a chill."

I smiled into his neck, my lips brushing his skin and tasting the musk of wolf and man. Katie's sensitivity to taste still lingered, despite the fact she no longer possessed my body.

"They breed us witches tougher than that, Aiden. I'll be right after a hot toddy and a long bath."

"Then let's—"

"We can't go anywhere until I release the protection circle." I took another deep breath that was filled with the warm, rich scent of him and then drew back. He didn't entirely release me though, and I wasn't about to object. If nothing else, it totally pissed off his mother. Although I guess the unhappy vibes could also have been the fact that she wasn't wearing a coat and was even more sodden than me.

I carefully unpicked the spell and released it, watching as both my magic and the wild faded into the silvery night.

"Right, it's safe to move." I raised my gaze to Karleen's. Her expression was set, and her eyes gave little away. Only the black swirl in her aura hinted at her agitation and annoyance. "Thank you for the pleasant evening, Mrs. O'Connor."

Her smile flashed but held little sincerity. "It was most... illuminating. Thank you for allowing me to speak to my daughter. Aiden, we'll talk later."

"Sure." His tone was flat. The annoyance was back, obviously.

As his mother strode back to her car, he rose and helped me up. Then he swung me fully into his arms and carried me to his truck, placing me carefully in the passenger seat and then grabbing a blanket from the back and tucking it around me. It went some way to warming my legs and feet. My shoes, I noted sadly, were not only wet and muddy, but were now missing several sparkly stones. A bin rather than my wardrobe was their next resting place.

Aiden jumped into the driver seat and started her up. "I take it you're heading back home rather than coming to my place now?"

I smiled, but it was filled with the weariness that beat through me. "Yeah. I'm sorry, but I'm just—"

"Bone tired, and perhaps more than a little sick of the whole O'Connor pack right now."

"Well, not the whole pack."

"I'll be having words with my mother—"

"Don't—not for me. It's not worth stirring up bad feelings for a relationship that has a limited time frame."

He was silent for too many seconds, and though his expression gave nothing away, his grip on the steering wheel seemed that little bit tighter. "What did Katie's warning to me mean?"

"You know exactly what she meant."

"Well, she obviously meant Mia, but she isn't exactly haunting me."

"Isn't she?" I said softly. "From what I can gather, you've avoided a long-term relationship with another wolf ever since."

He glanced at me, expression annoyed. "I haven't avoided them. I just haven't found anyone—"

"Who lived up to her standard."

His responding snort was a somewhat bitter sound. "And thank God for that, given she was a liar and a cheat."

And one who still held his heart. "Perhaps Katie simply meant it's time you stop hanging on to whatever feelings you have for her—be they anger, hurt, or something else—and start looking for the wolf who will be your future."

"I haven't finished with the present, thank you very much."

"And I, for one, am very happy to hear that." I hesitated. "I doubt your mother will be, though."

"My mother needs to stick her nose—"

"She's your mom," I reminded him gently. "Nose sticking comes with the territory."

He raised an eyebrow. "Speaking from experience?"

I laughed again, though it was a somewhat harsh sound. "Only from watching the interaction of my parents with my siblings. Mom no doubt loved me, but I was never her shining light, and I was always aware of it. I never had the same sort of interaction with her as my brother and sister."

"I never knew you had a brother."

I nodded. "His name is Julius, and he became the family's shining light after my sister was murdered. And from what Monty has said, he's done them proud by marrying into another powerful family and presenting them with four grandkids."

"Four? How much older is he than you?"

"Not that much. They had two sets of twins, apparently."

"Do they run in the family?"

"Yes, although my parents weren't blessed."

He glanced at me. "Why would twins be considered a blessing? I'd have thought multiple births would mean any

152

witch power would be split between them, and given how your parents reacted to you…"

He let the sentence fade, and I grimaced. "You'd think so, but apparently the opposite often happens, for some weird reason. It's why many lesser witch lines marry into families with a history of multiple births—they hope that, through them, they may improve their standing."

He snorted. "Which is really no different to what Mia's pack was attempting."

"It's a whole lot different, Aiden. For a start, there's no deceit or lies." There couldn't be when all the witch lines, royal or not, were carefully catalogued to inhibit any chance of inbreeding—as there had been, back in the darker ages. "But I have no doubt Juli's children will make advantageous marriages when they're old enough and further cement the hold on power my family has up there."

"That's still treating your kids as an asset, and I can't abide that."

"Neither can I, but not all witches can marry for love, Aiden. Not when there are only six bloodlines."

"A strange statement, considering what happened to you."

I shrugged. "My situation isn't common—"

"It seriously wouldn't *want* to be, given forced marriages are against the law."

Only if those doing the forcing are caught. There'd never been much hope of that happening in my case—not when my father and Clayton were so well respected in Canberra. I swallowed the bitterness that rose in my throat and tried not to think about what I'd do—how I'd react—when they finally caught up with us. Because they would, and sooner rather than later. I shivered.

Aiden immediately switched up the heating. "Did your sister make such a marriage before she was murdered?"

I nodded and rubbed my arms. My sister's killer had never been caught, and most believed his soul had been claimed by the dark entities he'd dealt with. And yet, for some reason, the prophetic part of me thought otherwise—though, as often was the case with such things, it gave no reason why.

"She was engaged, and while it was an advantageous match, she also loved him."

Not that it would have mattered if she hadn't. Cat had always been determined to get a firm hold on the wheels of power—something she'd been well on the way to doing when she'd been the first nineteen-year-old to ever be named successor to a seat on the high council. I presumed that position had instead gone to Juli, as my father certainly wouldn't ever consider me an option.

Aiden didn't comment, and for that I was grateful. I wanted to speak about my family about as much as he wanted to speak about his. In that, we were well matched.

He pulled to a halt in front of the café, then jumped out and ran around to open my door. Once I'd shed his blanket, he helped me down, but he didn't immediately release me. Instead, he wrapped his arms tightly around my body and kissed me with so much passion and heat that my pulse raced, my body ached, and my heart just about shattered. Rain dripped onto my head and dribbled down my neck, but it didn't matter. Nothing did. Nothing except this man and this kiss and the time we still had together.

I had a long habit of falling for inappropriate men, and history was definitely repeating itself here, but at least this time I'd gone into our relationship with my eyes wide open. As much as my heart might hanker for more, that could never be our fate. I simply had to settle for what I had and enjoy it while I could.

He broke off with a soft groan and then stepped back. "Are you sure you won't consider coming back with me? I can google the recipe for a hot toddy easily enough."

I hesitated and then shook my head. "While I'd like nothing more, I'm dead on my feet, Aiden. Can we make it tomorrow night?"

"Of course we can." He brushed his fingers down my cheek, then swung around and offered me his arm. "The least I can do is ensure you get to the front door without being attacked by flesh strippers or White Ladies."

I smiled and slipped my arm through his. "Let's hope both are silent tonight. I need the rest."

"Amen to that."

I dug my keys out of my bag; he took them from me and opened the door. I kissed him goodbye, and it once again turned into something hot and heavy. Perhaps Katie's words had impacted more than I'd suspected, even if he'd rather live for the moment than worry about the future.

He groaned again and pulled away. "You'd better get inside before I'm tempted to do something that'll get me arrested."

"You're the head ranger—no one would be game enough to arrest you."

"Maybe not, but report me for inappropriate actions? Hell yeah. I've been in the job long enough to have made a few enemies, and they'd love nothing more than to see me gone." He brushed his fingers across my lips, creating trailing spots of heat that had my insides quivering. "Get some rest. I'll see you tomorrow."

I kissed his fingertips, resisted the urge to do more, and then stepped inside. He spun on a heel and walked quickly away. I watched until he'd climbed into his truck and then closed the door and wearily climbed the stairs to our apartment.

Once I'd kicked off my shoes and dumped them in the nearest waste bin, I ran a bath, tossed in a mix of lavender, bergamot, and chamomile bath salts, then made a hot toddy to help warm the chill within. The combination of both did at least go some way to easing the fatigue.

Belle returned home just as the bathwater was beginning to cool. "Hey, I thought you were spending the night at Aiden's?"

"I was, but the glow of expectation was somewhat diminished when the surprise date turned out to be a meeting with his mother."

"Who obviously wasn't happy about your position in Aiden's life and who told you so in no uncertain terms." She crossed her arms and leaned against the doorframe. "What was Aiden's response?"

"That his relationships are none of her business."

"Then you've nothing to worry about." Her gaze narrowed. "But you're not actually worrying about that, are you?"

"No." I told her what Katie had said. "I've always known it would end, but having her basically tell him to look to the future was something of a kick."

"Did she give any indication whether said future love was days, weeks, or months away?"

"Well, no—"

"Then stop worrying about it. Just enjoy being with the man while you can."

"Oh, I intend to. I'm just wallowing in a moment of self-pity."

"Will another drink help with the wallowing?"

I grinned and held up my empty glass. "Another drink never goes astray."

She plucked the glass from my hand and headed out. I climbed out of the bath and, once I was dry, grabbed my robe and followed her into the small kitchen. "How was the date with Kash?"

"Disappointing." Her tone was gloomy. "He's totally focused on transcribing the damn books. I think I could have run around naked and shaken my maracas in front of his nose and he still wouldn't have noticed."

"The man's insane. Your maracas are magnificent."

"I know, right?" She handed me my glass, then took a drink from her own. "I've come to the conclusion he's simply more interested in the books than me."

"He definitely needs his head read."

"Yeah. I might stop going over there for a few days, just to see if he starts thinking with the little head again." Her gaze was troubled. "In truth, his interest in the books is getting a little too intent for my liking."

I frowned. Kash wasn't a witch, but that didn't mean there couldn't be a nefarious reason for his sudden interest. History was, after all, littered with the burned remnants of those without magical nous attempting witchcraft. "Do you think he might be tempted to use or sell the information?"

She hesitated. "Even if he was, I've now placed a block to prevent him either using the books or contacting anyone about them."

"What books have you been giving him?"

"A few of her earlier spell books, but mostly her notes on supernatural beings. I thought—given what's been happening here—they were probably the most urgent."

"At least it's nothing major." I accepted my drink with a

nod of thanks. "But if you're uneasy, then I think we need to find another means of transcribing the books."

"I agree. But rather than finding someone new, what if I investigated a means of doing it ourselves?"

"Wouldn't that be expensive?" The café was now making a little profit, but we still had to be careful, given our savings balance remained on the low side of things.

"If we got a system like his, yes, but we could buy a much simpler book scanner for under a thousand." She hesitated. "Of course, we'd also need another computer, given ours is devoted to ordering and wages. That'll add to the cost."

"It could still be a worthwhile investment, given just how rare your gran's books are."

"True. I'll do some more investigating."

"And Kash?"

She shrugged. "If he can't get his shit together, he's out the door. There's plenty of other fish in the sea."

"And one of them is named Monty—"

She swiped at me, and I jumped back with a laugh. "Do not mention *his* name and sex in the same sentence. Seriously, are you trying to give me nightmares?"

I grinned. "Hey, his physical prowess might be even better than his magic."

"I do *not* want to think about that. Ever." She downed her drink in several gulps. "I'm off for a shower—are you staying up?"

I shook my head. "I'm heading over to Aiden's tomorrow night, so I'd best get an early night."

"At least one of us is getting some action," she replied gloomily.

"Hey, plenty of fish, remember?" I tossed back the rest of my drink. The heated whiskey burned all the way down to my belly and sent a warm glow humming through the rest of me.

"Yes, but it would be nice to have a relationship that lasts more than a few weeks."

"Well, there's always—" I broke the sentence off with a yelp as she lunged for me, and then ran for my bedroom, laughing all the way.

"Your next revival potion is going to be revolting!" she called after me.

Which only made me laugh harder.

I stripped off my dressing gown, climbed into bed, and was quickly asleep. Unfortunately, it was a state that didn't last.

I wasn't entirely sure what woke me. The night was quiet, and the gentle pulse of the spells surrounding the building gave no indication that they were, in any way, being probed, let alone under attack. But I was lying in an almost fetal position, my legs tucked up near my chest and the top sheet loosely covering my head—something I used to do as a kid when prophetic dreams were distantly whispering and I had no desire to listen.

And yet it wasn't a dream that had woken me. It was more a presence—an awareness that something was out there, watching and waiting.

I opened my eyes. With the sheet over my head, I couldn't see anything, but I doubted there was actually anything to see. Not here in the bedroom, anyway.

I reached for my phone on the side table. It was twelve-thirty, which was smack bang in the middle of witching hour, a time when those who haunted the spectral edge of the world gained substance and reality. In truth, it wasn't so much the time that was important, but rather the position and strength of the moon. A full moon held far more power than a waxing or waning one, but in either case, midnight was when she reached her highest point in the sky and was therefore at her most powerful.

So, had some sort of supernatural activity woken me, or was something stranger going on? I suspected the latter, if only because of the continuing sensation of being watched.

And given there was no one and nothing in my room, that really didn't make much sense.

I silently cursed my psychic senses for not giving me the damn night off and climbed out of bed. After hastily pulling on jeans and a sweater, I headed out into the hallway, briefly looking right and left to pin down the odd sensation before striding through the living area and onto the balcony. The drizzle had finally eased, but an icy wind now whistled across the night, bringing with it the distant promise of more rain. I crossed my arms against the cold and stalked across to the railing. The street below was silent and empty. Nothing stirred, not even fragile wisps of wild magic.

Then a small movement caught my eye and I saw her—the White Lady. She stood near the corner where I'd caught my first true glimpse of her, and this time, she wasn't walking away. Instead, she stood her ground and motioned me down.

I remained exactly where I was. Katie might have told me to speak to her, but I couldn't do so without Belle being present, and I sure as hell wasn't about to put either of our lives in danger without first taking some precautions.

"I can't speak to you." It was softly said, but I had no doubt she'd hear me despite the half block distance between us. "That's not my talent. If there's something you want of me, then you need to relay it through my friend."

Her ghostly form shimmered, as if in agitation. After a moment, she nodded—a short, sharp movement that had the gossamer strands of her hair streaming behind her like long clouds.

"We'll also be well protected," I continued. "If you, in any way, try to harm either of us, we'll force you on and end any hope of you attaining the revenge you seek."

Again her form shimmered, though this time I suspected it was anger. Her second sharp nod didn't ease the tension within; in fact, it had the opposite effect. Given she was of magic, it was totally possible that—even in ghostly form—she was more powerful than either of us.

"Who the hell are you talking to?"

Belle's sudden question made me jump. I'd been so focused on the specter that I hadn't heard the door open. "Our White Lady. She wants to speak to us."

Belle stopped beside me and stared down the street. "She was definitely a powerful witch in her time—even from here, I can feel the thrum of her power. I'm not entirely sure speaking to her is the wisest course of action."

Spirits were Belle's domain, not mine, and I had no intention of gainsaying any decision she made when it came to dealing with them. "You think she's playing us?"

Belle hesitated, her gaze narrowing as she studied the ghostly figure in the distance. "I see no lie in her but there's a whole lot of rage, and I really don't like the feel of it. It could be covering a darker intent."

"What do you want to do?"

She glanced at me. "I do have one suggestion, but neither you nor she might like it."

I raised my eyebrows. "And that suggestion is?"

"We invite her in."

"Into the reading room?"

Belle nodded. "It would be far easier than trying to summon her, and no protection circle we could create on the fly would ever be as strong as the spells that now protect this place."

I frowned. "It would mean creating a temporary doorway through the magic to allow her entry—"

"Yes, but the 'can do no harm' rule would remain intact and unaltered."

Yes, but opening a doorway also meant we'd be vulnerable to attack in those few vital minutes between disengagement and realignment if there happened to be other White Ladies in the area. But she was right—this building was the one place we'd be utterly safe. "You think she'll go for it?"

"If she wants to talk to us, she will."

I glanced past her to our ghost and explained what we were going to do. "We promise no harm will come to you within our walls unless you attempt to attack us. This is the only way we'll communicate with you, now that we're aware just how powerful a witch you are."

For several seconds, she didn't respond. The wind stirred the insubstantial swaths of her gown, blowing them around her form like a foaming wave. Then she made a sharp 'whatever' gesture with her hand and nodded a third time.

"Give us ten minutes." I pushed away from the railing and headed inside, Belle on my heels. "You'll need to weave the temporary exception through the current spell threads— you've a better feel for her than me."

"That's if what I'm feeling is real. There's no guarantee with a magic-capable spirit."

I glanced back as we clattered down the stairs. "That's sounds like you've been reading up on them."

"A little. While I really do doubt she intends either of us harm, there're enough stories out there to emphasize the need for caution."

"And here I was thinking magic-capable spirits were a rarity." I strode into the reading room and began shifting chairs away from the center of the room.

"They are, but witches and spirits have been interacting for eons. That's plenty of time for deceptions to happen."

"I'm gathering most ended badly?"

"Very."

"Fabulous."

Her smile flashed, though it didn't do much to dispel the tension crinkling the corners of her eyes. "We'll be fine in here."

We probably would, but that didn't make what we were about to do any less dangerous. I helped Belle move the table, then rolled up the rug to reveal the spell work etched into the floor. We sat in the middle of it all and shuffled forward until our knees touched. Then, after taking a deep breath to center my energy, I narrowed my gaze and carefully began disengaging—but not deactivating—the multi-strand spell layers that shielded this place. Holding them tightly in one hand to prevent unravelling, I slowly and carefully pried away the threads that dealt with the more ghostly end of things and then glanced at Belle. "Your turn."

She immediately began to spell. Her magic wove through the existing strands, setting perimeters and adding time restraints. If, for any reason, we were rendered unconscious, the White Lady still had a limited time frame within our walls before the rest of the threads slammed down and evicted her.

Of course, if we *were* rendered unconscious and she *did* intend us harm, those time restraints probably wouldn't save us.

Once Belle had finished, I reconnected the main spells.

As the full hum of power once again flowed around us, I said, "How do you want to proceed?"

She hesitated. "The same way as we usually do for a hostile spirit. Me talking, you monitoring."

I searched her face for a second, seeing both her fear and determination. "If you'd rather not do this—"

"We need to find out what her link to both the shifters and the flesh stripper is, and this is the only way we can do it."

"Maybe, but your safety is more important—"

"Which is why you're going to forcibly disconnect us the minute she—in any way—attempts a takeover."

"What if she's more powerful than either of us?"

"That's totally possible, but there's no way she could be more powerful than the wild magic that now inhabits you."

I wasn't entirely sure the wild magic could be called upon in such a situation, but who really knew? There were already a whole lot of things happening that shouldn't be possible.

I held out my hands. She gripped them and squeezed lightly, as if I was the one who was stepping into danger rather than her.

"Ready?" she said, and then at my nod added, "Right, let's see what this bitch wants."

NINE

She took a deep breath, then reached for the specter prowling the pavement outside the building.

White Lady, we are ready. Her mental tone was both powerful and confident. *You may enter the building as long as you wish us no harm.*

The surrounding magic pulsed, and the hum of power briefly intensified as the threads reacted to the spirit passing through them. She wasn't immediately rejected, which was at least something.

Then she was in front of us. Thanks to my link with Belle, I could now see her very clearly. She remained in white, but there were flashes of crimson in her flowing hair, and her eyes were silver. Not just a witch, but also a royal one.

Do you have a name, spirit? Belle asked.

Names hold power. I do not wish to give you mine.

And yet you want our help.

Yes.

Why?

To stop the monsters that feast in this place.

Again, why? What is your connection to them?

They killed my child. They must be made to pay.

But in seeking such vengeance, you have paid a great price.

One I would pay ten times over to stop these creatures.

How is the shifter you killed connected to the flesh stripper? Are they working together?

No. They are one and the same.

Surprise rippled through Belle and echoed through me. *Shifters can't shred humans the way these things do.*

We are not dealing with shifters as such, but rather Empusae, a variation of the Empusa. They can attain several forms—that of Strix, and also a young woman. It is the latter with which they lure their prey to their deaths.

My heart began to beat a whole lot faster. I'd heard owls hooting a number of times over the last few nights—had it been the Empusae? Is that why the wild magic had surrounded me before I'd entered that tree tunnel?

Are they capable of magic? Belle asked.

Yes.

Given you've already killed one of them, Belle said, *why do you need our help?*

Because the other two are now aware of my presence. I will not so easily gain another opportunity to stop them.

How long have you been hunting them?

Decades.

And this is the first time you've managed to take one of them? Incredulousness filled Belle's mental voice. *Why, when you retain much of your witch power?*

Much is still not enough. The one I trapped was younger —foolish—and an easy target. The other two—one of them an elder—are not.

In case it's escaped your notice, neither of us are exactly powerful.

Perhaps not, but one of you commands the power of this land and the other can be a vessel through which I can move and act.

A chill went through me. *No, Belle—*

Let's not discount anything until we know more. To the spirit, she added, *Meaning what? Now is not the time to speak in riddles.*

The Empusae are aware of my presence. I have not been able to trace them since I bound and drowned the younger—

Which suggests, Belle cut in, *they might have simply left.*

They have not.

How can you be so sure? Belle's grip tightened on mine as she spoke, and strength began to flow from me to her. It was little more than a trickle, but the longer this went, the more help she'd need. Communicating with spirits didn't normally drain her so quickly, but this was a very different type of spirit to the ones we usually dealt with.

Because it ends here. I have foreseen it.

Have you also foreseen how that end will be achieved?

First you must trap and restrain them. Then you must stab them through the heart with blessed silver.

Which explained the needle Monty and I had found in the shifter's body. It hadn't been used to pin her to the owl form—it had been the means by which her soul had been evicted from her flesh.

And have you any ideas how we're going to trap them, given we can't even find them?

Most Empusae cannot be active during the day. They tend to hide in deep forest, in places well-protected from sunlight.

Why then was the one you killed in a cottage rather than a cave with the others?

She was foolish, as I said. But the Empusae do not roost together, only hunt. It is a means of ensuring the line goes on if one is caught.

That suggests the younger are the offspring of the elder.

They are. Many spirits are capable of reproduction, even if the means is very different to that of humans.

The breeding habit of demonic spirits was *not* something I wanted to think about. Ever.

This entire reservation is littered with mines, which gives them ample places in which to hide, Belle said. *It'd be helpful if you could provide a little more information about their roosting habits.*

Belle's pull on my strength grew; we'd have to end this soon before it became dangerous.

You will not find them in mines, unless they are the type that goes horizontally rather than vertically into the ground. They are not comfortable in deep earth, our spirit said. *And their roosts have a distinct aroma—one that is a combination of rotting meat and sickly perfume.*

Which was exactly what I'd smelled in the tree cave where we'd found the second lot of feathers—and that meant we needed to go back there and place a trap rather than just an alert.

And if we do find and trap them? Belle asked. *What then? What exactly do you want of me?*

You may kill the remaining younger creature, but I wish to inhabit your body while you stab the elder through the heart. I want to feel her blood pulse over my fingers. I want to watch as the light dies in her eyes and the realization of oblivion claims her. Only then can I rest in peace.

Belle's inner shudder once again echoed through me. *Allowing a spirit to claim his or her flesh is something every spirit talker is warned against.*

I guarantee, on my eternal soul, that I will not overstay or seek to claim what is not mine.

Your eternal soul was damned the minute you forsook moving on in favor of vengeance.

The White Lady's form shimmered, and her agitation sung through the air.

I have the goddess's blessing in this endeavor—my soul is not damned. Light will be my end, not darkness.

No goddess I knew would bless vengeance—unless, of course, she meant one of the many war goddesses. She was certainly old enough to be a follower of more ancient deities.

If I agree to this, Belle said, *how do I contact you? If they're able to sense your presence, you cannot simply follow us around.*

No. The White Lady hesitated. *If you call for Vita, I will hear its echo through the spirit world and respond. The name gives you no power over me, but there are few who bear it these days and none such who do reside in this place.*

Fine. Leave with our blessing, and we'll be in contact.

Vita immediately did so. A few seconds later, the time exception ran out and the full weight of the spell layers slammed down. We'd been in contact far longer than I presumed.

Belle took a shuddering breath, then released her grip on my fingers and fell into my arms. I held her while she shook, pushing energy into her body through our telepathic connection despite the ache flaring in the back of my brain.

"Enough," she said eventually, her voice etched with

weariness. "One of us needs to be mobile for work tomorrow."

"Work tomorrow is the least of my worries right now. Are you able to get to your feet, or do you want some help?"

"I think I can manage."

She pushed out of my grip, then slowly got up. I rose with her, keeping a hand on her elbow just in case. To say she was unsteady was something of an understatement.

"If this is how talking to her for ten minutes affects you, I hate to think what letting her spirit into your body is going to do." My voice was grim. "You can't—"

"It's not like we have many other options right now. Besides, didn't Katie warn you to give her what she wanted?"

I slipped an arm around her waist, providing support as we slowly made our way out of the reading room. "Yes, but—"

"Vita wants this. She *needs* this. And if she doesn't get it, the run of troubles we've had of late will seem like a party compared to the hell she'll rain down on us."

"But what she wants might well kill you—"

"Yes, and that means we have to find a way of preventing the force of her spirit overwhelming and destroying mine. There'd have to be spells—we can't be the only witches in the history of all magic forced to deal with a spirit this way."

"A comment that does not ease my fear in any way." I took a deep breath that also didn't help a whole lot. "Monty, Ashworth, or Eli might know, but in the meantime, we should check your gran's books."

"I'll do that tomorrow. You need to grab everyone else and figure some means of trapping these things."

A smile tugged my lips as we made our way up the

stairs. "My familiar has her bossy pants on this evening, it seems."

"Actually, I haven't got *any* pants on."

My grin grew. "Monty would be pleased to—"

The rest of that sentence ended in a grunt as Belle shoved her weight sideways and my shoulder hit the wall. "Tart," I muttered, smiling as I straightened.

"If you stop being a teasing bitch, I'll stop being a tart."

I chuckled softly. "One foul revitalization potion coming up."

"I'll be asleep before you finish making it."

"Then I'll wake you."

"You're evil, you know that?"

I chuckled again. Once I'd helped her into bed, I headed back down to make the potion. She was asleep by the time I returned, so I left the concoction on the bedside table for her to drink whenever she woke up.

When I checked her the following morning, the glass was empty but she remained asleep—and probably would be for a good part of the day, given just how drained she'd been.

I rang Monty and Ashworth and asked them to come over once the café had closed for the day, but I couldn't get hold of Aiden. I left a message and then got down to doing all the little things needing to be done before we opened. The day was steady rather than flat-out, which at least gave me time to run upstairs and check Belle was okay. She was only just beginning to stir by the time Monty and Ashworth arrived.

"Hey," Monty said. "What's up?"

"We had a visit from our White Lady last night, and Belle finally communicated with her."

Monty's expression immediately became concerned. "Is

Belle okay? I know strong spirits can seriously drain a talker's strength."

I placed a hand on his arm. "She's fine but she's sleeping it off."

His relief was evident. No matter what Belle might think, his flirtation was more than just a game. "Good. But if she needs a revitalization potion—"

Fuck, no, came Belle's somewhat sleepy comment. *He'd probably add some ever-loving herbs to it.*

I barely restrained my grin. *Even Monty wouldn't go that far. He wants to woo and win by fair means, not foul. Are you coming down?*

That would be another 'fuck, no.'

This time, the laugh escaped but I managed to cover it with a cough—though Monty's raised eyebrow suggested I hadn't done so too well.

"White Lady?" Ashworth said. "I gather I'm missing some information on this matter."

"Monty didn't fill you in?"

Ashworth scowled at him. "No, he did not."

Monty's grin was as wide as the Cheshire Cat's. "Must have forgotten. Sorry."

"A little more sincerity wouldn't go astray," Ashworth growled. "What has the specter got to do with the flesh stripper?"

"Everything. She's hunting them." I headed behind the counter to make us all a coffee.

"Them?" Monty said, voice sharp. "There's more than one?"

"There were three, but thanks to the fact she killed one—"

"The shape shifters are the flesh strippers?" he cut in excitedly. "That's awesome."

Ashworth gave him a dark look. "Only the greenest of witches would consider such a fact awesome."

"Hey, it's not my fault you're jaded, old man."

"This old man will clip you over the ears if you don't watch your manners."

Monty's grin widened. "Even on crutches, I could outrun you."

"I wouldn't bet on that."

"Neither would I." My voice was dry. I placed their coffees on the table, then sat down and quickly updated them on everything Vita had told us about the Empusae. "We've two problems—"

"One, how to find them," Ashworth cut in.

"And two, how to protect Belle if she does allow this spirit to share her body," Monty added.

"It's the second one that worries me the most—do either of you know any spells that can stop a hostile takeover?"

Ashworth frowned. "I know there are a few that can force a spirit out of a body, but I've only ever used the usual assortment of charms to prevent the spirit ever getting a hold. They won't work in a case like this."

"Not when the spirit is this strong or being willingly invited," Monty said. "I know uni had a course on spiritual possession. I'll contact the dean and see if he can give us something."

"Just tell him it's urgent," Ashworth said. "Deans are not well-known for their speed in answering questions."

Monty raised his eyebrows. "Speaking from experience?"

"Yes, and it's not one I want to repeat." His gaze came to mine. "Did Vita make any suggestions as to how to find their daytime hideouts?"

"We're in a werewolf reservation," Monty said. "Surely

Aiden can motivate the packs to do a thorough check of their compounds."

"I doubt the Empusae would be dumb enough to roost anywhere near the wolves," Ashworth said. "They'd surely know their scent would draw inquisitive noses."

"At least one of them was using that tree cave we found," I said. "So we'll need to set a trap around that."

Monty frowned. "If they're capable of minor magic, they might sense any spell we place and simply avoid the area."

Ashworth nodded. "Which is why we'd also run a concealment spell through it. If they *are* capable of only minor magics, they shouldn't sense it."

"Worth a shot," Monty agreed. "And the sooner we do it, the better."

I pushed to my feet. "Then let's go now, because I've a date with Aiden tonight."

"I'm rather surprised he's not here," Ashworth said. "Is everything okay?"

I gave him a somewhat wry look. "Yes, and don't start getting all grandfatherly on me."

A smile twitched his lips. "The local grump will never get all grandfatherly. He just doesn't want to see two of his favorite people falling out."

"Aiden will be shocked to hear you place him in such a category."

"Why? As werewolves go, he's pretty sensible, and there certainly isn't enough sensible around these parts at the moment."

"Gee, I wonder where *that* barb was aimed?" Monty said.

Ashworth's eyes twinkled, though his expression remained stern. "Shall I drive, or would you rather, Liz?"

I hesitated. Aiden still hadn't returned my call, so who knew what was actually happening tonight. "You can drive. Aiden can always swing past and pick me up if we get delayed."

"We'll have to detour past my place first," Monty said. "I haven't got my kit with me."

Ashworth made a disparaging noise. "That's slack, young man. Very slack indeed."

"Well, if someone hadn't been sitting on the horn in an attempt to hurry me up, maybe I would have remembered."

As they headed for the door, I ran upstairs to grab some clothes in case Aiden did swing by to pick me up, then raced down to the reading room to grab the backpack. Once I'd collected my keys and purse from under the counter, I said, *Belle, will you be all right alone for the next few hours?*

Other than a slight headache, I'm perfectly fine. I'll make another potion and then do some research, just in case Monty or Ashworth don't come up with anything.

Just make sure you eat something solid. We're going to need you at full strength.

It feels weird for you to be saying that to me; it's usually the reverse.

It is, and I personally hope it doesn't happen too often. I don't think I could stand the stress.

Welcome to my world. Her mental tone was dry. *Are you staying at Aiden's tonight?*

I presume so.

See you tomorrow then.

I locked the front door and then ran down to Ashworth's borrowed SUV. Once we reached Monty's, I ran inside to grab his kit. This apparently didn't please Eamon, who greeted me with a hiss and a flash of his dangerous claws. This time, though, he missed—deliberately, I suspected, if the glint in his eyes was anything to go by.

It didn't take us long to drive to the location of the tree cave, but getting through the forest with any speed with Monty on crutches wasn't easy. At least this time he avoided falling over.

When we did finally reach the clearing, Ashworth said, "Interesting spell."

I glanced at him sharply. "Why? It's a simple trigger spell."

"There's nothing simple about *that*. Not when the wild magic is present and concealing it."

I frowned. "How can wild magic conceal a spell? It can't act without direction..."

My voice faded. Except that some of it had, ever since Katie's soul had become a part of it.

"I suspect it's not deliberate concealment." Monty stopped beside me, the scent of his sweat stinging the air and his breathing a little ragged. "But rather the force of it overshadowing your spell and muting its power."

"Either way, its presence could be very useful," Ashworth said. "We'll use your simpler spell to hide our trap one."

I frowned. "Your trap has to be pretty powerful to contain the Empusae, and I'm not entirely sure the wild magic will conceal it."

"We'll run a second concealment spell through the weave," Monty said. "Between that and the wild magic, we should be right."

I hoped so, because right now this was our one and only hope of stopping at least one of the remaining Empusae.

"Can you disconnect your spell so that we can weave ours along the inside of it?" Ashworth said.

I did so, and then tried not to feel like a third wheel as they set up their protection circle and stepped inside it. This was the main reason why I couldn't be the reservation witch, no matter how deep my connection with the wild magic got. I simply wasn't good enough at spell craft.

Which didn't stop me learning from every spell they did. I might not have the knowledge, but I did have a good memory.

I crossed my arms and watched through narrowed eyes as their magic rose around the inside of my deactivated trigger spell. The two of them worked well as a team, and the spell was intricate and powerful. I wasn't entirely sure I'd ever be able to replicate the thing in full, but there were certainly bits of it I could apply to the spells I did know. Monty might have warned multiple times about the dangers of ad hoc spelling, but I'd been doing it for nearly half my life now. When you didn't have the training, you simply adapted.

Once they'd tied off and activated their trap, Ashworth glanced at me and said, "Right, your turn."

I immediately reconnected my spell, then silently studied it. Ashworth was right. Between the pulse of wild magic and the concealment spell they'd threaded through their snare, there was no outward evidence of our magics around the tree cave.

Ashworth helped Monty to his feet and then collected their spell stones. "Now it's just a matter of waiting."

Monty nodded. "Let's just hope the pair of them aren't out hunting for another victim to strip tonight."

"If they are, there's not a lot we can do about it." Ashworth glanced at me. "Give us a call the minute your spell goes off."

I raised an eyebrow. "I'm not daft enough to come out and confront this thing all by myself."

His expression was skeptical, though his eyes twinkled. "I'm not entirely sure that's true."

I snorted. "For that, you can pay for your next coffee."

"And I'm more than happy to do so, lassie." A smile tugged at his lips. "In fact, I think Monty should do his bit to support the café, too, and start paying for all those cakes he demolishes."

"I demolish the old stuff, not the new. I'm considerate like that."

I shook my head at their continuing banter and followed the two of them out of the clearing. Ashworth dropped us both off and then continued home to Eli. I didn't bother going back into the café—I simply went around the back to collect our SUV, headed across to the supermarket to grab some food, then drove down to Aiden's place.

Once I'd let myself in—again without setting off the alarm, which maybe meant I was getting the hang of it—I went upstairs for a quick shower. He still wasn't home by the time I'd finished, so I pulled on a loose-fitting summery dress and went back down to help myself to some of his rather fine whiskey. He rang just as I took my first sip.

"Have you got an alarm on your booze cabinet or something?" I said by way of greeting.

"No—why?"

His voice, I noted, was etched with weariness. "I just raided your Jameson Limited Reserve."

He laughed softly. "Tough day?"

"Yes and no." I took another sip and felt the happy burn all the way down. "It sounds as if you'll need a glass when you get home."

"Three or four, more likely. We've spent the day dealing with a murder in the Marin compound."

My pulse rate stuttered. "Not another flesh-stripper victim, I hope?"

"No. Just two men fighting over a damn woman. Things escalated badly before we could get there, and the victim died on the way to hospital."

"Oh crap, Aiden, I'm sorry." I hesitated. "Was it someone you knew?"

"I went to school with both of them."

"Oh God—"

"Yeah," he cut in softly. "He's looking at several years behind bars, at least, despite the number of people who've testified the death was accidental."

"And the families involved? How are they coping?"

I didn't know a whole lot about werewolf life within the compounds—no one did, outside the werewolves who lived there—but I had been into the Marin compound once as a guest, and I'd witnessed how pack leaders dealt with a suspected murderer. Or would-be murderer, in that particular case. Thankfully, the sharpshooter who'd actually been behind the attempt on my life hadn't banked on Aiden's quick reflexes.

"You've met Rocco Marin. You can imagine how well he's taking it."

"It wasn't one of his sons, was it?"

"No, but it doesn't matter. The alphas are responsible for the behavior of the entire pack, and something like this is a major stain on their reputation."

I frowned. "How? It wasn't intentional—"

"No, but the punch that knocked Terrell down and eventually killed him was thrown in a fit of anger, and no wolf pack needs anyone thinking they cannot control their emotions. We've spent too long fighting that image."

"I can't imagine there'd be many who believe the Hollywood version of a werewolf these days."

"Perhaps not, but that's not really the issue. Few other packs want to deal with those who cannot control themselves—and *that* hurts their prospects when it comes to mates."

Which was a major problem with a pack as small as the Marin—they needed outside blood to prevent inbreeding.

"Have you had dinner yet?" Aiden added.

"No, but I stopped at Woolies on the way here and got some supplies."

"Steak and chips, by chance?"

"Garnished with bacon and eggs, and no green shit for you."

He laughed softly. "You surely do know the way to a werewolf's heart."

I wish... "You showering before dinner or after?"

"Before. It's been a hot and sticky day, and I think the deodorant has given up."

I grinned. "I certainly have no desire to sit anywhere near a stinky werewolf."

He laughed again. "I'll be there in twenty."

I hung up and then walked across to the wall of windows, watching the ducks waddle around catching bugs in the grass, while I sipped the whiskey and waited for Aiden to arrive.

As the lights of his truck lit the driveway and scared the ducks away, I went back to the kitchen to prepare him a drink and top up my own. He walked in a few seconds later, looking weary and radiating sadness.

I walked over, handed him the glass, and then rose on my toes and kissed him, soft and lingering.

"A greeting a man could get used to." He tossed back the drink in one gulp. "I think a few more of each just might do the trick."

He snaked his free arm around my waist and pulled me closer. Our kiss was long and intense, filled with an aching hunger that came as much from his need to forget as desire. Even when the kiss did end, he didn't immediately release me. He just rested his forehead against mine and held me, obviously needing the comfort of contact to ease the inner turmoil so evident in his aura.

Eventually, he drew in a deep breath and released me. I plucked the glass from his hand and walked back to the kitchen to refill it. He followed me across and sat on one of the stools lining the counter. "Tell me about your day."

I did, knowing full well he simply didn't want to think about the loss of a friend and the necessary incarceration of another.

"I'll talk to the council in the morning and get them to order a full search through all the compounds," Aiden said. "But if they smell as bad as you've said, they would have been found by now."

"Which is exactly what Ashworth said." I leaned on the bench and took another drink. The loose neck of my dress ballooned open, and his gaze slid from my face to my throat and then down. I wasn't wearing any underclothes, and desire surged through his aura and stung the air. "How many mines are there in the reservation that match the horizontal criteria?"

"More than a hundred. But once the compounds are searched, I'll get them to check the surrounding areas. We might get lucky."

"Right now, luck might be all we have."

"Then here's hoping that trap you set works." He tossed back the remains of his drink. "I'm off to shower."

"Good. Even upwind, the smell was getting unpleasant."

A grin teased his lips. "The pong must be bad if your very human but delightfully cute nose is smelling it so strongly."

"It is, so get thee to a shower while I start cooking."

He grinned and headed upstairs. By the time he came back down—wearing loose sweatpants and a T-shirt that hugged his lean but muscular frame in all the right places—I was plating up our meals.

I poured us both another whiskey then moved across to the other side of the counter and sat beside him. We chatted as we ate, our conversation moving easily across a number of topics, all of them deliberately light. He really didn't want to think about what had happened during the day, let alone talk about it. Not any more than he already had, anyway.

Night had well and truly set in by the time we'd finished dinner and moved on to coffee. Though it was still relatively early, he yawned hugely.

"Sorry," he said. "I think the late nights have finally gotten to me."

I clucked my tongue. "My werewolf has no stamina. How sad."

His blue eyes twinkled. "I've more than enough stamina to tumble you, my dear witch."

"How about a massage first?"

His eyebrows rose. "Me or you?"

I placed a hand on his arm and felt his muscles twitch in response. Felt the tension of grief underneath. "I'm thinking you need it more than me tonight."

"Possibly." He caught my hand, raised it to his lips, and kissed my fingers. "I must, however, warn that having you sitting naked astride my buttocks while you massage my back could lead to a very thorough ravishing."

I grinned. "I'd be disappointed if it didn't."

"Good. Shall we retire upstairs?"

"Sounds like a plan to me."

He rose and, maintaining his grip on my hand, led me up the stairs. The cool light of the rising moon filtered through the vast wall of glass lining the lakeside wall of his bedroom and gave the masculine tones of the room a silvery glow. While he stripped off, I went into the en suite to grab the massage oil. It was one I'd made especially for him, and contained little more than the faintest whisper of sandal-wood, a scent I liked and that didn't overwhelm his more sensitive olfactory senses.

He was lying on the bed when I walked back into the room. I took a long moment to admire him in all his naked glory, running my gaze from his feet, up his well-toned legs, then over his hips and firm butt and up his spine to his slightly wider shoulders. Werewolves might generally be on the lean side, but his body was powerful and perfectly proportioned. Beautiful, even.

And, for this moment, totally mine to do with as I pleased.

Anticipation shot through me as I walked over. "Ready?"

"And raring," he murmured. "You might want to play, but with the scent of your desire riding the air, it's already taking every ounce of control I have not to haul you into my arms and make love to you."

I tsked. "All good things come to those who wait."

"As long as I'm not waiting too long," he said, his eyes filled with warm amusement when his gaze met mine.

I dolloped oil into my palm, then put the bottle down and started massaging his feet. He made a growly noise and then closed his eyes. I gradually made my way up his legs, letting my thumbs intermittently tease the inside of his thighs and brush across his balls; the growly noises became more constant. Grinning, I stripped off my dress and then sat naked astride his butt.

He groaned. Loudly. "Damn it, woman, are you trying to kill me?"

I laughed and slapped his back lightly. "Hush. I'm working here."

He muttered something incomprehensible and then closed his eyes and let me continue. I worked my way up his back, pressing my fingers into his muscles until the knots were released and the tension in him gradually eased.

"And now," I murmured, reaching for the oil again, "we need to do the front—"

He muttered something under his breath and then, after a flurry of movement in which the oil bottle ended up on the other side of the room, I was lying underneath him.

It felt good. More than good.

The glint in his eyes was decidedly wicked. "And now it's your turn to feel a little torture."

I raised an eyebrow, amusement teasing my lips. "Given the thick rod of heat currently pulsing against my stomach, I'm thinking the torture won't be lasting too long."

"Oh, I do so like a challenge," he murmured. "Consider it accepted."

He kissed me softly, tenderly, and then moved down, touching and tasting and kissing, all the while avoiding the one area that ached so badly for his touch. When his tongue did finally flick—ever so briefly—over my clitoris, a moan that was part pleasure, part frustration escaped. He chuckled softly, his breath fiery against my wet skin. "Had enough yet?"

"If you don't finish what you started, I'm going to—" I cut the sentence off and gasped as his tongue flicked again.

"Going to what?" he murmured.

"Finish it off myself!"

He chuckled again and then complied, his tongue an instrument of utter delight. My orgasm hit hard, and satisfaction rumbled up his throat as I shuddered and shook. The aftershocks had barely eased when he rose above me, his gaze holding mine, his eyes burning with desire and something that was almost proprietary.

Then, with tortuous slowness, he slipped inside me. The feel of him, so hard and hot, penetrated every fiber, enveloping me in a heat that was basic and yet so very powerful. He began to move, gradually at first and then more urgently, until his thrusts were so fierce the entire bed shook. Desire stirred anew, flooding swiftly through me, until every inch ached with desperate need.

"Oh God, Aiden..."

The plea had barely left my lips when the shuddering began and another orgasm hit. He followed me over that abyss, his lips catching mine, kissing me hard until bliss had ebbed and sanity returned.

"That," he murmured, slipping to one side and then gathering me in his arms, "was glorious."

"Hmmm," I murmured, unable to get anything more sensible out.

He laughed softly and planted a kiss on my shoulder. "Isn't it the male who's supposed to fall straight asleep after sex?"

"This is an equal opportunity relationship." I yawned as hugely as he had earlier. "Which means it's your turn to cook in the morning."

"Done." He tucked me a little closer, his body warm against my spine. "Night, gorgeous."

"Night," I murmured, and for the first time in days, fell into a deep, untroubled sleep.

We were deep in the midst of the lunchtime rush the following day when unease prickled down my spine. I collected the empty plates on the table I was wiping down and surreptitiously studied the nearby ones. There were a few new faces interspersed between the old, but none of them set off my internal radar. I frowned and walked back to the kitchen, handing the plates to Frank—our kitchen hand—before joining Belle behind the counter.

She took one look at my face and said, "What's wrong?"

"I don't know." My gaze swept the café. From here, all the tables were visible, and not one of them had anyone that in any way spelled trouble. "I'm just getting this weird vibe that shit is about to hit."

Belle placed two lattes beside a slice of honeycomb cheesecake and a chocolate brownie, and then shoved the tray forward for Penny—our full-time waitress—to collect. "The reservation, the café, or us personally?"

"Undefined."

"Unhelpful."

I smiled. "That's not exactly unusual when it comes to my prophetic abilities."

"True." She briefly scanned the room. "I'm not sensing anything or anyone untoward—"

She stopped abruptly and her gaze widened. *Fuck, get upstairs. Now.*

Why? I said, even as I turned and bolted for the stairs.

An unknown witch is about to step inside the café, Belle said. *And she's protected telepathically.*

I silently swore. While there could be a number of logical reasons for a witch to be wearing such a band, both trepidation and instinct were warning her doing so as she was about to step into our café was no accident.

I was halfway up the stairs and out of immediate sight when the small bell above the door chimed. A tremor ran across the lines of magic protecting the café as the unknown witch stepped inside; that reaction, however minor, said that while her intent wasn't malicious, our spells were nevertheless uncertain as to her actual purpose for being here. But it obviously wasn't just for coffee and something to eat.

I scooted around the corner and then stopped, leaning against my bedroom door and sucking in great gulps of air.

Goddammit, she has the coloring of a Sarr, Belle said.

Someone you know? Or worse—at least from a secrecy point of view—someone from her family?

I don't immediately recognize her, but I've lots of cousins and she could be any one of those. If you connect on a deeper level, you'll be able to see—

If she's a tracer sent here to suss us out, she might well sense my presence in your mind.

If she's a tracer, she's going to sense your presence even with all the additional spell layers on the upper floor.

True, but it's still a risk I'd rather not take. I paused. *Has she spotted you?*

Not yet. I'm standing behind the coffee machine. She's currently just looking around.

I'll contact Monty and see if he's been advised of her presence.

He would have warned us.

Unless she spelled him into silence.

She doesn't feel strong enough to have pulled something like that on him.

Then maybe it was Canberra itself.

Not even the strongest witch on the council could place a restriction spell on another witch over such a long distance.

The strongest witches on the council were my damn parents and husband, and I wouldn't use the word 'couldn't' in any sentence when it came to the three of them.

I got out my phone, then quietly moved away from the stairs so there was no chance of my conversation being heard downstairs—no matter how unlikely that even was given the clatter of cutlery and plates and the overall buzz of conversation.

Monty answered second ring. "If you're wanting an update on the flesh strippers, talk to your ranger. He hasn't given me squat so far today."

"That's not—"

"So there's been another murder?"

"No, and will you just let me finish?"

He must have heard the anxiety in my voice, because all humor fell from his voice. "What's the problem?"

"Did you get any sort of notice from Canberra about a tracer being sent here?"

"No, and you know I would have told you if I had. I take it such a witch has arrived?"

"She's in the café right now."

"And you're certain she's here to snoop?"

"My sixth sense is."

"I'll be there in ten."

"Thanks, Monty."

I wasn't sure what he could do, but he was the reservation witch and should have been advised of this witch's presence if she was here at the council's behest.

I shoved my phone away and resisted the urged to pace. I needed to keep calm and not do anything that could be felt along the magical lines by the woman below. I didn't know much about tracers aside from the fact they were basically magical bloodhounds able to pick up the 'scent' of a spell and trace it back to its originator. If she was here for me, then the one thing in my favor was the fact that none of the spells I'd created before I'd fled Canberra would be active now—and even if some were, the signature of those spells would be vastly different to the ones I created now, thanks in part to the presence of the wild magic.

Fuck, Belle said. *She's got an old photo of you and is asking Penny if she's seen you. Says you're believed to be working here somewhere.*

I closed my eyes against the surge of panic. This was it. This was the first step in us being found. And there was nothing I could do to avoid it—not now. Even if we did attempt to alter the tracer's memories, it would do no good. Belle might be a powerful telepath but even she couldn't entirely erase her mental 'fingerprints' in someone else's mind. Another telepath would see the signs even if they couldn't undo what she'd done. It might even be enough to draw Clayton out of his Canberra cave to reclaim his bride and fully consummate the marriage.

The memory of cold hands on unresponsive flesh stirred, and a deep shudder ran through me. I swallowed against the bitter rise of bile and said, *And Penny's response?*

189

That it's illegal to employ anyone that young in this reservation.

Despite the tension, I couldn't help but smile. *Has the tracer spotted you yet?*

She's headed my way now.

The impending sense of doom ramped up several degrees. I closed my eyes, trying to remain calm, trying not to panic.

Succeeding to do neither.

Then, after what seemed like an eternity, Belle said, her voice echoing my panic, *Oh fuck, Liz, she* is *a goddamn Sarr.*

TEN

A cousin?
Probably, because Daniela is a very popular name in my branch of the family tree.

But you don't immediately recognize her?

No, but I've a bad feeling she knows who I am.

It was usually me getting the bad feelings. If Belle was getting them, then things were catastrophic. *If there's one thing in our favor, it's the fact that you no longer resemble that scrawny teenager.*

Yeah, but how many Sarr witches hang around a witch who looks like a Marlowe?

Not many at all. *Except she's looking for a witch with green eyes, not silver. It's something.*

I'm not sure it'll be enough. She's obviously done some research on our fake identities.

There was another long stretch of silence. I knew Belle was answering the woman's questions, but tension sawed at me. I wanted to know what was happening—needed to know what was happening—but I dare not touch Belle's thoughts any deeper because I had no idea just how sensitive tracers were. If Ashworth had sensed the merging of our magics when we'd been standing together, then it was logical a magical bloodhound would be more than capable of such a feat—and maybe even be able to do so when neither of us were in the same room, but simply connected mind to mind.

She knew who I was before I said anything, Belle commented eventually. *So she has done her homework.*

Meaning she'll also be well aware your partner is one Elizabeth Grace.

Most likely. And I never thought I'd ever be happy to see him, but Monty just arrived.

And?

He's hobbled straight up to the other witch and asked what the hell she was doing in his reservation.

I smiled. *I can just imagine the indignant tone and expression.*

Oh yeah, he's putting on a full show. She paused. *Daniela is apologizing profusely for not advising him of her presence and purpose. She says she was unaware the reservation position had been filled.*

You buying that excuse?

Nope. And neither is Monty.

He was no fool, even if he sometimes acted it. *Is she quizzing him?*

Yes. She showed him the photo and said she's looking for Elizabeth Marlowe, who disappeared from the capital a few years ago.

Fabulous. I scrubbed a hand through my hair and dislodged the hairband holding my ponytail. I swore, picked it up, and looped it back into place. *The photo can't be a recent one.*

If there was one thing Belle and I had been very careful about, it was putting up photos on social media.

It's not—you're probably thirteen or fourteen in it.

Meaning there was a small chance she wouldn't take one look at me and make the connection. I'd been a late developer, and my curves hadn't really blossomed until I was nearly eighteen. Add that to the eye color change and there was a hope—a small sliver of hope—that she wouldn't make the connection. Although the silver eyes did make me look like my mother.

And at least half a dozen of your cousins, Belle commented. *But as far as anyone in Canberra is concerned, your eyes are green. Eyes generally don't change color, so it may be our saving grace.*

Except for the fact I'm obviously a blueblood and you're obviously a Sarr, and she's looking for one if not both.

True. Belle's uncertainty and fear ran down the mental line, sharpening my own. *She and Monty are sitting down for a coffee and a friendly chat.*

I bit back the urge to swear. I knew well enough that he intended nothing more than to ease the tracer's suspicions about the café and its owners, but the longer she spent here, the more time she could study the magic protecting this place and pick out the deeper similarities to whatever spell she was using to trace me.

If she *was* using a spell, that was. It was always possible she was here thanks to the Interspecies Investigations Report that had been submitted to Canberra some months ago. That report—a summation of the actions taken after a vampire had killed a human within the reservation—had apparently mentioned our presence, however offhand it might have been.

I scrubbed my hands across my eyes. *If I don't appear, she's going to think it suspicious.*

Yes. Belle paused. *Monty's giving me a weird look. Hang on while I connect.*

Monty wasn't telepathic in any way, shape, or form, but he didn't have to be. Belle could simply skim his thoughts to get the gist of what he wanted. I switched my weight from one foot to the other and tried to curb my impatience.

Okay, Monty's also of the opinion you need to come down, but he suggests I disappear upstairs so we're not seen together.

I took a deep breath and released it slowly. I could do this. I *had* to do this. But first, a few changes. I spun and ran for the bathroom. After sweeping my hair into a tight bun, I hurriedly applied some eyeliner to alter the appearance of my eyes and then eye shadow to enhance the color of them. The result certainly made the color of my eyes pop, but would it be enough? I crossed mental fingers and then said, *Meet you on the stairs, then.*

I resolutely strode toward them. Belle touched my arm on her way up, an encouragement that didn't help much. I plastered a smile on my face then walked around the counter to take care of the waiting orders.

Penny appeared and slid another one across the counter to me. "It's for Monty's table, and they'd like to speak to you when you have the chance."

"Thanks, Penny."

She nodded, then picked up the latte and hot chocolate I'd just made and whisked them away to their waiting table. I finished the rest of the orders, then made Monty's and Daniela's. After another deep breath that didn't do a whole lot to calm the sick churning in my gut, I picked up the cups and walked across to them. Monty's welcoming smile was bright, but his eyes were filled with all sorts of warning.

He wants you to be calm and casual, Belle said.

Like I'm normally not?

Not when it comes to your family. He says your panic is often visible in your eyes.

Nothing much I can do about that. I placed their cups on the table and then said, "You wanted to speak to me?"

"This is Daniela Sarr," Monty said smoothly. "She's here searching for a missing witch."

"There's not many of us in this res; if any were missing, you'd know about it more than me." I glanced at Daniela, my smile pleasant enough. Her eyes narrowed a little when her gaze met mine. She'd been expecting green, not silver. "I'm not sure how I can help unless you think she might be one of our customers."

"Possibly." Her voice was a familiar echo of Belle's deep, rich tone. She pushed the photograph across the table toward me. "Have you seen her around?"

I studied the photo, outwardly calm, inwardly a screaming mess. It had been taken on a family outing on a yacht owned by a politician trying to curry favor with my dad, and it was a day I remembered clearly simply because of how seasick I'd gotten. Even in this photo, as old as it was, I looked rather green around the edges.

But there was no point in avoiding the obvious.

"Other than her eyes, she could almost be my sister."

"Eye color can be changed easily enough with contacts. Lean forward."

I hesitated then obeyed, and hoped like hell she couldn't hear the hammering of my heart. Her gaze searched mine for several, very long seconds, and then she grunted. Her expression was an odd mix of suspicion and confusion.

The latter did nothing to ease the inner fear. "I take it the woman in the photo is not a full-blood?"

"Quite the opposite," Daniela said. "Her parents are in fact Eleanor and Lawrence Marlowe."

"Who I presume are persons of significance in Canberra, given the gravitas you've placed on their names."

Her eyebrows rose. "You don't know them?"

"Why would I? I grew up in Darwin." I shrugged. "Either way, I don't think the woman in the photo has been here."

"Are you sure?"

"I think I'd remember seeing someone who looks like me." My voice was dry, the inner turmoil absent. "But if you can grab something personal of hers—something she wears everyday—I might be able to track her for you."

"That is an impossibility, I'm afraid."

"Then I'm not sure how else I can help." I hesitated, wanting to run but resisting the urge. "Anything else I can do for you?"

"Yes," she said. "The spells around this café? They have an unusual method of construction."

I smiled, even as my stomach flip-flopped. "So Monty and every other witch who has walked in here has said."

"They *are* your spells, then?"

"Not just mine. I wove some, Belle wove some, and somehow, the wild magic got mixed up in it all."

"The wild magic has a habit of doing that," Monty said. "I've sent reports back to Canberra about it."

She nodded and leaned back in her chair to study me for a second. "According to your birth certificate, your parents were human. You shouldn't be capable of any magic, let alone magic this strong."

I raised my eyebrows, feigning alarm. "You've been checking up on me? Why? What have I done?"

She waved a hand, a motion that was meant to be reassuring. "Nothing. I simply did some research on all witches who currently inhabit this reservation. One can never be too careful."

One couldn't—it was a motto I'd lived the last twelve years by.

"Why?" I gestured at the photo she'd yet to pick up. "Do you think we're responsible for this woman's disappearance?"

"No. But hiding secrets? Most definitely."

Which we are, Belle said.

Yes, but just how deeply into the puzzle we present is she willing to go?

Deep enough to make her dangerous.

I take it you've managed to get through her shields?

Only enough to catch emotions more than distinct thoughts, Belle said. *This psi protection band is far stronger than the ones the IIS or even Monty had on.*

"When Elizabeth disappeared," Daniela was saying, "her friend and familiar—Isabelle Sarr—went with her. I find it a rather large coincidence you and your friend have the same first names and family coloring of our missing witches."

"Elizabeth and Isabelle aren't exactly rare names." Monty's voice was dry. "Last time I was up in Canberra, the place was littered with witches bearing those names."

"You will also have noted how rare it is for a Marlowe witch to be hanging around with a Sarr."

"I'm not a Marlowe," I said, voice even despite the increasingly violent churning in my gut, "no matter how much I resemble one."

Daniela's expression was disbelieving.

"Well, if the other Elizabeth *is* here," Monty said, drawing her attention away from me again, "she might be hard to find. There're plenty of places within the reservation where a person intent on remaining unfound can hide."

"We suspect her hiding is being done in plain sight," Daniela said. "And we've traced her as far as Peak's Point."

It was all I could do to stand still, to not react. We'd been driven out of Peak's Point by the Fitzgerald brothers—who were more carnival tricksters than actual witches—and had left them with a parting gift involving rats. Their response had been to send a sharpshooter after us—and if he'd managed to track us here, then it was no surprise a tracer had.

Something neither of us even thought about, Belle said, mental tone gloomy.

If she talked to anyone, it would have been the brothers rather than the sharpshooter. He's locked up in Melbourne. They're not.

Ashworth had never really told us how much prison time the brothers had been given, but they'd certainly be serving it in Canberra, as that's where the main witch jail was located.

"Pike's Peak is a fair way from the Faelan Reservation," Monty commented. "Why are you so certain she came here?"

"I interviewed the two men who hired a sharpshooter to take Ms. Grace out." Her gaze flicked to me. "And they swear you are the person in the photo."

A cool smile touched my lips. "Meaning you're choosing to believe two charlatans convicted of attempted murder over both my statement *and* the evidence of your own eyes. In which case, I guess there's no point in me saying anything else, is there?" I glanced at Monty. "If you need anything else—or if you find something belonging to the missing woman and want me to attempt a tracing, you know where to find me. In the meantime, I'd better get back to work. Pleasant meeting you, Ms. Sarr."

Oh, pleasant and yet catty at the same time, Belle said. *Bravo.*

Nothing I say or do is going to make a difference now. As the old quote goes, 'the end is nigh.'

I turned and walked away. And, no matter how much I wanted to race back upstairs and down the bottle of Glen-fiddich I had stashed in my wardrobe, I forced myself to remain behind the counter and serve as if there was absolutely nothing wrong. As if my safe little world wasn't on the brink of utter collapse.

Monty and Daniela stayed for another half hour, the two of them chatting in a friendly enough manner. Things had quietened down by the time they departed, so I left Penny with orders to call me down if things got hectic again and headed upstairs.

Belle handed me a large glass of whiskey. "Whatever happens, happens. It's no use worrying about it now."

I gulped down half the drink, felt the burn all the way down to my stomach. It didn't entirely calm the churning but it did go some way to easing it.

"I've spent most of my adult life worrying about it, Belle. I doubt that's going to change now."

She laughed softly. "No. But at least we're not alone."

I couldn't help smiling. "No, because Monty will definitely use any excuse, big or small, to stand by your side."

She took a swipe at me, and I jumped back with a laugh. Whiskey sloshed, threatening to spill over the sides of the glass. "Hey, careful, we can't waste good booze on the floor."

"If you're not careful," she said, her expression severe but her eyes filled with amusement, "I'll tuck the bottle on top of the highest cupboard possible, where you'll never reach it."

"There are such things as ladders, you know." I took another drink, my smile fading. "I know we can't avoid what's coming, but I really would like to get some warning of it."

The last thing I wanted or needed was to walk into the café one morning to find my father or husband waiting for me.

"That's not likely to happen, given they definitely mean us harm."

I waved my free hand around. "And do you really think these spells will stand up against the combined might of two of the strongest witches in Canberra?"

"If it was just our magic, no. But it's not, is it?"

"True." I finished the remnants of the whiskey and held out the glass for a top up. "As much as I know Monty will pass on any information he has, I seriously doubt he'll be informed of either my father's or Clayton's movements."

"No." Belle pursed her lips. "You know, now might be an ideal time to come totally clean with Ashworth. He and Eli have a lot of contacts in Canberra that aren't related to either of our families, and they could just be the eyes and ears we need up there."

I took a deep breath and released it slowly. "You're right, but after so many damn years of hiding—"

"It's nice to have people to confide in," Belle said softly. "Nice to have people we can trust."

It was. "I guess if the shit does hit the fan and we come out the other side okay, you can finally contact your mom again."

"Yes." She paused. "I do miss her."

I knew, and felt guilty about that, even though I was well aware Belle had never regretted any of the choices she'd made. Not then, not now.

I finished the second glass of whiskey. "I'll ring Ashworth and see if they're available for a chat tonight."

Belle squeezed my arm. "It'll be all right. Really, it will."

I smiled and nodded and didn't believe a word of it. Ashworth answered on the fifth ring. "If you're calling for an update, I've got squat. You need to talk to your ranger rather than me."

A smile touched my lips. "That's a statement I've heard before."

"Monty?"

"Yes. And it may just be that there is no more information for Aiden to share."

Ashworth grunted. It was not a happy sound. "To what do I owe this honor, then?"

I hesitated, and then said in a rush, "I was wondering if you and Eli were available after dinner. I need to talk to you both about something."

"That sounds serious."

"It is."

"Wouldn't happen to have anything to do with that stray tracer witch I saw Monty with, would it?"

"You don't miss much, do you?"

"I may be getting old, lass, but there's nothing wrong with either my eyes or my senses."

I smiled. "I never said there was. I'll bring the cake if you provide the coffee."

"Done deal. Any time after eight will be fine—Eli should be finished teaching the kids by then."

Eli had fully thrown himself into reservation life and

was now helping to coach the local kids' cricket and football teams. Apparently he'd been pretty good at both when he was younger and had only quit playing regional cricket in his forties after a rather nasty fight with two rogue witches had left him with a shattered right hip and a warning from the doctors that high-impact sports were now out of bounds.

"I'll be there. Thanks, Ashworth."

"I think it's way time you started calling me Ira, lass."

I smiled. "It just sounds... wrong."

He snorted. "You're a strange one sometimes."

"Which is why you like me so much. See you soon."

I hung up and met Belle's gaze. "Are you coming?"

She hesitated. "I think it better one of us stays here. I don't trust that witch one iota."

I raised my eyebrow. "You think she'll break in magically and snoop?"

"Yes, if only because she's a Sarr, and we're not exactly well known for following the rules."

"True." Although Sarrs not following the rules had been a major factor in our escape. "I wish there was some sort of spell to stop prying magic."

"If there is, Monty would know it."

My eyebrows rose again. "Are you actually volunteering to contact the man and ask for help?"

"I wasn't volunteering to do any such thing." Her voice was dry. "And he'll need to teach us both, as it'll take the two of us to weave it through the current connections."

I nodded. "Of course, there's no saying such a spell would keep my father or Clayton out."

"Probably not. In fact, it might be better if it didn't, simply because we've a chance of holding our ground within the café thanks to the multiple layers of spells and wild magic. I'm not sure that'll be the case outside."

I doubted it would be the case inside, but I guess we'd find out soon enough. I finished the rest of my drink and rinsed the glass out. "I'd better head downstairs and help Penny close up."

"I'll finish checking Gran's indexes for anything else on Empusae, then head over to the storage to grab the books. That way, the SUV is free tonight if you want to use it."

"I've had two large whiskies in short order—I think I'd better walk."

She raised her eyebrows. "You're not going to Aiden's tonight?"

"He's got another meeting with the council, so depends on what time that finishes. If it's too late, he'll just stay up at the compound."

Amusement touched her lips. "We're talking about a werewolf with an extremely high sex drive. It won't be too late."

"It might be for me."

"Yeah, right. Believing *that*."

I grinned and went downstairs. By the time I headed over to Ashworth and Eli's, flags of red and gold were staining the evening skies and the night air was crisp, holding a vague promise of rain. Their place was a beautiful old miner's cottage that still held all of its original features, even though it had been fully renovated and contained all the mod cons, including solar panels and central heating. I knocked on the gorgeous old paneled front door and heard the echo of footsteps approaching.

"Perfect timing," Ashworth said as he opened the door. "Eli's just put a fresh pot of coffee on."

He stepped to one side and waved me in. I walked down the central corridor—the walls of which were soft gray with white accents on all the lovely old fretwork—and entered the kitchen living area that dominated the entire rear of the house.

Eli swooped in, gave me a hug, and then relieved me of the cake box I was carrying. "And what sweet delights have you brought us to drown our sorrows in?"

"Banana bread cheesecake, Toblerone cheesecake, chocolate caramel slice, and a couple of slices of black forest cake."

"Damn, this witch must be very bad news indeed." Ashworth pulled out a chair to seat me, then walked over to gather plates and forks.

"She is. Or will be."

Eli raised his eyebrows. "Meaning this visit is due more to your prophetic abilities than anything she's said or done?"

I grimaced. "It's a mix of both."

"Well, wait until we all get comfortable, and then you can tell us everything."

Which, once we all had a strong cup of coffee laced with a dram or two of whiskey, was exactly what I did. About my family, my forced marriage, how Belle had been my savior, and what we'd done since then to conceal who we really were.

Everything.

Neither of them immediately said anything by the time I finished. Then Ashworth—big, gruff, grumbly Ashworth—walked around the table, pulled me to my feet, and wrapped me in the biggest, sweetest bear hug I'd ever had. Tears filled my eyes and tumbled over my lashes. Belle was right. We weren't alone. With Aiden, Monty, and now Ashworth and Eli, we'd not only a safe harbor and people who would stand with us, but I'd found the family I'd been searching almost my entire life for.

"Dear God, lass, to think the two of you had to go

through all that when you were still so young," Ashworth murmured. "After such a betrayal, it's no wonder you were so reluctant to trust anyone."

I nodded, then took a deep, somewhat shuddering breath and pulled back. Eli silently offered me a tissue, and then wrapped me in a hug before I could use it.

"We're here for you," he murmured. "No matter what it takes. No matter what we have to do. You know that, don't you?"

His words heralded in another round of tears. "Sorry," I hiccupped eventually. "I think all the booze I drank earlier has weakened my emotional control."

"Lass, you've been so wound up—so guarded—these last twelve years, it's a wonder you're not a crying mess on the floor. I would be."

It was an image that had amusement bubbling. "I seriously doubt it."

Eli grinned, produced another tissue, and lightly patted my cheeks to soak up the remaining tears. "Believe it. He's a softy at heart—cries in movies all the time."

I smiled. "So do I. Maybe we're related somewhere in the distant past."

"Given the intermingling of Ashworth and Marlowe blood over the decades, it's quite possible. Sit, lass, and I'll grab us all another coffee."

"And I'll serve up the rest of those cakes," Eli said. "Because this is definitely a two-cake problem."

I smiled and reclaimed my chair. Once our coffees were refreshed and the additional cake had been served, Ashworth said, "Right, first things first—we need a means of tracking their movements."

"They'll fly rather than drive," Eli commented. "And they'll no doubt get their secretaries to make the bookings."

"Unless they want to keep their visit to Melbourne secret," I commented. "Few people know about my marriage, remember."

"It'd be interesting to discover just how they managed to bury the documents," Eli said. "All marriages by law have to be entered into the witch registry, and that's an open document that's regularly checked to ensure there's no close blood ties. If your marriage was buried, then they either bribed or spelled someone—and the latter would be an extremely dangerous step for someone who values their reputation as much as either Clayton or Lawrence."

"I have no doubt my father is arrogant enough to believe his actions would never be questioned."

"While it's true both he and Clayton hold great power, they are also not without enemies, and some of those are not to be messed with." Ashworth scooped up the last bit of black forest cake and munched on it contemplatively. "All the same, I have a friend who works in the registry office; might see if he can discreetly follow it up. It'll be a handy thing to know come the confrontation."

A shudder ran through me, and I hastily gulped down whiskey-fueled coffee. It didn't do much to chase the chill away.

Eli reached across the table and briefly squeezed my hand. "The other thing we need is a warning they're on their way, and that may be harder."

"Unless, of course, we can discreetly rope in the Black Lantern Society," Ashworth said.

"Who are?" I asked.

"Basically, a secret society of witches, werewolves, and vampires who work behind the scenes to right wrongs and bring justice to those who escape it."

"Sounds more like a vigilante group than anything else."

And while I wanted Clayton and my father out of my life, I didn't want them dead. Even if, in the deepest of my dreams, I imagined Clayton dying in a thousand different, horrible ways.

"It's... whatever it needs to be," Ashworth said. "They mostly don't go as far as vigilantism, though."

Mostly also meant it wasn't totally off the books. "It can't be too secret if you and Eli know about it."

"We know because my sister is one of its matriarchs." Ashworth grimaced. "Of course, she doesn't know *I* know."

"She will if we ask for her help," Eli said, amused. "And she won't be pleased."

Ashworth waved his hand. "She owes me a favor or two."

I frowned. "I don't want either of you to get into—"

"Lass, I took an oath to uphold the law. What happened to you is not only against the law, but also against common decency. Even if we weren't friends, I'd be helping you."

I blinked once again against the sting of tears. "Thank you. Both of you."

Eli nodded. "We'll start putting out feelers tomorrow. We can formulate a plan of action once we've got everything in place."

"What about Monty?" I asked. "He'll want to help—"

"No doubt," Ashworth said, "but he's your cousin, and given they obviously suspect you're in this reservation, any move or request he makes will be analyzed and checked. It's far better if he remains out of the loop as far as this goes."

"He won't like that."

Amusement crinkled the corners of Ashworth's eyes. "Aye, he won't, and I can't say that makes me unhappy."

I smiled and scooped up the last of my cheesecake. "He spent a good deal of time with Daniela today, so I'll get the lowdown on her from him tomorrow. He might have picked up something useful."

"Unlikely," Eli said. "Aside from the fact tracers are very good at playing their cards close to their chests, she'd have come here knowing who all the players are, what their relationships were, and who she needed to keep an eye on."

"Meaning she'll be watching the café?" I asked.

"And most likely tracking your movements. At least for a few days in order to confirm or deny her suspicions."

I snorted. "I don't do a whole lot more than work in the café and spend time with Aiden. Spelling isn't a major part of my life."

"If she's a strong tracer, she doesn't need to see you perform magic; she just needs to be close enough to see it within you. The deeper kernels of your power signature haven't altered—"

"Well, they have," I cut in, "because the wild magic is now a part of me."

"And if you're right about the reason for your ability to use it," Eli said, "It means it was there from the day you were born. It's just that no one ever picked it up. But a tracer's specialty is seeing the power grid within every witch— she'll see what others have missed for so long."

"Which is just another nail in the coffin of any failing hope I might have of avoiding what I sense coming."

"Together, we'll get over this, lass. Have no doubt of that."

I smiled, even as doubt stirred deep within. But that doubt was based on fear—on the memories of a sixteen-year-old betrayed by the man who should have protected her. I wasn't that child, and it wasn't just Belle and me facing this threat now. Whether in the end it would be enough, I couldn't say. Not even my prophetic abilities, as vocal as they'd been about this looming confrontation, could envision the outcome. But we had a chance, however slight, and that was what I had to hang on to now, not the fear twelve years in the making.

I finished the rest of my coffee and then rose. "I'd better get back before it gets too late."

"Do you want a lift?" Eli asked.

I shook my head. "It's only a short walk. I'll be fine."

They escorted me to the door, then stood on the small porch with their arms around each other, watching until I'd turned the corner. I couldn't help smiling. The pair of them coming into my life really was one of the best things to happen to me.

Aiden called just as I entered the café. I pulled my phone out of my pocket and said, "How'd the meeting go?"

"As well as can be expected given the situation." His reply was terse. "I'm going home, and I'd really like your company. I know it's late but—"

"I'll be packed and ready in ten."

"You really do need to start leaving some of your clothes at my place. It would make things a whole lot easier."

And a whole lot harder when I had to leave. "I'll consider it."

"I guess that's one step in the right direction." His amusement was evident in his voice. "I'll see you soon."

I shoved my phone back into my pocket and ran up the stairs. Belle was already asleep, so I wrote her a note and then packed some clothes and shoes for tomorrow. Aiden pulled up just as I locked the front door.

He leaned across the truck to open the door, then kissed me long and hard once I'd gotten in. "Hmmm," he said. "You taste like banana, coffee, and whiskey."

I smiled. "That's because I've been overindulging in all three."

He pulled out onto the road, then glanced at me. "Any reason for said overindulgence?"

"You could say that." I quickly filled him in on everything that had happened.

"If either your father or your husband makes any attempt to harm you, in any way, I will tear them to shreds." His voice was grim. Dangerous.

I reached across the truck's cab and placed a hand on his thigh. His fingers wrapped around mine, warm and strong and fierce. "I appreciate the sentiment, but the last thing I want is you up for a murder charge."

"Then maybe I'll settle for tearing off a limb or two."

I smiled. "You know, there's a part of me that seriously wishes to see that, but... not at the cost of destroying your own life. And it would, you know that."

His breath hissed through clenched teeth. "Yes, but the sentiment applies. I will do whatever I can to keep you safe."

"I know that."

He nodded, just the once, as if a contract had been made. And it was a contract that was later sealed in his bed, when he made me feel so cared for and so damn precious that it rocked me to the core.

And afterwards, as we drifted to sleep, I was forced to admit the one thing—if only to myself—I'd been avoiding like crazy these last few months.

I hated the man I was married to, and loved the man I could never marry.

Life was never going to be the same for me, no matter what happened in the next few months.

A sharp ringing woke us many hours later. Aiden muttered a number of obscenities and spent several seconds groping for the phone.

"Aiden O'Connor," he said eventually, his voice husky with sleep.

"Sorry, boss," a familiar voice said. "But you said to ring if we had another situation."

Byron, I realized after a moment. Aiden flicked the loudspeaker on so I could hear.

"The flesh stripper?" he said.

"Yeah. I'm afraid it's struck again."

"Where this time?"

"Up in the Campbell Creek plantation."

"Which is rather close to where the second victim was found," I murmured. "They have to be roosting in that area somewhere."

He glanced at me and nodded. "Who reported the find?"

"Jeni. She was returning home after a night out with one of the Sinclair boys."

Aiden grunted. "She okay?"

"Not really. I've managed to calm her down, but she's still a bit of a mess."

"You called in the crew?"

"I will, after this call. I might get Ciara to pick Ashworth up first, as this place is a maze and we don't want him lost." Byron hesitated. "Can Liz come out with you? Neither Ashworth nor Ciara are much good at calming hysterics."

Being a calming influence was certainly a skill I wouldn't have attributed to myself, although I guess I had become adept at talking down the occasional client who wasn't happy with the outcome of whatever psychometry search they'd asked me to do.

Aiden glanced at me, an eyebrow raised in question. I nodded, then threw off the sheets and headed into the bathroom. I had no idea what time it was, but the moon's power was well on the wane, meaning it had to be at least four in the morning.

"We'll both be there ASAP," Aiden said.

"Good, because I'm not liking the feel of this area right now."

Unease prickled down my spine. I stopped and looked around. "Tell them to get into the truck and stay there until we arrive."

Byron obviously heard me, because he said, "You think the killer could still be in the area?"

"Are you hearing any owls hooting?"

He paused, obviously listening, and then said, "In the distance, but yes."

"Then get into the truck, lock the doors, and don't get out for any reason, no matter what you see, even if it's a distressed, naked female."

"Will do."

Aiden hung up, then climbed out of bed and began getting dressed while I quickly jumped into the shower.

"Will they be safe in the truck if the owls he's hearing are the Empusae?" he asked.

"Maybe. There are a few spirits who don't like iron, but cars these days are more aluminum and plastic. It really doesn't have the same effect."

"Then how likely is it that the Empusae will attack them so soon after feeding?"

"That, I can't say."

I quickly dressed and then clattered down the stairs, grabbing my purse off the counter before following him out the door. Once we were on the main road, he hit the siren and lights and pushed the truck as hard as he could. We made it to Castle Rock in record time, the blue-and-red lights washing the empty streets with color as we sped through them.

It took another eight minutes to reach the plantation area. Aiden slowed and turned into a dusty road dividing two orderly rows of pines, and then picked up the radio. "Byron? You out there?"

There was no response. My pulse rate jumped several notches, and fear stirred. And yet, why would the Empusae bother coming back? Despite my earlier warning, it really didn't make any sense—not when dawn was closing in fast and they'd obviously fed for the night.

Aiden tried the radio again; when that didn't work, he tried the phone. The response was the same. He swore, pressed some app, and then shoved the phone at me. On the screen was a map of the area with two small flashing dots—the blue was obviously us, as it was the only one moving, and the red one Byron.

"You've trackers in your cars?"

He nodded. "Had them installed before Christmas. Thought it might be a good idea, given what you'd said about the shit headed our way." His expression was grim. "And just as well, given this place is a warren of roads. You can be my guide."

I nodded, my heart pounding with ever-increasing speed the closer we got to that red dot that was Byron's SUV.

"He should be just past the next corner," I said as the

213

two dots were almost on top of each other, "close to the intersection of another two tracks."

Aiden grunted and slowed down. Dust bloomed around the truck and momentarily cut vision. Then, gradually, an SUV appeared out of the shadows. It was parked sideways, blocking the road. The door was open, but there was no movement, no sign of life, in either the SUV or the surrounding area.

But there *was* blood, and chunks of flesh, and bones that gleamed white both on the ground and all over the car itself.

I covered my mouth and uttered a sound that was part horror, part disbelief.

And then the headlights pinned one last atrocity.

A head. Sitting in the middle of the front seat, still oozing blood and gore.

Byron.

ELEVEN

"Oh God, no..."

The words were all but torn from me. Aiden didn't say anything; he simply picked up the radio and called in the rest of his team. Then he rang his sister.

"Ciara, did you get a call from Byron?" His voice was very controlled; none of the fury that vibrated through his body could be heard.

"Should I have?"

"He was meant to call but obviously didn't get the chance. We need you and Luke out here immediately." He gave her the coordinates and then added, "And pick up Ashworth on the way through."

"What about Monty?"

Aiden hesitated. "He's on crunches, and they'll present problems given the scatter pattern of the kill. We'll update him tomorrow."

Monty would not be happy with that decision, even if it was the right one.

"Fine." She hesitated. "I take it our flesh stripper has struck again?"

"Yes. And this time, Byron is one of the victims."

"Oh fuck, Aiden—"

"Yeah," he cut in, "so get out here as fast as you can."

"Will do."

She hung up. Aiden took a deep breath, and the anger eased a bit. His expression, when he finally met my gaze, remained controlled, but his eyes burned with frustration and fury.

"We need to find these things," he said. "We need to kill them."

"We will." Somehow.

I reached across and touched his arm. His muscles jumped under my touch, and after a moment, he wrapped his fingers around mine and squeezed them.

"I need you out there in case the Empusae are still in the area—are you going to be okay?"

He meant with the gore, not the Empusae. I swallowed heavily and nodded. "The crime scene is too large for me to create a protective circle around though, so I'll have to shadow your movements, just in case."

He squeezed my hand again, then got out of the truck. I followed suit and studied the area with my 'other' senses. The night was utterly still; there were no owls hooting, no animals moving through the underbrush, and no growling or grunting from the possums that were undoubtedly in the area. It was almost as if the night itself had been struck numb by the ferocity of these murders.

And while the feel of both evil and death lingered heavily in the air, I didn't think the Empusae remained in the area. But then, they could well be watching from on high and simply attack the minute we let our guard down.

But as brutal and as ugly as these deaths were, they'd obviously been ordained by fate, as neither man's soul lingered. They'd moved on—hopefully to a far longer, far happier life.

My eyes were drawn, against my will, to the front seat of the SUV and the bloody remains sitting there. Byron's eyes were wide and terror forever etched into his face. Why had he gotten out of the car? Or was he given no choice? Had the Empusae simply spelled open the door and then ripped him apart?

And where on earth was Jeni?

My gaze swept the bloody remnants, and my stomach's churning increased. I swallowed heavily against the bitter rise of bile and tried my best to clinically examine rather than react. While there were a lot of body parts strewn about, I couldn't see anything that looked female. And maybe I wouldn't, given the utter destruction, but still...

"Aiden, I don't think Jeni was in the SUV when this happened."

"She wasn't. Her scent runs off into the trees." He handed me a pair of shoe protectors. "Put these on so you don't wreck another pair of shoes."

I had absolutely no intention of wrecking another pair, simply because I had no intention of stepping in or on anything that even vaguely resembled a body part. But given the utter mess... I shuddered. "Aren't you going after her?"

"I will as soon as the others get here."

"But—"

"If the Empusae chased her, she's as dead as Byron and the victim he found. If they didn't, then she'll be back at the compound by now. I'll contact—"

The sharp ringing of his phone cut the rest of his words off. He glanced at it, then hit the answer button and said, "Has Jeni appeared up there?"

If the relief that briefly lit Aiden's expression was anything to go by, she had.

"I'll be up to talk to her as soon as the others get to the crime—" He paused, listening. "No, I can't fucking come up straight away. I've a dead ranger, another unknown victim, and a crime scene to lock down. I'll get there as soon as Tala arrives and can take over."

I couldn't hear the exact reply, but the tone was somewhat conciliatory and also male. Aiden grunted. "Get the doc to sedate her, then. I'll bring Liz up to do a reading if you'll clear it with the other alphas—that way, we'll see what she knows without her reliving the trauma."

There was another short pause, then Aiden grunted again and hung up.

"Your dad?" I guessed.

He nodded. "Impatient, as usual."

"You realize I'm not going to be of much use up there, don't you? Belle's the telepathic witch, not me."

"If you can retrieve memories from a dead person's mind, surely you can retrieve them from someone who's simply sedated?"

I hesitated. "I actually don't know, because I've never tried."

"But theoretically, it should be possible, right?"

"I guess, but—"

"Liz, if nothing else, this will remind my mother just how vital you are to this reservation."

If it worked. If it didn't, it would only confirm her opinion we were nothing more than charlatans. "I suspect me using psychic powers won't really make much of an impact on her current opinion."

"Perhaps not, but neither of my parents has seen you in

action, and this will back what Rocco has already said about you."

Meaning Rocco had discussed me with either the council or Aiden's parents? Interesting, given I really hadn't done that much in the way of magic when I'd helped uncover Larissa's—who was at the time my suspected assassin—lies.

"We can try," I said. "But don't be surprised if it doesn't work."

"When you state something probably won't work, it generally does." His smile was fleeting and didn't do much to lift the anger. "Watch where you step if you're going to follow me around."

I nodded and rubbed my arms. The last thing I actually wanted to do was watch him catalog the various remnants of humanity. I certainly didn't want to see anything more than what I already had. The churning in my stomach was bad enough; too much more and I *would* be sick. In fact, if I'd had any damn choice, I'd be as far away as possible from this crossroad and the deaths it held. But I had no idea if the Empusae were still in the area, and no desire to leave Aiden to their bloody ministrations if they were.

He began photographing. I shadowed his movements, my eyes on the ground, watching where I placed every single step. The silence stretched on, broken only by the soft clicking of the photo app as we slowly moved around the SUV. It was then the other victim came into view. His bones had been picked clean and then piled neatly on the edge of the small crossroad, his skull gleaming in the beam of moonlight that caressed it. The Empusae had had the time to deal with him 'properly', which suggested Byron might have come onto the scene after they'd left.

So why return and tear him apart?

Was it, perhaps, some sort of retribution—a life for a life? One of the elder's offspring had been killed, after all, and while Vita had been responsible for that rather than Byron, maybe the elder simply didn't care.

Was this, perhaps, a macabre warning? A bloody and violent form of a 'kill one of mine, and I'll kill one of yours' note?

Trepidation stirred even as chills ran down my spine. While we were all at risk if vengeance was her intent, I couldn't help the sudden notion that I'd somehow made the top of her hit list. Which made no sense and was probably more my tendency to expect the worse than anything else. But still...

I quickly looked around, senses on high alert. But the night remained absent of anything other than the scent of blood and death. The Empusae—and any other evil or magic, even the wild kind—were nowhere near this area.

As Aiden began to unroll the crime scene tape around the entire area, the sound of sirens finally cut across the silence. Minutes later, four SUVs pulled up behind Aiden's truck; Ciara, Luke, Ashworth and—surprisingly—Eli were in the first one. Tala, Mac, and Jaz were in the others.

"Maggie and Duke are on their way," Tala said as she exited her SUV. Then her gaze ran past us and she stopped in shock. "Oh God—"

"I need two teams to deal with all this," Aiden cut in. "Eli, thanks for coming along. We're not sure if the Empusae remain in the area, so between the two of you, will you be able to set up some sort of protective circle or magic repellant to protect everyone?"

Ashworth nodded. "Although we might have to set up two separate circles and merge them at a set point to allow movement between the two if the kill zone is large."

"It is," I said.

"Ah. Then perhaps it'd be better if the three of us—"

"I need Liz's help up at the compound." Aiden's tone suggested he'd brook no arguments on that. "We're going to interview our survivor—Jeni—to see if she witnessed anything that might help us track these things. Tala, you're in control here. I want two separate teams on this. Ciara, we'll need an ID on the first victim ASAP."

"As has been noted before, we'll do our best but we can't work miracles, Aiden."

"I know. Just do what you can." He glanced at me. "Ready?"

I nodded. Anything was better than remaining here amongst the utter destruction.

We climbed into his truck and he carefully reversed out. Tension, anger, and sorrow radiated from Aiden's body, and his aura was a turbulent, unreadable mix. But that was understandable—he was head ranger, and a werewolf besides. They didn't like losing and, right now, with this case, that's all we seemed to be doing.

We reached the boundary for the O'Connor compound and were quickly waved through the checkpoint. The truck's engine growled loudly as we climbed the steep incline. Trees closed in, shutting out the fading light of the moon and leaving nothing but inky blackness either side of the twin headlight beams.

We continued to wind our way up the mountain, and eventually the trees receded, revealing sheer mountain walls. We were entering the mouth of a canyon. Above us, dawn painted the sky with flags of red and gold.

We reached another checkpoint. Aiden slowed, but a wolf appeared and we were once again waved on. The growing daylight caught the quartz reefs running through the canyon's walls, making it appear as if ribbons of stars surrounded us. Of course, given that much of the gold found in the area surrounding the compound had been found in quartz reefs, some of that glitter might have been very precious indeed.

Buildings appeared—some large, some small, but all of them resembling longhouses of old—and, thanks to the stone they were made of, were absolutely beautiful. Every building shone, and all of them had earthen rooftops filled with masses of different grasses and wildflowers. There was same proliferation of green technologies here as there had been in the Marin compound, though, with every house having a combination of solar panels, wind turbines, and battery storage.

The farther we moved into the encampment, the more the canyon widened out, and the larger and grander the longhouses became. Eventually, we entered what looked to be the remnants of an old crater. The canyon walls soared high above us, unadorned by trees, but nevertheless beautiful thanks to the quartz reefs and the proliferation of wildflowers.

Aiden slowed as we rounded a corner. Up ahead, in a wide clearing, was a grand hall. Unlike the Marin one—which resembled a relic of medieval times—this hall was circular with an angular earthen roof pitching up to the chimney in the center of the structure.

Around the perimeter of the clearing were three two-story longhouses, each one separated from the next by a path that ran back into the forest. While these buildings were also made of stone, the reefs that ran through them looked to be pure gold, because they gleamed like fire under the red skies of the morning.

Aiden's statement that the O'Connors were wealthy

was something of a misnomer. They would never be merely 'wealthy'—not with the amount of gold on show here. The three packs might be plowing all tourism profits back into the day-to-day operation of the reservation, but the O'Connors, at the very least, would never be left wanting for money, no matter what happened.

It could also be another reason why no humans were allowed up here. It wasn't just about privacy, but rather the wealth on show and the greed it often sparked in humans.

Aiden stopped the truck in a parking area on the right edge of the clearing and then glanced at me. "Ready?"

"No." I took a deep breath and tried to calm the nerves. "But let's get it over with."

We climbed out of the truck. A wolf appeared out of the trees to my left; if not for the fact he was much younger than Aiden, I could have been staring at his twin. Same eyes, same facial features.

Aiden walked around the rear of the truck and pressed a hand against my spine, lightly pushing me forward. "Liz, meet my brother, Dillon."

Dillon had to be at least fifteen years younger than Aiden, but he'd nevertheless mastered the art of giving nothing away with either his eyes or his expression. "Nice to meet you, Liz." His gaze flicked to Aiden. "They're waiting for you both in the infirmary."

His voice was ultra polite. I wondered if that was instinctive, or if he'd been warned to keep his distance and his manners.

"Thanks, Dillon," Aiden said, amusement evident.

Warmth briefly speared the blue of Dillon's eyes. He nodded politely my way, then turned and trotted away.

I glanced up as Aiden pressed me forward. "Is he the youngest in the family?"

He had two brothers, I knew that much, as well as five sisters—six, if Katie was included. I had no idea if such a large number was normal or not for a wolf pack.

"Yes."

His tone was clipped, and annoyance instinctively rose. "I'm gathering I'm not to ask too many questions about your family?"

His gaze shot to mine. "That's not what I meant to imply. It's just—" He hesitated, and half shrugged. "I'm not used to talking about my family to anyone outside of the pack."

And that was something I always would be, no matter how long we were together. I looked away, studying the gold-wreathed buildings and ignoring the inner sadness. "Then can I ask which of these longhouses belongs to your family?"

"It's the one on the left with the ivy-leaved cyclamen on the roof."

Which was one of the largest here. I wondered how many generations lived within its golden walls, and where his bedroom was... "It's pretty."

"It is, thanks mainly to the long hours Mom spends on the roof to ensure weeds don't overrun the flowers." He shook his head, his love for her evident in his expression despite the lingering swirls of annoyance in his aura.

We walked through the pathway between his home and the next. The buildings immediately behind were obviously communal, as there were blacksmiths, stonemasons, potters, and woodworkers all working in the area. The large infirmary building lay at the far end of the lane, and behind it, lying in the shadows of the canyon's walls, were smaller longhouses.

"Given a werewolf's ability to self-heal by simply

shifting shape," I said, "I wouldn't have thought such a large infirmary would be necessary."

"The ability to shape shift comes with puberty. Until that point, there's all manner of cuts and broken bones needing attention. Werewolf children are no different to human when it comes to pushing boundaries, but their belief in their own immortality is probably much higher."

"Well, they probably do bounce better, given the strength of their bones."

Amusement teased his lips. "True only to a certain point—trust me on that."

Though dawn had barely risen, there were already a number of people moving about this area. Most pretended they weren't interested in us, but their curiosity nipped at our heels. I ignored it and studied the two-story building instead. Unlike most in the compound, the grayish stone here was unadorned by reefs of either quartz or gold. The flat roof was also stone, and it gave the entire building a dour, hunkered-down appearance. But maybe that was intentional; maybe they wanted it to be the sort of place young werewolves preferred to avoid.

Aiden opened the door and ushered me inside. A silver-haired woman glanced up and immediately motioned to the stairs on her left. "They're waiting in Ward C."

She didn't bother explaining who 'they' were, but I guessed it would, at the very least, be Aiden's parents and Jeni's. Our footsteps echoed as we climbed the stairs, making the place seem empty. And, aside from Jeni and whoever was in the ward with her, maybe it was.

The corridor on the upper floor ran the visible length of the building. There were a number of doors running off either side and, down the far right end, a double set of secure doors and a sign saying Surgery and Intensive Care.

Which surprised me, given Castle Rock's hospital was fully equipped and only ten minutes away by car.

We went left. Ward C was three doors down. Aiden ushered me in; the four people inside immediately glanced around. Two of them were his parents—while I'd never been officially introduced to his father, I'd glimpsed him when we'd entered the compound's outer forest to rescue Ashworth from the dark sorcerer intent on making the well-spring—and the wild magic—his own. But even if I hadn't seen him before, I would have still known who he was. When it came to looks, the males in Aiden's family didn't fall very far from the DNA tree.

The other two were obviously Jeni's parents—their auras were an agitated mix of anger and deep grief, the latter surprising me a little, given she'd at least escaped the destruction the Empusae had visited on the two men. But I guess they feared that the trauma of what she'd witnessed would probably be with her for a very long time to come, possibly even causing serious mental problems. It certainly wasn't an unknown phenomenon.

Aiden stopped at the end of the bed. I did the same and studied the sedated girl. She was tall and slender and looked to be in her late teens. Like her parents, her hair leaned toward the darker end of the spectrum for the O'Connor pack, being almost brown rather than a shade of blonde or silver.

"Liz, this is Joseph and Karleen, my mother and father, and Sean and Ryanne, Jeni's parents."

Obviously, Karleen wanted her husband kept unaware that she and I had already met—why else would Aiden be reintroducing her?

Ryanne's red-rimmed gaze met mine. "Can you do anything for her?"

"If you mean erase or hide her memories to ease her trauma, then no, that's not—"

"Why we're here," Joseph cut in. Though there was no censure in his tone, it was nevertheless a warning. He glanced at me. There was absolutely nothing in his expression to clue me in as to what he might be thinking, about either my presence here or me. Even his aura gave nothing away. "Aiden said you can read her memories without having to put her through the stress of questioning—is this true?"

I nodded, even though it was something I hadn't tried before. "I'll have to connect with Belle, though, just in case the memories are so strong they drag me down."

Joseph frowned. "I don't understand—"

"What Liz is about to try isn't telepathy," Aiden said. "It's more an immersion in Jeni's memory—she'll see and feel what Jeni did."

"That sounds... dangerous," Ryanne said.

"It can be," I said. "Which is why I need to connect to Belle."

"She's the telepathic one, isn't she?" Joseph said.

"Yes. She'll monitor my thoughts and drag me out of Jeni's mind if I go too deep and get caught up in her emotions."

"Why would that be dangerous?" Sean asked.

"Because, as Aiden said, I'll be fully immersed in her mind, and I'll see and feel what she did. But if those memories overwhelm me and I lose my control, it's possible neither of us will come out of it whole."

"That's a bit of a stretch, isn't it?" Karleen's expression was skeptical. "I mean, how is something like that even possible?"

"I was deeply immersed in Karen Banks's mind, trying

to discover where she was and what she was doing when the vampire took her life. Her death could have been mine, because my body was reacting to what was happening to Karen as if it was happening to me. It's only thanks to the fact that Belle got me out in time that I'm standing here now."

"Ah."

One word that somehow managed to convey understanding while still sounding skeptical.

"Is there anything you need to do in preparation?" Joseph asked.

"I'd normally raise a protective circle to keep evil out, but that's not necessary in this case."

Mainly because Jeni was alive rather than dead.

"Then please proceed when you're ready."

Joseph stepped back from the bed, as did Jeni's parents. Karleen remained exactly where she was. Not giving ground, not even for something like this. I took a deep breath to calm my nerves and then walked to the front of the bed. Jeni's face was pale, but her breathing was even and her aura relatively calm. The drugs they'd given her had been strong enough to soothe both mind *and* soul.

"Aiden, can you pull the bed away from the wall for me?"

He immediately did so. I slipped into the space between the bed and the wall, and then carefully placed my hands either side of Jeni's head. No images stirred in response. The drugs had done their job.

I took another deep breath and—keeping mental fingers crossed that Belle was awake—reached for her.

There was no immediate response, which meant she was probably asleep. While I could break the spells that protected her room from the constant buzz of my thoughts, it would take more time and energy than I really wanted to expend right now. Which meant that I might have to go on alone—

You called? came her thought.

Yeah—did I wake you?

Nope. I had to pee. What's the problem?

There have been two more murders, but this time, we have a witness. She's been heavily sedated, so I'm going to directly connect with her mind and relive her memories.

And you want me to monitor, just in case. Wait a sec while I get comfortable. There was several seconds of silence, then, *Right, go for it.*

I immediately closed my eyes and pushed into Jeni's mind.

Nothing happened. Not straight away. All I felt were the muted echoes of her horror and disbelief. The deeper I went, the greater those two emotions became, until they crawled across my senses and dragged tears from my eyes. It was warning enough that the memories I was about to access were very bad indeed.

I pressed past another layer. While the drugs still held sway here, images were now flickering. They were fragile wisps that spoke of blood and gore and horror, but they fragmented and spun away the minute I reached for them.

Then, with an abruptness that had my breath snagging in my throat, I was in... *Saw Byron, who should have protected me, reduced to bits in an instant. Blood... and body parts... everywhere. On the ground, on me. It's all I can smell, all I can see...*

"Liz," Aiden said softly. "You need to tell us what you see."

I jumped and fought to place a layer of distance between the thick heat of her emotions and me. "She was on her way home when she heard the screaming. It sounded like her friend Jimmy, so she ran to help him. What she saw instead..."

I paused, and swallowed heavily as the images once again flared thick and fast across my senses. *Jimmy with two women who were both beautiful and naked. Women who attacked him, shredded him with claws and teeth, their bodies slick with his blood as he screamed and writhed. The abrupt silence as he died, and yet remained upright and still as the women stripped him of all humanity before finally licking his bones clean. Bones that were unnaturally white in the gleam of the moon. Oh God, oh God...*

Lizzie, came Belle's warning. *Pull back.*

I shuddered and did so. As distance returned, I was suddenly aware of my rapid breathing and the thick churning in my stomach. I swallowed heavily, and then said, "She saw the two Empusae attacking Jimmy... and then she ran."

Back down the forest, away from the destruction. And yet, for all of her terror, for all of her fear, she had the presence of mind to call the rangers.

"Can you describe these women?" Joseph asked. "Give us facial composites?"

"Yes, although I'm not sure they'll do much good, given Empusae also have owl form and can basically hide anywhere."

"We've already organized a reservation-wide search for possible dens," Joseph said. "If these things are hiding in any of our forests or compounds, we'll find them. It's the possibility of them hiding within our residential areas that worries me."

"From the little we've learned of them, that's not likely."

"What about Byron?" Aiden said. "Why did he get out of the SUV?"

I took a breath and went back into Jeni's memories.

"They were both in the SUV, as ordered. Byron was trying to calm Jeni down, without a whole lot of success. Then someone else began screaming... a woman, in the forest behind them rather than at the crossroad ahead where Jimmy died."

I paused as Jeni's panic washed through me—her fear that Byron was going to leave her in the truck alone. Her begging him to stay, to not get out and investigate. The screaming intensifying, and then the door being wrenched open. And then, and then...

"Lizzie," Aiden said, again softly. "Tell us what you're seeing."

"Byron didn't get out of the car." Tears slipped past my closed eyelids. I could not only see his death through Jeni's memories, but also feel Byron's horror, his confusion, and the utter, mind-numbing agony he'd so briefly suffered in those few brief minutes of sensation between life and death. I swallowed heavily, my voice quavering a little as I added, "He was distracted by the screaming of one Empusae while the other snuck up and wrenched the door open. Jeni fled as he was being torn apart."

Dear God, what she's witnessed... Belle said. *I have to help her, Liz. It's the only way she'll get through this.*

I know. I removed my hands, swiped at the tears, and then raised my gaze to Jeni's parents. "My friend Belle can mute her memories of this event if you wish. It may help her recover."

Ryanne frowned. "Wouldn't it be better to totally erase them?"

"Full erasure really isn't possible." Which wasn't

exactly the truth; a strong enough telepath *could* do so, but it wasn't something that was either recommended or often even tried, as it left the recipient extremely confused and sometimes unable to fully function. "But we can certainly cloud her memories of the event. She'll know what has happened, but it'll no longer have the same immediacy or effect."

"When can your friend get here?" Ryanne immediately said.

I glanced at Karleen rather than replying. Her smile was tight—she did *not* want another outsider in the compound. Especially when that person was linked to me. "It would perhaps be better if Jeni is taken out of the compound to be treated."

"But surely—" Sean began, only to be cut off by a look from Aiden's father.

"Is there anything else in her mind that could help?" Aiden said.

"No." I returned to the end of the bed and then glanced at Jeni's parents. "If you want to give us a call at the café later this morning, we can make arrangements for Belle to come and see Jeni. I'd keep her sedated though—her memories are... harrowing."

They both nodded. I flicked my gaze over to Karleen. "Thank you for allowing me up here today."

"You're quite welcome."

Her reply was as insincere as my thank you, and amusement stirred. Hopefully, I managed to keep it in check. I glanced up at Aiden. "If you want to get back to the crime scene, just drop me off outside the compound, on the main road. I'll get Belle to come pick me up."

"After all the help you've been giving us, the least I can

do is take you home." He glanced at his parents. "I'll update you when I know more."

With that, he touched a hand to my back and guided me out the room. He didn't say anything until we were back in his truck and heading out of the compound.

"I'll drop by later this afternoon to get a composite of the two Empusae. The likelihood of them hiding in plain sight might be remote, but I don't think we can risk it."

I nodded and rubbed my arms. While the morning air held a bite, the chill was more an inner one, its source the wash of Jeni's horror and terror still echoing through my brain.

Which is not dissimilar to what happens when you go too deep with a psychometry reading, Belle commented.

And means it's something I don't need to be doing too often.

With that, I agree. Ask Aiden if he'd like a coffee and an egg and bacon sandwich to be waiting for him when he gets here.

I passed the message on, and got a brief but bright smile in reply. *That would be a yes, thanks, Belle.*

Once we were out of the compound, Aiden hit the accelerator. It didn't take us long to get back to Castle Rock. Belle was waiting, as promised. Once I'd handed him the coffee and sandwich, I leaned across and kissed him. He brushed the hair out of my eyes and then gently ran his fingers down my cheek. "Are you going to be all right?"

"Yeah."

He didn't look convinced, but didn't comment. I climbed out and, once he'd left, followed Belle back into the café.

She came out of the kitchen with two mugs of coffee. "The council isn't going to keep this one quiet."

"No. And are you sure you've put enough alcohol in those coffees?"

She raised her eyebrows. "You can't possibly smell it from there—I wasn't that heavy-handed."

I accepted the mug and took a sip. The whiskey was evident but it certainly wasn't overpowering. "Maybe my great love for the malted stuff has made me hyperaware of its presence."

"Maybe." Belle's expression suggested she doubted it. "Anyway, I got a call from Monty about ten minutes ago. The tracer is staying in town for the next couple of days."

"Is she intending to question us some more?"

"She didn't say, and he wasn't certain. He did suggest we keep our spelling to a minimum though."

"As long as the Empusae don't decide to attack, I'm good with that."

"Even if they do attack, it might be better if you leave the magic stuff to Ashworth and Monty."

"A very sensible suggestion."

"And one you may or may not follow." Her voice was wry.

I grinned. "You know me too well."

"I'm your familiar. It's part of the job description to know your thoughts before you have them—not that many of them are worth knowing."

"Deliberately so—such eccentricity stops you from getting bored."

"I'll certainly admit boredom has never really been a problem over the years." She drank some coffee and sighed in appreciation. "Monty's heard from his source in Canberra. Apparently, he's got some snippets about the tracer and the Empusae we need to hear—although when it comes to the latter, I suspect it won't be much more than what we've already found."

"Meaning he's using it as an excuse to get a decent meal and to do some Belle watching."

"I suspect so." She shrugged. "As long as he keeps his amorous thoughts to himself, we'll be fine."

I raised an eyebrow. "Do I sense a slight softening in attitude?"

"You do not."

"Believing it."

"You should."

"Totally."

She gave me the look—the one that said I was dead if I didn't shut up. I grinned, but resisted the urge to tease her any further.

We finished our drinks and then concentrated on the day's chores. Custom was steady rather than busy, and Byron's murder was very much the topic of conversation. Which was interesting, given there'd been four other murders before the Empusae had lashed out at him.

Monty came in as things were quieting down and walked over to the table we generally kept reserved for Aiden, Ashworth, and him if we knew they were coming in. We'd placed a basic 'mute conversation' spell around it when we'd first begun dealing with the rangers, initially to prevent any unwanted information about either Belle or me from getting out, and then later to stop the gossip brigade hearing any tantalizing tidbits about the investigations we were helping with.

Penny took his order and, once it was ready, I delivered it and silently activated the spell as I sat down opposite him.

"So, what did you learn about our tracer?"

He grimaced. "Not a lot—she's playing her cards close to her chest."

"So you don't know who sent her?"

He picked up his cutlery and began to eat. "No, but I suspect the order comes from Clayton rather than your father."

"Why?"

"Because I contacted a few friends and asked them what they knew about a tracer being sent to my reservation. Their replies were... interesting."

My stomach flip-flopped. Interesting wasn't good. "In what way?"

"Apparently, Clayton is desperate to have children but the numerous lovers he's had over the years have been unable to conceive."

That might have something to do with the hex I put on him, Belle said.

Hex? That's the first time you've mentioned that to me. To Monty, I added, "And how does that relate to the tracer being here?"

You were pretty out of it at the time, Belle said, *and there was little point in mentioning it afterward.*

Hexes can bounce back rather badly—

Unless they're used to save oneself. Your trauma is mine, remember, and it was pretty damn fierce that night.

"There's rumor currently doing the rounds up there," Monty said. "That he married in secret but the woman disappeared not long after."

"I take it my name isn't on the short list of possible suspects?"

"As far as I can tell without pressing too hard, no."

"Because why would he marry an underpowered witch —even one with the best family connections—when there were plenty of other women who'd be willing to step into the breach?"

He nodded. "The rumor has been given weight by the fact the records are sealed—no one can gain access to them. Clayton, of course, denies the rumor and the fact he had anything to do with said records being sealed."

"Of course he would. What he and my father did was against the law." To Belle, I silently added, *What sort of hex did you cast?*

A limp willy one.

Laughter silently bubbled through me. How very appropriate. *Is there seriously a spell that can do that?*

Yes. And in Clayton's case, I didn't add a time limitation, which means his dick will never man up—and it serves him right.

That will explain why he hired the tracer. Given he certainly didn't have that problem when he tried to rape me, he obviously suspects we're the source of his problems.

Yes, although it doesn't explain why he's left it so long to try and find us.

Maybe it wasn't until the Fitzgerald brothers were jailed and blabbed their mouths off that he suspected where we were. We might have changed our names, but I don't think there's another green-eyed royal witch who hangs out with a Sarr. It wouldn't be hard to put two and two together.

It wouldn't have been hard to do a finder spell using some of your personal items, either, Liz. As I've noted before, if they seriously wanted to find us, they would have.

And yet they've resorted to a tracer rather than a spell. Perhaps we were better at covering our tracks than we thought.

"Which is why the records were no doubt sealed," Monty was saying. "I've asked my friends to keep me updated on the goss, so hopefully they'll let me know if and when Clayton suddenly leaves town."

If Clayton did leave town, I had no doubt it'd be so well concealed no one would be any the wiser. "And the Empusae? Anything new on them?"

"Well, there *is* one textbook that suggests the best way to get rid of Empusae is to swear at them. Apparently, insults send them screaming away."

"Somehow, I can't see the rangers accepting that as a suitable method of dealing with them—especially after Byron's death."

He straightened. "What?"

I quickly filled him in on the two murders and on what I'd seen in Jeni's mind. He swore and thrust a hand through his hair. "Shit, Liz, this is bad."

"Considering we've currently no leads on these bitches and five dead people, that's something of an understatement."

"What about the White Lady? She must have some way of locating the Empusae if she's been dogging their heels for decades."

"She's already told us she hasn't been able to trace them since she bound and drowned the younger."

"Well, that's terribly inconvenient."

"Indeed." My voice was dry. "In fact, I haven't seen her since Belle talked to her."

Which was rather weird. If nothing else, she should have been there last night, because the Empusae had taken two men rather than the one; even if she'd been some distance away, she would have had time to get there. Besides, whether they were watchful or not, she was capable of killing them.

She killed the weakest of the three, Belle commented, *and only then because she caught it off guard.*

It's still surprising she wasn't there last night.

Maybe our chat took as much out of her as it did me—and spirits don't recover as easily as us.

Maybe. I still think it's odd, though. To Monty, I added, "Did you get any practical information on killing Empusae?"

"Nothing much more than what Vita has already given us. One book did suggest they can be killed the same way as you'd kill a vampire—stake through the heart, burning, or chopping off their heads." He paused. "I suggest we avoid burning—vampires can't regenerate, but these things are shifters and might be able to."

"After our confrontation with the soucouyant, I don't even want to think about creatures on fire."

"A sentiment I can certainly get behind." He mopped up the last bit of tomato sauce with his burger bun. "I might get one of the rangers to take me up to the crime scene and check it over myself."

"Why? If they'd left anything in the way of a magical fingerprint, Ashworth would have found it last night." Anything else, the rangers would have found.

"I know, but I'd still like to investigate the area myself. Then I'll head over to the coroner's and ask if I can view the bones of all the victims."

I frowned. "Why the bones specifically?"

"To see if any trace of magic remains."

"Why would there be magic on their bones?"

"I don't know, but I remember a uni professor once mentioning that some supernatural creatures leave traces of magic behind in their DNA. Given you said the Empusae licked the bones clean, it's possible their saliva left such an imprint. If that *is* the case, we might be able to use it to work up a tracking spell."

"That's a whole lot of ifs."

"Maybe, but they're better than what we currently have."

Which was another of those understatements. "Let me know if you find anything."

He raised an eyebrow. "Like you let me know about last night?"

"Hey, I suggested you should be contacted. Aiden decided your crutches would be a problem given the wide kill splatter."

"The sooner I can get rid of the damn things and walk properly again, the better," he muttered. "But, if the Empusae hit again, I'd like to be advised at the time, even if it is impractical for me to be present."

"If I'm there, I'll do so."

"Better than nothing, I guess." He got out his wallet. "How much do I owe?"

"Nothing. You may be distant family, but you're all I've got." Or wanted. In the odd low and emotional moment, I might want to see my mother again, but that came with all sorts of dangers—especially when I had absolutely no idea whether or not she'd agreed to either the use of the spell that had made me sign the marriage certificate, or the subsequent drugging that had forced submission to Clayton. Better by far to avoid them all. "And I'm surprised you let Ashworth's poking get under your skin."

"The one thing I don't like being accused of is being a freeloader, so—"

"Do you really think Belle would let you get away with freeloading?"

A reluctant grin touched his lips. "Well, no—"

"So just put the wallet away—at least when the café is doing well. If that changes, you'll soon be asked to ante up payment."

"Okay, then." He shoved his wallet away and rose. "I'll talk to you later."

I nodded and collected his plate and coffee mug, taking them into the kitchen as he left. Once the café was closed, Belle headed out to smudge Jeni's memories, while I cleaned up and did a bit of prep for tomorrow.

Belle returned around five. I made us both a coffee and then sat down opposite her at a table bathed in sunshine.

"How did it go?"

She scrubbed a hand across her face. "About as well as could be expected. She'll always remember the horror—it simply went too deep to risk hazing it—but I did at least manage to put some distance between her and it."

Meaning she would view it as something that had happened some time ago rather than just yesterday. "And you?"

"Okay." She paused and shuddered. "But dealing with memories that heartbreaking and foul is not something I ever want to do again."

"Hopefully, we won't have to." I drank some coffee. "How are Jeni's parents holding up?"

"Okay. They're going to go away for a few weeks."

"A good move." Especially given the Empusae might just decide to go after our one and only witness. "What do you think about Monty's suggestion we contact Vita again?"

"If she'd known a way to easily find the Empusae, she would have mentioned it. She wants them dead as badly as we do, remember."

"Any idea as to why she's not been sighted, then?"

"No." She paused to sip her latte. "The spirits do say

your guess about her strength is right. They also state there's a stirring to the south of Castle Rock."

"I don't suppose they'd care to define stirring." My voice was dry. "Or perhaps give a more definite location? To the south isn't exactly helpful."

She grinned. "They suggest we start looking in the area around the old Garfield Water Wheel. The stirring will become evident."

"As much as I'd like to grumble about the continuing lack of information, I guess that *is* far more than they've given us previously."

"And they appreciate your acknowledgement of this fact."

"While they're in such a good mood, I don't suppose they want to track down the Empusae for us?"

"That would be going against the rules."

I raised my eyebrows. "There's rules for spirit guides?"

She hesitated, obviously listening to her guides. "It's more things they can and can't do. Their main purpose is to guide and provide advice. They cannot directly intervene, which is what providing such direct information would be."

"Suggesting they do know where the Empusae are."

"They can neither confirm nor deny that."

"Then they remain in my 'annoying' category."

Belle's expression was momentarily intent. "They say this pleases them, as they wouldn't know how to cope with you actually being friendly toward them."

I chuckled and drank some coffee. "Have they at least got a suggestion as to when we should check?"

"They suggest you put your coffee in a travel mug and depart straight away."

"Then I shall do so." I pushed to my feet. "Can you call

Ashworth and tell him what's going on? I might pick him up on the way through if he's not busy."

"Wise plan."

"Is that your thought or the guides'?"

"Both. Going anywhere by one's self is not something they suggest doing right now."

"Great. Even the spirits are spooked by the Empusae."

"They're not spooked. They're just not liking the current trajectory of kills."

"No one does." I paused. "You'd better ring Monty, too, and let him know the spirits have sent me on a wild goose chase."

"News he won't take well."

"Yeah, but he won't grumble as much at you."

"An annoying truth."

I poured my coffee into a travel mug and then made one for Ashworth. Once I grabbed my purse and keys, I said, "Any plans for tonight?"

She nodded. "Kash rang and asked if I wanted to go out for dinner. I'm not sure he realizes I'm annoyed at him, though."

"Well, considering most of your dates have been within the confines of his place, this is at least a step in the right direction."

"That is very true, and why I said yes."

I slung my purse over my shoulder. "I'll see you later, then."

"Yes. Just... be careful."

I flashed her a grin. "I always am."

Her snort of disbelief followed me out the door.

Ashworth was waiting out the front of his place, a backpack slung over his shoulder. "That extra coffee for me?"

He dumped his pack on the floor and then pulled on the seat belt.

I nodded. "Did Belle fill you in?"

"Yep." He took a sip and sighed appreciatively. "You two have a knack for coffee. And cake."

"The latter is absent today, I'm afraid. How did the investigations go last night?"

He grimaced. "Exactly as you'd expect. The Empusae know what they're doing—there wasn't much in the way of magic or spells to be found."

"Was that because they would have faded by the time you arrived, or because they're not using magic to trap their victims?"

"The latter, I suspect. From what I've read so far, Empusae use their bodies to entice their victims into their arms, and that gels with what you saw in Jeni's mind."

Meaning Aiden had updated him. "I don't suppose you've any idea how many people they kill in an area before they move on?"

"No, but that is perhaps a question Belle could ask your White Lady. If she's been tracking these things for so long, she surely must have some idea." He studied the road ahead for a second. "I ran into your tracer today."

"Oh, really?"

"Hmmm. She had a heap of questions about what I knew about you and your past. I repeated the guff you told me when we first met."

"Was she convinced?"

"Doubt it. I suspect her spider senses are tingling, and that's always dangerous when it comes to a tracer."

I shrugged, pretending a calm I wasn't feeling. "There's nothing we can do about her. Not without setting off her senses more."

"Oh, I know that. All the same, Eli and I created a redirection spell for you." He reached into his backpack and pulled out a palm-sized wooden disk deeply etched with witch runes. Though the magic was inactive, the thick lines of it swirled around the disk, providing intriguing glimpses of the power and complexity of the spell. "It'll haze your aura and stop the tracer from using it to track you. All you have to do to turn it on and off is touch the disk."

"How did you tune it to me?"

"I didn't. It's a general spell that'll work for anyone who happens to be within the small set radius."

"What if she's actually following the SUV? Red Outbacks aren't exactly a dime a dozen around these parts."

"Which means you'll just have to pay more attention to what's behind you."

"Any idea what she drives?"

"A white Corolla hatch."

My gaze automatically flicked to the rearview mirror. Nothing. "Given how many of them are on the road, I could spend the next few days desperately avoiding totally innocent Corollas."

He chuckled softly. "I'd offer the use of Eli's car, but I'm afraid that hair of yours will give the game up as easily as this SUV."

"I could use a glamour spell in combination with your anti-tracker disk—it would at least buy me some time."

To do what, I wasn't entirely sure. But the mere fact the prophetic part of me thought I might need it made me more than a little uneasy.

"That's a good idea. We can swap cars later tonight, if you'd like."

I raised my eyebrows. "Hadn't you better check with Eli first?"

Ashworth waved the comment away. "Your SUV is brand new—he's not going to forsake the chance to test her out, trust me on that."

"I thought you were the car nut in the family?"

"Only in that I enjoy rebuilding them. In every other way, he's as keen on them as me, no matter what he says to the contrary. Did you not know he used to be a rally driver when he was much younger?"

"Before or after all the sport?"

"During."

"How in the hell did he ever find time to hold down a job or a relationship?"

"Good time management." His smile flashed. "Let me regale you with some of our rally misadventures."

He proceeded to do so, making me laugh as we headed out of Castle Rock. At Louton, I turned left onto North Road and carefully wound my way through the various tracks until the GPS told me we'd arrived at the wheel. I stopped the SUV and surveyed the deserted and rather scrubby-looking parking area.

"I'm not seeing anything that resembles a water wheel here."

"That's because we have to get out and walk." He pointed to a sign on the left. "Or so that says."

"Huh." I climbed out, locked the car, and walked over to the path indicated by the sign. "You sensing anything?"

Ashworth shook his head. "But I'm not the one with the trouble radar."

"That radar is mute right now."

"And I can't say I'm sad about that, lass. I've a date to see a very old movie and it's only on tonight."

I raised my eyebrows. "What movie?"

"*Singin' in the Rain*, which is the best musical ever, no arguments."

I raised my hands. "You won't get one from me, but you do know it's out on Blu-ray, right?"

"Of course, but there's something special about seeing it on a big screen in a grand cinema older than the movie itself."

The Royal was certainly grand, even if some of its art deco edges were looking a little tired these days. I shoved my keys into my pocket and led the way up the path. The water wheel soon came into sight, though all that actually remained was the massive stone foundations that—according to the nearby sign—had once supported one of the world's largest water wheels. I stopped at the top of the old wooden steps leading down to the flat clearing that held the foundations and studied the area. Belle's guides might have advised us to come here, but there was no immediately obvious reason as to why.

Ashworth stopped beside me. "Well, isn't that a pretty impressive remnant?"

"It's bloody huge, but it's not exactly what we're here for."

"No." He scanned the area. "I'm not sensing any—"

He cut the rest of the sentence off and frowned.

"What?" I immediately said.

"It may be nothing, but there's a tremor of energy coming from the right."

"Magical energy or something else?"

He hesitated. "It's too far away to be certain."

"Then let's get closer."

He took the stairs two at a time then strode across the clearing with such speed that I had to scramble to catch up with him.

We were soon well away from the old wheel, but the area remained scrubby; after a long, dry summer, what little grass remained was brown, and the scattered trees were sad-looking. Piles of tailings and waste pocked the area, evidence of the sheer number of mines that had once existed here. It was a thought that had me watching where I walked more closely. I'd already fallen down an old mine shaft once. I did not need to repeat the experience.

After another ten minutes or so, Ashworth slowed. I immediately scanned the area with my 'other' senses and finally caught the tremor Ashworth had sensed earlier. It was definitely magic, and it was definitely foul.

"Have you any idea yet who or what is behind that tremor?"

"No." Ashworth's reply was remote, his expression distracted. But the force of his magic burned through the air; he was inspecting that distant caress. "But it doesn't feel human in origin."

My heart began to beat a whole lot faster. "Do you think it could be one of the Empusae?"

"It's possible. Belle's guides did say it was imperative we got out here."

"Yeah, but they also said they couldn't directly interfere with an investigation or point us toward them."

"Well, if it is the Empusae up ahead, then they haven't done either. The wheel is a long way behind us."

"A technicality that doesn't really apply here."

"Technicalities matter when it comes to guides."

After another few minutes, we came into a clearing littered with rocks and debris—all waste from the small mine that had been dug horizontally into the hill directly opposite us.

It was just the sort of place Vita had said the Empusae

preferred.

Fear surged, but I resisted the urge to form a repelling spell around my fingers and took a deep, calming breath instead. As usual, it didn't do a whole lot to help.

Ashworth motioned toward the mine. "The tremor of magic is coming from within that, but I'm not getting a sense of anything supernatural, so it may be an older roost."

"Surely we wouldn't be picking anything up if that were the case, though?"

"'Wouldn't' and 'shouldn't' aren't words I often use in conjunction with the supernatural world."

I eyed the mine's entrance nervously. "So what are we going to do?"

"Investigate, of course."

"If you get flesh stripped, Eli is going to kill me."

He chuckled softly. "Aye, he will, but it won't come to that. I've a blessed silver knife with me and a couple of freezing potions ready to go. And it's still daylight, which gives us the advantage."

Not if we went deep into that mine, it didn't.

On the off chance that things were about to go ass-up, I sent a quick text to Aiden just to let him know where we were and what we were doing, then followed Ashworth across the clearing. The nearer I got to the mine, the more my gut churned. The entrance wasn't particularly large—at five-eight, I couldn't be considered tall, but I had to bend down to look into it.

Ashworth's expression was intent as his power ran before him again, a wave that tested and probed the interior of the mine. "There's definitely been some sort of supernatural entity using this place, even if they're not currently here."

"Do you think it's worth setting a trap?"

He nodded. "But not here, at the entrance. She'd probably sense it too easily."

"If she's going to sense it out here, why wouldn't she sense it inside?"

"Because I'll bind the remnants of her own energy to the spell. It'll camouflage it long enough to entrap her." He swung his pack around and pulled out a flashlight. "You keep watch out here."

He disappeared inside before I could argue. I squatted on my heels, my back pressed against one edge of the mine's entrance, a position that allowed me to keep an eye on his progress while also watching the clearing.

"It's actually not that deep," he said after a few minutes. "It probably only runs thirty meters or so into the hill, and she's not nesting that far in."

"Vita did say they don't like being too deep underground."

"Remember those teeth the victims were missing? They're all here, from the look of it."

"I suggest you leave them there."

"Intended to."

A wave of power washed over me as Ashworth began his spell. I studied the distant sparkle and wished I were closer to watch the spell unfold. I'd probably learned more in the few months Ashworth, Eli, and Monty had been here than I'd ever learned at school.

The spell's power reached its crescendo and then quietly faded away as Ashworth incorporated the remnants of the Empusae's essence and then tied off the spell. A few minutes later he appeared, sweating and dusty.

He straightened his back with a groan. "I don't know how the miners of yesteryear survived working in conditions like that."

"Many of them didn't." I pushed upright. "I guess we now just have to keep our fingers crossed that one or both of our traps catch these bitches."

"And that they don't kill anyone else off in the meantime. I did suggest to Aiden the council put a curfew order out for the forests immediately surrounding Castle Rock."

"That might only push the Empusae into another area. Besides, we're dealing with werewolves, who tend to think they can handle anything."

"Byron aside, none of the other victims were wolves. I think these things have a penchant for human flesh."

A possibility, given they'd torn Byron apart rather than eaten him. "The council have been averse to issuing such orders in the past—they've never wanted to panic the public."

"There's five bodies in the morgue. It's time they worried about saving the public rather than panicking them."

I agreed. I just wasn't sure the council elders would.

Once we'd gotten back to the car, I sent Aiden another text and got a thumbs-up and a kiss emoji in return. By the time we got back to Ashworth's place, the sky was ablaze with pinks and yellows. But with all that color came the distinct feeling of being watched. I glanced around casually, but couldn't see anyone or anything that looked out of place. Nor was there any sort of shimmer to indicate Vita was out there—though there hadn't been on other occasions, either.

"When do you want to exchange cars?" Ashworth grabbed his pack and jumped out of the SUV.

I hesitated. "Not tonight—it'd be too obvious. Perhaps we can do a swap somewhere out of town, and a little more private."

He nodded. "We'll change over the number plates, too. That'll help the confusion factor."

I raised my eyebrows. "That's illegal."

"We're in a werewolf reservation, and you're dating the head ranger. I'm thinking he'll give us a pass on this, especially when it helps keep you safe. Talk to you tomorrow."

With that, he slammed the door shut and headed inside. I returned home. The sensation of being watched got no stronger; it was just a steady pulse of awareness that was distant enough to prevent me picking up who or what it was.

I frowned and headed inside. The shadows were closing in and the café was hushed. Belle had already left, so I tossed my purse on the counter and headed into the kitchen to make myself some dinner. Aiden rang an hour later to say he was heading home to grab some sleep, and that he'd see me in the morning.

With nothing else to do, and nothing interesting on the TV to watch, I went to bed early.

Only to be woken many hours later by the thick sensation of being metaphorically punched in the gut.

TWELVE

I t wasn't an outside source attacking me magically. It was my own magic—something had just triggered the alert spell I'd placed around the tree cave.

I threw off the sheets and quickly got dressed, then grabbed my phone and scrambled down the stairs as I rang Ashworth.

"Lizzie? What's the prob—"

"My alarm around the tree cave just went off," I cut in. "I'll pick you up in a few minutes."

He swore and hung up. I raced into the reading room, grabbed the backpack, and threw in everything I thought I'd need, including a few additional charms designed to ward against demons. While the one around my neck would protect me from all manner of evil, the Empusae were capable of at least some minor magics, and I had no idea whether that would make it possible for them to get past my defenses.

"I wouldn't think so," came Belle's somewhat sleepy comment from the doorway.

"Always better to be safe than sorry." I closed the last of

the storage cupboards and then swung the pack over my shoulder.

She stepped aside to let me pass. "You want me to come with you?"

I shook my head. "I'm picking up Ashworth. You could ring Monty for me, though. I promised to keep him updated."

"He'll want you to swing by for him."

"Yes, but speed is of the essence here. We have no idea how these things communicate, and whether the one we haven't snared will be able to free the one we have."

"He helped set that snare, remember. He might be needed to unravel it."

I swore softly. "I'd forgotten about that bit."

"I'll go ring him now. That way, you can pick him up after Ashworth." She hesitated. "What about Aiden?"

"He can't do anything up there." Nothing other than become a target for the free Empusae if she was around the area. "I'll ring him once we're up there and have dealt with the problem."

"Be careful."

I nodded, swept my purse off the counter, and ran out the back door. It only took me a few minutes to get across to Ashworth's, and he wasn't waiting alone. Eli was with him.

"Have you called Monty?" Ashworth said as they both climbed inside.

"Belle has." I took off. The tires squealed, the sound echoing across the otherwise silent night. "How are we going to proceed?"

"There's no 'we' in this," Eli said. "You and I are going to stay back and—"

"These things are powerful," I cut in. "It may just take the four of us to deal with them."

"Perhaps," Ashworth said. "But unless we've managed to snare both, that still leaves one free to attack. You and Eli are the backup team. If the other bitch does come at us, it's up to you two to deal with her."

I wasn't entirely sure 'dealing' with her would be an option given she'd no doubt be winged and also well aware that she was dealing with witches. And if she *was* capable of minor magic, then it was more than possible she'd conceal her presence until it was absolutely too late to do anything to counter her attack.

But I kept my fears to myself and concentrated on getting to Monty's as fast as possible. He was hobbling out his front door just as we pulled up. Eli flung the rear door open and then slid across to the other side of the seat.

"Where's your crutches?" I said as Monty climbed inside and slammed the door shut.

"They're too damn awkward in the bush. I'm better off without them."

"If you fall over, none of us are stopping to pick you up," Ashworth grumbled.

"I'm not going to fall over. I wouldn't give you the pleasure of seeing me do that, old man."

"One more 'old man' comment, and I really will clip you over the ear."

"As will I," Eli said, amusement evident in his voice. "Especially given I'm the oldest here."

"Yeah, but you don't look it. Ashworth is all weather-beaten and wrinkly."

Their banter continued. I let it roll over me and drove on, pushing the SUV to its limits in an effort to get to the area that held the tree cave as fast as possible.

When we could take the SUV no further, we continued on foot. Monty managed to both keep up and not fall over, and we made good time through the trees. But we were not alone in the forest. My watcher was out there, in the distance, tracking our progress.

Vita.

It had to be. It certainly couldn't be the tracer—not when the presence was ahead rather than behind. It made me hope that if we *had* caught one of the Empusae, it wasn't the elder one. Belle wasn't here, and the last thing we needed or wanted was to piss off our magic-capable White Lady by depriving her of the kill she'd waited centuries for.

We reached the clearing. Shadows wrapped the semi-circular mound of rocks and dirt that supported the tree cave, and there was no immediate sense that anything or anyone lay within it.

Nothing except the smell.

It was ten times stronger now than it had been the first time we'd been here, and it was so damn putrid I started to gag.

"Fuck," Eli whispered, a hand over his nose. "Why did no one warn me these things smell like—"

"Meat left too long in the sun and cheap, cheap perfume." Monty hobbled past Eli. "Shame your partner didn't think to bring nose plugs, like some of the smarter portions of this outfit did."

Eli shook his head at Monty's back and stopped several yards inside the clearing. "I take it the smell is confirmation that we have indeed snared one of the Empusae rather than some other kind of demon?"

"Not entirely, as the spell we set was a general demon snare rather than Empusae specific," Ashworth said. "But there's few who have this particular scent."

"And isn't that a good thing."

I stopped beside them both. The glittering threads of

wild magic that powered my spell moved in a lazy circle around the tree cave. Despite the fact I'd only set the spell to raise the alarm once, the underlying magic remained strong. It was yet another example of the wild magic changing the intent of my spell.

Monty stopped close to the edge of my spell and bent to inspect the cave. "I can't see any movement—are you sure we've actually caught—"

Something flew out at him; something that was all flesh and talons and howling rage.

He jumped back instinctively, but lost his balance and would have fallen had Ashworth not lunged forward to grab him.

His naked attacker hit the invisible boundary of the snare and tumbled back into the darkness of the cave.

"I think that rather succinctly answers your question," Eli said, his tone dry.

"Yes." Monty nodded his thanks to Ashworth. "They're rather fearsome-looking things, aren't they?"

"That they are." Ashworth swung his pack around. "Let's create a double protection circle around the cave. We can then force her out and kill her."

I handed Monty his pack. "How are you going to do that? A stake isn't practical, because if you get within arm's reach of that bitch, she'll tear you apart."

"The youngster here can freeze her. I'll handle the staking and decapitation part."

I raised my eyebrows. "Why both?"

"When it comes to demons, I always work on the theory that more is better."

"What are you going to do if it's the elder we've caught? Our White Lady isn't going to be pleased if you steal her vengeance."

"It's not the elder," Monty said. "It doesn't feel that strong."

"Agreed," Ashworth said. "Which means if the other one does attack, you two are going to have to capture her rather than kill."

"You do know how to spin a demon snare, don't you?" Eli asked.

I nodded, and didn't admit just how recently I'd learned or that my knowledge came from watching Monty rather than formal training. I didn't think either he or Ashworth would appreciate that sort of information right now.

Ashworth began placing his spell stones onto the ground. Monty followed, weaving his in and out of Ashworth's. It would double the strength of the protection circle when it was raised.

Once the circle fully encompassed the tree cave, the two men stepped inside. Ashworth looked at me and said, "Take your spell down. We can't risk the wild magic interfering with what we're about to attempt."

I nodded and immediately dismantled my spell. As the threads faded and the wild magic floated away, the night seemed darker. More volatile.

I scanned the trees, unsure whether the inner tension was simply nerves or a not-so-subtle warning from my psi senses that things were about to hit the fan big time. And maybe part of that certainty rose from the fact that it had been a little too easy to snare this Empusae—especially after the death of the younger one. It would have warned them they were dealing with witches—even if the source of the magic for that first death had come from a dead witch rather than a live one—and it should have made them more cautious.

So why would this one have flown—or even walked—so easily into this trap?

I could perhaps understand it if dawn had been close and she was desperate to get undercover, but sunrise was at least an hour and a half away yet.

And that suggested the Empusae might well be using this trap against us. After all, it was doubtful they'd be aware there were four witches in this reservation rather than the usual one.

I flexed my fingers and resisted the urge to reach for the wild magic. I couldn't use it against the demons, not if we were going to kill them. The wellspring might now be well protected, but we still risked staining it if it was used in such a way.

"I'll set up on the far side of the tree. You watch from this side," Eli said. "And keep alert. If the other one is out there and realizes what we're doing, her attack will be hard and fast."

I nodded and moved into the center of the clearing. After placing my pack on the ground, I drew out my silver knife and the charms and placed both on the ground in front of me. Then I carefully set out my spell stones and raised a protection circle, making sure I wove in exceptions that allowed me to throw spells or even my knife without shattering its magic. Then, finally, I wove the demon snare, fashioning it into a ball that could be easily thrown. But I didn't completely tie off the spell or activate it; I just placed it on the ground, ready to be grabbed. There was nothing else I could do then but sit and wait.

And hope like hell that inner certainty and the growing sense of anticipation coming from Vita would amount to nothing.

Monty and Ashworth activated their circles. The intertwined threads were bright against the shadows of the night, but if the captured Empusae felt their magic or in any way feared what might be happening, she gave no sign of it. Maybe she'd been knocked unconscious when she'd hit the snare barrier. Or maybe she was simply waiting for the right moment to attack.

"Right," Ashworth said, his voice loud in the surrounding hush. "Let's contract the snare and force this bitch out into the open."

As the two of them picked up the outer layers of their containment spell and began to reel them in, I cast an anxious gaze skyward. There was no immediate sense of threat, no sign of any bird, no indication that there were any other supernatural beings in the area beyond Vita or the trapped Empusae. I felt no easier. We knew so little about these demons; we had no idea if they were capable of telepathic communication or simply had a sixth sense of when the others were in trouble. In reality, it didn't matter either way. The elder would be up there somewhere, waiting for the right time to attack.

As the containment spell continued to retract, the spell's energy grew. It stung my skin and made the small hairs on my arms stand on end. I risked a look at the cave. There was no sign of the Empusae as yet, and still no indication that she was aware of what was happening. Maybe she *had* been knocked out—

A scream of fury rent the air. It was a sound so fierce and otherworldly that goose bumps ran across my skin. It wasn't anger; it was a call for help.

The other Empusae had to be close.

My gaze jumped skyward again, but there was nothing to see beyond stars and darkness. In the trees to my right, energy stirred, something I felt rather than saw. It wasn't the

Empusae. It was Vita. Coming closer and staining the air with her anticipation of a kill and her need to be a part of it. I wasn't sure how she was going to achieve the latter without Belle here to aid the process. I was too well-protected for her to take me over, and Eli too canny to allow it.

I can catch a cab out there if need be, Belle said. *The three of you should be able to hold her in a snare until then.*

I hesitated. *Best wait until we do actually catch her. Vita's more powerful than she makes out, and I don't trust her.*

She gave us a guarantee she wouldn't overstay. She won't break that. She dare not.

We're dealing with a spirit who has been seeking revenge for decades. I very much suspect she'll say or do anything to get it at this point.

Perhaps. Belle's mental tone was filled with doubt. *But we have little other choice except to trust her, especially if she is as powerful as you suspect.*

Which was also totally true.

The trapped Empusae screamed again. Dust plumed out of the cave's mouth, and the thick stench of rotting meat sharpened abruptly. I could see the far edge of the containment net now, even though the Empusae remained invisible. She had to be using some sort of concealment spell, but any hope she had of convincing us of her absence was somewhat dashed by her screams.

The net contracted until it was roughly six feet high and little more than four or five feet wide. Dust swirled within it, briefly framing the feminine form.

"Right, Monty, freeze her." Sweat gleamed on Ashworth's bald head and trickled down the side of his face. "Then I'll do the deed."

Monty nodded and the tempo of his magic rose. However much he might jest, however much he might claim not to be powerful enough for Canberra, there was no doubt he was stronger than either Ashworth or Eli.

His magic reached a crescendo, and all movement within the snare stopped. The Empusae screamed again.

This time, the sound didn't come from the one in the snare.

I swore and readied the demon net. Its light pulsed across the night, a mix of silver and gold that was both my native magic and the wild. It might have been a sleeping element of my magic until I'd come into this reservation, but now that it had awakened within me, there was no keeping it out of my spells.

I scanned the sky again. There was no shadow hiding up there; nothing to indicate she was near.

Nothing except the growing sense of danger.

The caress of Ashworth's magic rose as he climbed to his feet, a silver knife in one hand. The Empusae might be pinned, but she wasn't silenced, and her screams of fury now filled the air as she fought Monty's hold on her, trying to get free, trying to attack.

Monty hissed, a sound almost lost to the noise the Empusae made, and the stink of his sweat stung the air as his magic rose another notch to counter her movements.

Then, from out of the trees behind Eli, shadows moved.

"Eli!" I yelled. "She's behind you!"

He swung around and slashed with his silver knife. The shadow dodged away then a claw appeared, raking the air. Eli's protection circle shimmered in response but held firm. The shadow melted away as quickly as it had appeared.

Tension pulsed through me. I scanned the trees, looking for some sign or sense of her. Then Vita's energy surged, and a ball of light that was so damn bright it brought tears to my eyes shot out of the trees and arrowed past me. My head snapped around and I caught a brief glimpse of a shadowy, feminine shape before it dissolved into feathers and flew upwards, out of the path of the fiery ball. The bright energy didn't follow. It simply melted away.

Vita's frustration flooded the air, a force so strong it momentarily overwhelmed my senses. I gasped and slammed down more mental shields—and barely in time. My psi senses screamed a warning even as something hit my protection shield. As the threads of my magic bent and then responded, trying to keep the intruder out, counter-magic surged, its feel foreign and dark. The Empusae's claws broke through my shields and she swiped at me, forcing me to jerk back to avoid my face being shredded. I swore and reached for my knife; she swiped again, this time more desperately. Her claws raked my arm, drawing blood as I grabbed the knife. I twisted it up, lashing at her, slicing two bloody talons even as she screamed and withdrew.

Power surged again, this time familiar. Eli, casting a counterspell to force her away from me even as he threw his demon snare. She jagged sharply sideways, somehow avoiding it. I grabbed my net spell with a bloody hand and threw it after her; again, she sensed it, but not quite soon enough. One wing caught and, for a second, I thought we had her. Then she twisted away, tearing free from the net before it had the chance to spread across the rest of her body.

She disappeared into the night, leaving behind a drifting cloud of bloody feathers that burned away long before they hit the ground. The elder had obviously learned from earlier mistakes.

But why was she retreating? It made no sense— The thought stalled as my gaze went to the tree cave.

Ashworth stood alone within the snare. The other Empusae was dead.

I took a deep, shuddering breath and then looked down at my arm. Three of her claws had raked me, and the wounds were deep and bloody. I reached into my pack, grabbed a bottle of holy water, and poured it over the wounds. It immediately began to bubble, suggesting it was fighting either magic or infection, and it hurt like blazes. My breath hissed through clenched teeth, and tears stung my eyes.

Eli appeared in front of me. "Are you okay?"

I nodded and carefully dismantled my protection circle. He immediately took my hand and inspected the wound.

"Looks like the holy water is basically sterilizing the wound. Infection won't be a problem, but the wounds are deep enough that you might need—"

"I'm not going to the hospital for stitches. Butterfly bandages will hold it together just fine."

He sniffed. It was not a happy sound. "Can you wiggle all your fingers okay?"

I did so, and he nodded, his relief evident. "You, my girl, are damn lucky. Wait here while I go get my first aid kit."

As he rose and moved away, I picked up my spell stones and placed them back into their bag. Then I used another bottle of holy water to rinse the blood from my knife. I had no intention of letting it stay on the blade—I had no idea if a demon's blood was capable of either permanently staining the blade or maybe even rendering it unusable. Better to be safe than sorry, especially when I simply didn't know enough about demons.

My gaze went to the trees. Vita was still there, but her

presence was muted. Obviously, creating those energy balls drained her to the point of exhaustion.

Which is obviously why she wants our help, Belle commented. *She might be able to interact with this world, but it's an ability that is somewhat limited.*

Limited isn't a word I'd use to describe those energy balls.

And yet it was incapable of adapting to the Empusae's movements.

True. I took a deep breath and blew it out. *Let's just hope the trap Ashworth set around that cave produces results, because I have no idea how we're going to capture the remaining bitch otherwise.*

If she's in any way sensible, she'd get the hell out of here while she still can.

Except that we've now killed two of her offspring. Would you?

She sighed. *No. I'll head into storage and collect more of Gran's books. She's got one on tracer spells, so we might be able to jury-rig something.*

Worth a shot.

I glanced up as Eli returned. Behind him, Ashworth and Monty had dismantled their magic and were walking around collecting their spell stones. Both looked gray—containing and killing the Empusae had taken a lot out of them, and it made me wonder how in the hell we were ever going to cope with the remaining one, who was not only stronger but far older and cannier.

Eli insisted on spraying antiseptic over my arm, even though the holy water had erased any chance of infection, then placed a number of butterfly plasters over the wounds to draw the skin together. Once he'd bandaged my arm from elbow to wrist, he packed up, then rose and offered me a hand up. "You okay to drive?"

I hesitated, and then pulled the keys from my pocket. "You'd better—at least until we get to your place. I can manage the short distance from there."

He accepted the keys, then glanced across to the other two men. "Ready to go?"

"Yes," Monty said and then hesitated. "Should we set another trap around this place, just in case she comes back here?"

"I'll do it," Eli said. "You three start making your way back to the SUV. I'll catch up."

"You're not staying here alone," Ashworth immediately said. "That bitch is pissed off, and there's no telling where she is at the moment."

"I'll stay," I said. "You two are so drained a gnat could overpower you right now."

Monty's smile was a pale echo of its usually robust self. "Only if said gnat has superpowers."

But he didn't argue any further. He simply turned and hobbled away. Ashworth hesitated, obviously torn between the need to protect Eli and the knowledge that he wasn't going to be of much use if the Empusae did hit us again. Common sense prevailed, because he nodded and followed Monty into the trees.

Eli quickly constructed another demon snare, weaving in an exception that would allow the local wildlife to seek its shelter without setting off the trap. Once he'd finished, I said, "Do you want me to lay another concealment spell around it?"

He shook his head. "I doubt the Empusae will come back here—not now that she's aware we know they've been using it. She's too canny for that."

I nodded, and we headed out of the clearing. Vita's essence faded in the opposite direction. I guess her need to recover overran the desire to follow me about.

Once Monty had been dropped off, Eli drove home. As both men walked inside, I jumped into the driver seat and headed back to the café.

Belle was waiting with a reviving potion, a couple of strong painkillers, and the demand I head upstairs and rest. I didn't argue. I might not have been the one performing the harder magic in that clearing, but I nevertheless felt drained.

It was close to ten the next morning by the time I woke. I grabbed the plastic wrap from the kitchen to protect the bandages from water and then had a quick shower.

Aiden just walked in came Belle's comment. *And he's not happy.*

Feed the man a brownie and tell him I'll be down in a sec.

I don't think a brownie is going to cut it.

Meaning he's probably heard of our little adventure last night.

Probably. I can tell him you're still sleeping if you can't be bothered facing questions right now.

Which will only make him more annoyed. Especially given he was well aware that I only overslept when I'd overdone it magically.

I pulled on a sweater to hide the bandage and then slipped on jeans and some shoes. Every movement made my arm ache, but there wasn't really a lot I could do about that aside from taking more painkillers.

I clattered down the stairs and spotted Aiden waiting at his usual corner table. Though his expression wasn't giving much away, his aura spoke volumes. As did the untouched brownie slices sitting in front of him. I grimaced and delayed the inevitable confrontation a few seconds longer by first making myself a coffee, then cutting several bits of thick banana and caramel cake. It wasn't what dietitians might recommend for breakfast, but right then I wasn't caring.

"Why didn't you ring me last night?" he said, the minute I sat down.

I squashed the instinctive rise of annoyance and raised the muting spell so those at the nearby table wouldn't hear our conversation. "Because you would have been a liability."

"It was my duty—"

"It's your duty to maintain law and order and to keep both the human and wolf population safe," I cut in bluntly. "It's Monty's duty—and Ashworth's, while he's acting reservation witch—to take care of any supernatural nasties that are endangering said population."

"That doesn't negate the fact—"

"That you would have been a fucking liability out there. The four of us barely coped, and we were all well prepared and well protected by magic. Having you there—having to expend extra time and energy protecting you—might have gotten one of us killed. So stop with the alpha bullshit, Aiden, because I'm really not in the mood for it this morning."

He stared at me for several seconds, his expression unreadable, then reached past the plate of brownies and gently took my hand. "How bad did you get hurt?"

I scowled at him. "Why do you always presume it's me who's hurt?"

"Because now that I've been so rightly told off and have calmed down, I can smell the antiseptic." He carefully pushed the sweater sleeve up to reveal the bandage. "What happened?"

"The Empusae used her magic to counter my protection spell—something I wasn't aware was possible. She missed my face, but got my arm."

His gaze jerked upward and scanned me, searching for wounds that weren't present. "I'm glad that was all."

I smiled. "So am I, trust me."

His fingers tightened on mine, then he leaned across the table and kissed me. It was soft and sweet and filled with caring, and made we wish he could simply take me in his arms and hold me forever. Kiss me forever.

"Well," I murmured, ignoring the regret that rose when his lips left mine. "That's sure to set a few tongues wagging."

"I'm not sure why—it isn't exactly a secret that you and I are going out. Hell, they were all placing bets on the possibility."

I smiled. "Yes, but public displays of affection have been few and far between."

"Because I generally refuse to give the gossips fodder. But they're not here today, and you looked as if you needed a kiss."

I raised an eyebrow. "So if they had been here, said kiss would not have been forthcoming?"

"Possibly." He picked up a brownie and took a bite. "Ashworth tells me that he and Monty killed another Empusae last night."

I nodded. "We've also set a trap around a cave we found up near the Garfield Water Wheel, so keep your fingers crossed that we catch her sooner rather than later."

He nodded. "A thorough search of all three compounds has now been completed. We didn't find any onerous scents that would indicate the presence of this demon."

I started in on my cake. "I didn't think you would. These things are too clever to make a mistake like that."

"And yet they're not beyond making them—as evidenced by the fact two are now dead."

"Yeah, but the most dangerous one still lives, and I've a suspicion she'll raise some hell before we manage to stop her."

"I can always rely on you to bring a bit a reality to the discussion."

I waved a spoon at him. "Hey, you're the one that wanted honesty in this relationship."

"Which I appreciate greatly, even if it sometimes seems otherwise." He paused. "My father sends his thanks for your help up in the compound yesterday."

"And does that thank-you also come with a warning not to expect further invites?"

"No. Though it would be appreciated if you kept what you saw to yourself." He hesitated and glanced toward Belle, who was plating up an order at the counter. "Well, between you and Belle, anyway."

"Because of all the sparkle?"

He nodded. "You can imagine what would happen if its presence became common knowledge."

"There'd be carnage."

"Yes, because wherever there's gold, there're humans who risk all to get at it."

"Your pack's secret is safe." I hesitated. "Is it only the O'Connor compound that so ostentatiously displays its wealth?"

"The Sinclairs' gold runs through internal ceilings and walls. The Marin compound have several thick veins of gold running underneath their building, but for the most part, it remains untouched."

"So why has your pack put it so openly on display? I know few humans are allowed up there, but it's still an unwarranted risk."

He shrugged. "You have to remember, we've held this land almost as long as white settlement has been in Australia, and for a good part of that history, this area was totally closed to all humans. It was only when the forced resettlement happened and the treaty was struck that humans were allowed entry."

And even then, only in certain portions of the reservation. "Then the gold rush struck."

A smile touched his lips. "Yes, and that influx of humans also meant an influx of coin. Humans might hunger for gold, but they cannot live on it alone."

Which was why the wealthiest people in any gold mining town of old were often those who provided services —the traders, the publicans, the landlords, and sometimes even the whores.

"How's Jeni?"

"Good—she's come off sedation, and the murders she witnessed are nothing more than a distant dream—troubling but not mind-destroyingly terrifying. Belle did good work there."

"It's lucky that Jeni was so young—her mind is a little more malleable than that of a full adult." I finished the last bit of cake, then picked up my coffee and took a sip. "Are you on late shift tonight?"

"I finish at eight—why?"

"I feel the need to have your arms around me and your body pressed close as I fall to sleep."

A smile twitched his lips. "If I'm pressed too close, sleep might be a little... hard."

"Careful lovemaking would not be unappreciated. You'll have to do most of the work, though—the arm is still rather sore."

Concern crossed his expression. "You should have a doctor check it."

"The wounds are sealed, and there's no sign of infection. It'll be fine."

He didn't look convinced but he knew me well enough now not to argue. Instead, he finished his coffee, leaned across the table to give me another kiss, and then stood. "I'll pick you up when I finish tonight, then."

I watched him leave, then rose and moved back to the counter. My arm protested vehemently the minute I tried lifting anything heavier than a mug, so I manned the coffee machine and plated up cake orders for the rest of the day.

Aiden picked me up a few minutes after eight and, once we'd arrived at his place, made me dinner, ran me a sweet-smelling bath, and generally cosseted me. When we finally did make love, it was sweet and gentle and filled with such deep passion that my heart sang. I went to sleep with his arms wrapped around me and a contented smile on my lips.

Only to be woken hours later by a shrill ringing.

Even as Aiden reached for his phone, I threw off the sheets and began to dress. I had no doubt what this call was or what it meant.

"I'll be there in twenty," Aiden said. "Call Ashworth and Monty and get them out there ASAP."

"The Empusae?" I asked when he'd hung up.

He nodded and climbed out of bed; the moonlight streaming in through the windows silvered his muscular body and made him look almost otherworldly. He caught my sweater before I could pull it on and tugged it out my hands.

"You need to stay here."

"What? No—"

"Liz, be sensible. If this attack follows the pattern of the others, the Empusae will be long gone."

"What if it's another trap? What if she's waiting up high and does to you what she did to Byron?"

"Then you can tell my ghost 'I told you so.'" He tossed the sweater onto the bed and stepped closer, catching my chin with his fingers and lifting my lips toward him. "Ashworth and Monty will be there. They'll cope. You need to rest and recover."

"I need to be out there—"

"That is *not* your job." His voice was gentle, but held a hint of steel. "To be as blunt as you were earlier, you are not this reservation's witch and you do not have unending reserves of either strength or magic. You need to rest."

I took a deep breath and released it slowly. What he said was totally sensible. I just didn't feel sensible right at this particular moment. "Remind Ashworth that he and Monty need to capture this thing, not kill it."

Aiden frowned. "Why?"

"Because of the White Lady. She's here for vengeance, as I said earlier, and if she doesn't get it, all hell will break loose."

"Oh, things just keep getting better, don't they?" He kissed my nose. "I'll call you if we do snare the Empusae. Until that moment, however, you need to rest. I can smell your weariness."

"You can't—"

He raised his eyebrows. "I'm a wolf, remember."

"But still basically human, and our noses aren't capable—"

"Except that they are. Even in this form, we have millions more olfactory receptors in our noses than regular humans do. So stop arguing and get back into bed so I can leave."

I grumbled unhappily but did so. He left a few minutes later, and despite my anxiety and frustration, I quickly fell to sleep.

It was close to six by the time he crawled back into bed. I turned around and snuggled closer. He wrapped an arm around me and gently caressed my spine.

"Bad?" I said.

"Yes. But we're not entirely sure it was the Empusae."

His touch moved down to my butt and pressed me closer. I slipped a leg over his and rubbed myself against him. Teasing him, readying me, although neither was really needed. Not if the desire surging between us was any indication—its scent was so strong that even I could smell it.

"Why?"

"Because while it was brutal, no one was flesh stripped. And I really don't want to be discussing this right now."

I raised an eyebrow, a smile teasing my lips. "Then what would you like to be doing?"

"You."

He slipped inside. From that moment on, there was no talking, only rising desire and utter satisfaction.

Afterwards, when he was asleep, I rose and had a shower, then left him a note and caught a cab home. As much as I would have liked to remain in bed with him, I had a business to run.

It was a slow morning in the café, which was probably just as well given I was basically restricted to one arm.

Monty hobbled in just after one and claimed the corner table.

I wandered over. "You here for lunch?"

"And to update you."

I raised the muting spell again. "Aiden said you weren't sure the murder last night was the work of the Empusae."

He wrinkled his nose. "It had some of the hallmarks, but none of the bodies were eaten."

I blinked. "Bodies? Plural?"

"Yeah—the victims were an old couple who lived on the outskirts of Dundoogal."

Which was one of the border towns, if I remembered correctly. I frowned. "That's out of the Empusae's hunting area—do you think she did it as a parting gift?"

"I don't know." He scrubbed a hand across his face and, for the first time, the cheerfulness fell. "I'd like to think so, but I've a suspicion that's not the case."

"The White Lady might be able to tell us." Belle placed a plate of steak and vegetables in front of him. "Felt you coming and asked Mike to cook this up for you."

"Anticipating your man's desires is a sign of true—" He stopped, his gaze running past us. "Daniela, what are you doing here?"

My head snapped around. She strode toward us, her expression giving little away, and her aura a vivid orange that oozed satisfaction.

I had a bad feeling that meant bad news for me.

Her brief smile was as remote and cool as her expression. "I just wanted a final word with Ms. Grace before I leave the reservation."

I tried to quell the instinctive rise of annoyance and fear and forced a smile. "What about?"

She hesitated. "Perhaps somewhere more private would be best?"

I waved a hand toward the table. "There's nowhere more private than here."

Her gaze narrowed, then she nodded and sat down. "The muting spell is clever. I would still prefer, however, if it was a one-on-one conversation."

"That would be my cue to get out of here." Monty picked up his food and rose. His gaze met mine, full of warning.

I didn't react, simply because Daniela watched me. Belle touched my shoulder and followed Monty across the room.

I sat down opposite Daniela. "To repeat, what do you want to talk to me about? I've already told you I don't know the woman you're looking for."

"Does the name Clayton Marlowe mean anything to you?"

Somehow, I didn't react. Somehow, I kept my fear to myself, even though it exploded inside of me.

"No," I said, voice even despite the inner storm. "Should it?"

Her gaze scanned me. I had no doubt her other senses were, as well, even though the charm around my neck remained mute. "I suspect so."

"You can suspect anything you like, Daniela, but that doesn't make it the truth, no matter how much you might wish otherwise."

She smiled coolly. "Indeed."

The sense that twelve years of running, of careful lies and mistruths, was about to come to a crashing halt sharpened abruptly. My heart raced so hard it was all I could hear, all I could feel.

I licked my lips and said, perhaps a little hoarsely, "Is there a point to this? Because I really need to get back to work—"

"I thought you would be interested in knowing that I'll be leaving this afternoon. My report should be on my employer's desk within a few weeks."

If I'd thought my heart couldn't race any harder, then I'd been wrong. "Must be a damn long report if it's going to take that long to write it up."

"There are still a few things I need to check first."

"Huh." I paused, not sure what to say to the woman who was about to destroy my whole world. "And why would I be interested in knowing any of that?"

"Because," she said softly, "my report concludes that you fit the description I was given in all ways except for one."

How I held still—how I managed to present a calm front when the confrontation I'd spent twelve years avoiding had just became inevitable—I'll never know.

"And just what is that?" I somehow managed to say. "Eye color? Because that's pretty damn major."

"Yes," she said calmly. "Which is why I will be recommending that Clayton Marlowe come to this reservation and judge for himself."

THIRTEEN

I stared at her.

I couldn't do anything else.

Not for several minutes. Clayton was coming. Here. To see me. To get me. To make Belle pay and to force on me what he'd been unable to have with other women.

It felt like there was a fist around my heart, squeezing tight. I couldn't seem to get enough air, and Daniela's face swam in and out of focus.

Then something within me twisted, and a fiery strength rose—one that had been a part of me since before I was born, but had somehow awakened within this reservation. Calm descended. There could be no more running. Not now. This reservation was to be the final battleground, the place where my fate and my future would be decided, for good or for bad. But this was my home ground, not his. He might be more powerful than all of us combined, but was he stronger than the wild magic that now burned through me?

I guess we'd all find out soon enough.

Something flickered through Daniela's gaze—an awareness of the power now burning within, perhaps. As much as

278

I wished she hadn't caught that surge, it really didn't matter anymore. Her report would be sent, her recommendations would be made. The fate I'd spent twelve years running from was now in motion. There was nothing I could do to avoid it.

I could only wait and prepare.

"You've nothing to say?" Daniela said.

Nothing to admit, was what she was really asking.

I smiled, though it held little in the way of warmth or friendliness. "What do you expect me to say?"

"Nothing, I guess. But I find the fact you haven't even asked who Clayton Marlowe is rather odd."

"I simply gathered he is somehow related to the missing woman."

"He's her second cousin, and also her husband."

"Was she abducted or something?"

"Or something." Her smile was every bit as cool as my own. "Thank you for your time, Ms. Grace."

She rose and left. I closed my eyes and clenched my fists against the scream that broke past the calm and threatened to erupt.

Damn her. Damn her to *hell*...

Hell is too damn good for her, came Belle's comment.

A cup of coffee appeared in front of my nose. The rich scents that teased my nostrils suggested it was heavily laced with whiskey. I accepted it gratefully and took a sip. If I kept this up, I thought glumly, I'd be well on the way to becoming a lush.

Belle plonked down beside me. Monty took Daniela's seat, his expression grim. "You could take this fight up to him, you know. You could approach the courts and ask for an annulment. The records might be hidden, but they do exist."

"He won't give me an annulment. He wants revenge. He wants what we've denied him for twelve years."

"There's no doubt in my mind that Clayton can hold a grudge with the best of them, but I doubt even he would step beyond the boundaries of the law—"

"Except this is about more than the loss of face he suffered that night," Belle cut in. "It's about revenge. It's about the fact he probably hasn't been able to get an erection for the last twelve years thanks to a spell I might have cast in anger as we fled that night."

Monty blinked, and then something close to awe entered his expression. "You did that? To a blueblood possessing ten times your power?"

"I was a little angry at the time."

"Then I shall endeavor never to make you angry enough to cast such a spell my way." His amusement fell away. "That does put a more dangerous spin on things, however."

"Yes." I drank some more coffee. "Both my father and he broke the law when they forced that marriage on me, Monty. What makes you think they won't do so again to get me back?"

He grimaced. "That means it's perhaps even more vital you take the fight to him. If knowledge of what happened that night becomes public—"

"It's my word against two of the most powerful witches on the council," I cut in. "Who do you think they're going to believe?"

"Yes, but if the marriage at least became public knowledge, his actions over the last twelve years will come under some scrutiny. He'll also have to watch what he says and does in regard to you."

"I don't think it'll help—"

"But it can't hurt," Belle said. "Not now that the tracer's

report is about to be filed. The minute he sees us, he'll know the truth of our identities. At least if the marriage is outed before that happens, there'll be questions about why we disappeared and why he and your father went to such lengths to hide it."

It went against every instinct; went against the need for self-preservation, and the desire to grab the few precious moments of life and love I had left to me before it went to hell.

And yet, it made utter sense. To hold on to secrecy now would be playing into Clayton's hands.

I glanced at Monty. "I don't suppose you know anyone up there who might have the pull to get the marriage certificate released?"

He hesitated. "I could perhaps ask my father. He and Clayton have what can only be described as a rocky relationship, and I have no doubt he'd jump at the prospect of causing Clayton a little embarrassment."

"It's a start. I'll also ask Ashworth—he already has people up there keeping an eye on Clayton's movements."

And if the Black Lantern Society was as powerful and as righteous as he implied, then two of the most powerful witches in Canberra forcing an unwanted marriage on a minor was something they'd surely want to investigate.

Monty reached across the table and caught my hand. "You know I'll do everything in my power to protect you, don't you?"

"Yes." My voice held a tremulous note. Monty might be distant family, but he was also the only family who meant anything to me.

"And you know Ashworth and Eli, and even Aiden, will do the same. All of us will get you both through this. It's a promise."

I smiled, even though my heart wasn't really in it. "Remember that old saying? The one about making promises you can't keep?"

"It doesn't apply here. Believe that, if nothing else."

I nodded. There was nothing else I could do. The dice had been thrown, and the game was now in motion. There was nothing we could do to stop it.

My only real hope was that when Clayton made his move, he did so openly and honorably.

But I seriously feared that would not be the case.

The rest of the day crawled by. I called Ashworth once we'd closed for the day and told him what had happened. He immediately said he'd get the Black Lantern Society onto it. It didn't make me feel any easier. Nothing would now. Not until this mess was all finally sorted, one way or another.

As evening began to stain the skies, I settled down to read the book on tracking spells Belle had retrieved from our storage locker earlier.

She came out of her bedroom, looking glamorous in a red dress that skimmed her curves and only barely flirted with her upper thighs. I raised my eyebrows. "If your plan is to make Kash realize exactly what his inattentive manner has caused him to miss, I think you've got it spot-on. But I'm not sure that dress will be legal in many places."

She grinned. "We're off to Émigré, which has a 'less is more' policy on certain nights."

"I wouldn't have thought Émigré would be Kash's thing."

Belle snorted. "He is, above all else, a player, even if his nerdy self came to the fore when he was scanning Gran's books."

"Then I won't expect you back home tonight. Have fun."

"Oh, I very much intend to." She swung her purse over her shoulder and headed out.

I spent the next hour or so reading the book, marking a couple of pages that had spell possibilities, although I didn't find anything designed specifically for Empusae. Not yet, anyway.

With a frustrated sigh, I put the book down and then headed downstairs to make myself something for dinner. I'd barely finished eating when someone knocked loudly on the front door.

I frowned and glanced across to the old clock on the wall. It was just after eight, so it surely couldn't be a customer, and anyone we knew would have rung us first.

"Who is it?"

"My name is Judy Rankin. I need your help."

I hesitated, studying the closed door for several seconds, feeling her out with my 'other' senses. Unfortunately, they were giving me squat.

"If you need help, Mrs. Rankin, you should talk to the rang—"

"I can't," she cut in. "Please, can we just talk?"

I thrust a hand through my hair and juggled the need to help with the desire to tell her to go elsewhere. As usual, the former won out. My sister's death had certainly affected me in more ways than one.

I walked across to the door but didn't immediately open it. Instead, I peered through the bullet holes that we'd never bothered to repair. The woman standing on the other side of the door was tall, with pinched cheeks and a long nose.

Not a wolf, I thought, even though her coloring was similar to the Sinclair pack.

There was no one else within immediate sight, so I opened the door and let her in. "I gather you're after some sort of psychic help if you believe the rangers can't help."

She walked into the middle of the room and then stopped, her expression a mix of curiosity and desperation. "This is not what I was expecting."

Meaning she wasn't one of our regular customers. Certainly I couldn't remember seeing her before. "What do you want, Mrs. Rankin? It's been a long day, and I'm really not in the mood to be mucked about."

"Oh. Sorry." Her gaze jumped to mine, her expression slightly contrite. Not the brightest bulb in the box, I thought. "My son and his three mates have gotten themselves lost, and I was wondering if you could help me retrieve them."

It seemed to be the month for boys getting lost. I could only hope they hadn't fallen down an old mine shaft as well. "Do you have any idea where they are?"

She nodded, her annoyance obvious. "Up in the Manton's Gully forest."

"And they have their phones with them?"

She was obviously aware of the point I was about to make, because she immediately said, "Yes, but they've wandered into an area not covered by Google Maps and they've gotten themselves lost."

Given Google Maps covered pretty much everywhere, that was quite a feat. "So why come to me rather than the rangers? You've a reasonable idea where they are, so it shouldn't take long for a ranger to find them."

"I know, but I don't want to land the boys in trouble." She hesitated. "They're a little too near the Marin compound, you see, and I don't want to draw any unwanted attention to them."

"Because they've been warned about trying to enter the Marin compound several times before?" I guessed.

She grimaced. "Yes. They don't mean any harm, but the elders don't see it that way."

"Would you still feel that way if it was a bunch of teenagers raiding your home?"

Surprise flitted across her expression. "Well no, of course not, but it's hardly the same."

It was, but she obviously was never going to get that. I sighed. "If you want me to find them, I need something of your son's—something he wears every day. I also won't be doing it for free."

Not when I didn't like the woman.

"Oh," she said, somewhat surprised. "How much would it be?"

I gave her our general rate for personally finding things, and she blinked. "That seems overly high to me."

"Mrs. Rankin, if you want me to work outside of my usual hours, then you pay penalty rates. Or go to the rangers. Your choice."

"Oh," she repeated. "Well, I guess I have no option. We could use his school shoes—"

"I'll need something that has had constant direct contact with his skin."

"Which they do."

I blinked. "He doesn't wear socks?"

"No. Apparently, it's a fashion statement."

"In my day, a fashion statement like that would have landed you in detention." Which made me sound older than Methuselah, I thought, amused.

"Oh, it still does, but it's considered a badge of honor."

One that obviously didn't bother his mother. "Fine. Go get a shoe and I'll see if I can get any vibes off it."

"And if you can't?"

"Then you'll have to do things the old-fashioned way and organize a search party."

"That would take far too long," she said, her tone cross. "And, as I've already said, I can't afford to have this brought to the attention of the elders. It might get us thrown off the reservation."

If her son couldn't be bothered following the rules, then perhaps that was for the best. But I bit back the comment and simply told her to go get the shoe. As she did, I walked down to the reading room and filled the backpack with the usual assortment of holy water and potions, and then grabbed my knife and its sheath. There was no way known I was going anywhere at night without a little extra witchy protection behind me. The Empusae might not have been active last night, but that didn't mean she wouldn't be tonight. Didn't mean she wasn't circling the whole reservation, just waiting for the right moment to swoop and attack.

With that cheery thought lingering, I threw the pack over my shoulder then grabbed my phone and keys. Mrs. Rankin reappeared just as I was making a coffee. I didn't bother offering her one. I wasn't in the mood to be that generous right now.

I screwed the cap onto my travel mug and then walked over to the table on which the shiny black shoe sat. I picked it up, opened the psychic gates, and immediately felt a response. It was distant, but nevertheless strong. There was no sense of danger coming with that pulse, no sense of urgency. Her son might be lost, but he and his friends weren't overly concerned about it.

"Okay, I'm getting a clear response—"

"Oh good, let's go."

No way, no how. Not together. I cleared my throat and somehow managed politeness. "It'll be easier if we take two cars—that way, you can take the boys straight home once we've found them."

"So I just follow you?"

"Given you know their starting point, it'll be quicker and easier if you lead the way there. I'll use the shoe to locate them from that point on."

"Oh. Okay. I'm parked out the front."

"I've a red SUV around the back. You can't miss it."

"Oh. Okay," she repeated, and headed out. I locked the door behind her then pulled out my phone and called Aiden as I left via the rear door.

"I take it this is not a social call," he said.

"Yes and no. I just thought I'd inform you that a Mrs. Rankin has just asked me to find her wayward son. If I'm not here when you come to pick me up, I shouldn't be too far away."

"Let me guess, said son is missing up near the Marin reservation."

"Yeah."

He swore. "They've been warned multiple times about that. I'll contact Rene and tell him you'll be in the area."

"Thanks." Mrs. Rankin wasn't going to be pleased, but I'd rather face her ire than a werewolf intent on protecting his compound's boundaries any day.

"There is a sliver of self-interest in my actions, you know." His amusement shimmered down the phone line.

"Oh, of that I have no doubt, your sexual drive being what it is and all."

He laughed. "Be careful out there. Call me if the psychic senses don't land a result."

"I have his shoe. We'll be fine."

"Meaning he's walking around the bush with one bare foot?"

I smiled. "No."

"Shame. The little brat needs some discomfort in his life. I'll catch you later."

I shoved the phone away and started the SUV. Mrs. Rankin pulled away from the curb as I nosed out onto the street, and led the way through Castle Rock and out toward the Marin reservation. Darkness had closed in by the time she turned left into what looked to be little more than a goat track and then stopped.

I grabbed the flashlight out of the glove compartment then swung my pack over my shoulder and climbed out. The stars were bright in the sky, and the nearby forest filled with the song of cicadas. If they were singing, then there was little in the way of threat in the area.

I locked my SUV and walked over to hers. "Why on earth would you drop four boys off here?"

She seemed surprised at the question. "Because it's a good area to practice their orienteering skills for a comp that's coming up."

If this little adventure was any indication of said skills, they had no right to be entering any sort of competition. "And there were no other places further away from the Marin boundary that would have done?"

"Of course, but this area—"

I held up a hand to stop her excuses. "Just give me the shoe."

She did so. Life pulsed across my fingertips, a strong beat I'd have no trouble following. "Okay, let's go."

"What?" she said. "You want me to come with you? Into the bush?"

It's your fucking son, lady. I took a deep breath and said, "Yes. I'm a stranger—they might just run."

"Oh. Right." She sniffed, a sound that was somehow filled with displeasure. "Let's go then."

I switched on the flashlight; the bright beam pooled out in front of me, silvering the nearby leaves and muting the call of the cicadas. The pulse coming from the shoe led me to the left; after squeezing past a number of thorny bushes, I found a slight path. Mrs. Rankin followed close behind, her annoyance staining the air. Hopefully, this little adventure would impress on her the need to stop overindulging her damn son.

It was a good hour before the signal coming from the shoe jumped into sharper focus. I stopped and swept the light across the trees. There was no sign of the teenagers, but they were nevertheless close.

"Call your son, Mrs. Rankin."

"Charlie? You out there?"

"Mom?" The voice came from our left.

I swung the light around. A slender figure popped up out of the scrub and flung a hand across his face to protect his eyes.

"What the hell are you doing all the way out here?" he said.

"What the hell do you think I'm doing? Rescuing you, you idiot."

"I thought you'd just send the rangers."

"What? And get us all in trouble again? That would be bright, wouldn't it? Where are the others?"

Three "We're here" followed this question, and all four boys stepped onto the path. There was little contrition on their faces—they'd enjoyed every minute of being 'lost', and that alone made me wonder if it had been deliberately done.

"We'd better get you lot home," Mrs. Rankin continued. "Before your mothers start wondering where the hell you are."

If their mothers weren't already wondering that, I'd be seriously surprised.

"So who's she?" Charlie said. "And why is she carrying my shoe?"

"She's the psychic who helped me find you."

"By using my shoe?"

"Yes. And the cost of hiring her is coming out of your allowance, Charlie, I can assure you of that."

"Oh, *Mom*—"

"Don't 'oh Mom' me. You were warned to keep to the marked tracks and you didn't. Just thank the lucky stars it was us that found you rather than the Marins."

"We're not that close to their boundary."

A comment that all but confirmed my suspicion they weren't as lost as they'd made out. I shook my head, then turned around and led the five of them back to the SUVs. Mrs. Rankin ushered the boys into the back of her vehicle, then grabbed her purse and handed me the fee. She obviously wasn't lacking for cash if she carried that sort of change around.

"Thanks for your help." She hesitated. "I'd appreciate it if you didn't mention this little adventure to your ranger friend. I wouldn't like it getting back to the wrong ears."

A request that had come way too late, and one I wouldn't have obeyed anyway. "I suggest you get back into town without delay, Mrs. Rankin. There's been some trouble around these parts recently."

"That seems to be a running theme in this reservation. Might be time to move again, I'm thinking."

I made no comment; I just nodded, climbed into my

SUV, and reversed back between the trees so she could get past. Then I followed her back onto the gravel road that wound its way out of the area.

I'd barely gone a mile or so when there was an odd thump. The steering became sluggish and unresponsive, the wheel began to vibrate, and there was an odd flapping sound coming from the rear of the vehicle. I pulled off the road and jumped out. The rear left tire was flat.

So much for the sturdiness of new tires.

I opened the rear door, pulled up the floor mats, and then tugged out the spare and the tire-changing kit. Only to discover the wheel nuts had been done up by Superman himself and there was no way I was ever going to get them undone. Not even by jumping up and down on the lever thingy.

I blew out a frustrated breath, then grabbed my phone and called the auto club for help. Twenty minutes, they informed me.

I glanced at my watch and made another call, this time to Aiden. "I am going to be late back."

"Haven't you found the boys yet?"

"Yes, but the SUV now has a flat tire, and I have to wait for the RACV to turn up."

"You don't know how to change a tire?"

"Of course I do." My tone was indignant. "I just can't move the damn wheel nuts."

"Ah. Do you want me to come up there and keep you company?"

"As tempting as that offer is, it'll probably take you as long to get here as the RACV."

"True enough. Shall I wait outside the café or will you drive straight back to my place?"

"The latter makes more sense. But I expect a hot chocolate to be waiting for me when I get there."

"I'll throw in some marshmallows, just to sweeten the deal, if you like."

"I'm aquiver with excitement."

He laughed. "See you soon."

I shoved my phone into my pocket then leaned against the SUV and crossed my arms. Mrs. Rankin's SUV was no longer visible, but even if it had been she would probably have been too busy discussing the day's events with her darling Charlie to even notice I no longer followed her.

I shook my head and hoped that, when I finally did have kids, I had the good sense to set a few more boundaries and rules.

Of course, a daughter born to a witch and a werewolf was likely to be strong-willed in the extreme... I smiled. Talk about wishful thinking.

I pushed away from the SUV and began to pace, suddenly unable to stand still. Or, if I was being at all honest with myself, unwilling to think about a future that didn't involve Aiden.

Fifteen minutes later, headlights appeared, pinning me briefly in brightness before the driver dropped the high beam. I covered my eyes and saw the yellow paintwork and the lights on top of the cabin. The RACV.

"Hey," the driver said as he jumped out of the vehicle. "Got yourself into a bit of a pickle, I hear?"

"The wheel nuts are too damn tight."

"Yeah, that's a common problem with new cars. We'll have it fixed in no time."

He retrieved a heavy-duty hydraulic jack and a battery-powered wheel nut wrench from the back of his van and in very little time had my tire changed.

He hefted the flat into the back of my SUV. "I have to say, I don't think this was an accident."

My pulse rate briefly stuttered, and then leaped into a higher gear. "What makes you think that?"

"This." He pointed to what looked like a burn mark. "Someone's deliberately weakened the wall of the tire so that it would blow out under stress. If you've been driving along any of the rough old tracks that run off this one—"

"And I was."

"Then that explains it. We'd best check the rest, just in case."

He immediately did so. I ran my fingers across the damaged bit of the tire and felt the faint caress of energy. No human hand had done this. A chill rose, and I quickly scanned the area. The sooner I got out of here, the better.

Thankfully, the rest of the tires showed no sign of damage, though that might not mean anything given the source of the attack was supernatural in origin. Once I'd signed his paperwork, the repairer jumped back into his van, turned around, and drove away.

I did a quick check just to ensure there was no more magic to be found, then quickly jumped into the SUV and followed him down the road. But as it curved around to the right and took the van from my sight, the SUV shuddered a second time, and then the vibration and flapping sound started again.

I tried not to panic; after all, while the tires had been checked, it was possible that something had been missed, especially if the weakness was on an inside wall.

Possible, instinct whispered, but not likely.

I pulled to the side of the road and immediately locked all the doors even as the memories of just how little it had protected Byron stirred. In the twin beams of the headlights, dust stirred, but there was little else to be seen in the night.

And yet...

I grabbed my backpack then climbed out of the SUV and walked around to the back. It was once again the left rear tire—the one we'd just changed.

I looked around in alarm. While I couldn't sense or see anything untoward, I had no doubt she was out there, somewhere close. Watching. Waiting.

I swallowed heavily and got out my phone. Aiden answered second ring. "If Joel hasn't arrived yet to change your tire, I'm going to kick his butt tomorrow."

"He's been and gone, but I've got another flat."

Something cracked in the trees to my right. I jumped around, magic dancing like fireflies across the fingers of my free hand. Again, there was nothing to see, but that sense of danger was growing.

"They're new tires—this shouldn't be happening."

"I know, and I don't think it's an accident."

"I'll ring Joel immediately and get him back—"

"And put him in the firing line? No way, Aiden."

He swore softly. "Then I'll grab Ashworth and be out there in twenty minutes. Have you got your spell stones with you?"

"Yes." But they wouldn't do any good. The elder Empusae had already proven capable of breaking into my protective circle. I rather suspected that, after getting a feel for my magic, she'd be even more prepared the second time around.

"Then use them. Just keep safe until we get there."

"I will."

He hung up. I stared at the phone for several seconds, suddenly feeling very alone and out of my depth.

Which was ridiculous. I might be alone, but I wasn't powerless. I shoved my phone back into my pocket and then carefully wove a spell around my fingers, one that was a demon net and tracker combined. This time, if my net did hit her in any way, a couple of threads would latch onto her feathers and give me a means of tracking her. Monty might frown at the way I mixed my spells, but as yet they hadn't failed me.

I crossed mental fingers that *this* spell would not be the first.

I pressed back against the SUV and studied the trees on either side of the road. Aside from that sharp crack a few minutes ago, there was little in the way of movement or sound. But the fact that the cicadas were so quiet suggested something was indeed out there.

I flexed my fingers, the movement stretching the spell twined around them and sending a rainbow shimmer of light across the nearby shadows. Just for an instant there was an answering glimmer in the trees.

A glimmer that looked like eyes.

Eyes that were round and golden.

Owl eyes.

Empusae eyes.

Oh fuck...

Energy sparked around my other hand, enriched with the glittering threads of wild magic—the stuff that came from within rather than the stuff native to this reservation. Which had been strangely absent over the last few days, but I guess it couldn't be everywhere. And it certainly wasn't logical to expect it to handily turn up whenever I needed it —even if part of me wished it would do exactly that right now.

The eyes disappeared. The sick churning in my gut

intensified. I remained still, every sense I had wide open in an effort to catch the slightest hint of movement or magic.

Nothing.

The night remained, at least on a surface level, free of sound and threat.

But she was out there, watching and waiting.

For what?

Are you okay? came Belle's comment. *I'm getting all sorts of weird vibes from you.*

I've had two flat tires. Aiden's on his way out here.

That doesn't explain the weird vibes. What's wrong?

I think the Empusae might be stalking me.

Well fuck, where are you? I'll come get you—

There's nothing you can do. And no way she'd get here in time if something *did* happen. *It might be nothing.*

Even as I said that, another crack rang out, jangling my nerves and making my heart skip unevenly for several beats. The bitch was playing with me...

We both know the latter part of that statement is an outright lie. I'll head home and—

Belle, don't wreck your night—

Leaving Kash to party on without me in the club is not wrecking my night. You dying on me totally would. I'll get home and get comfortable, just in case you have to pull on my reserves.

I drew in a deep breath and released it slowly. *Thanks, Belle.*

Energy stirred. Not mine. Not even the Empusae's. It belonged to Vita. She might have told us she couldn't track this demon, but she had an uncanny knack of showing up just before the bitch attacked...

The thought had barely crossed my mind when a figure came out of the trees and arrowed toward me. I swore and flung my net spell. It spun through the air, spreading out as it did so, providing an ever-widening area in which to capture the demon. She screamed in fury, a sound so fierce it made my ears ache. In the blink of an eye she went from flesh to feather form and then soared upwards. I flicked my spell after her; one edge caught her tail and threads of magic spun from the net to her feathers and lashed around them tightly. She screeched and twisted violently one way and then the other even as her magic surged and attacked mine. I quickly unraveled the net spell and let it fall away, hoping against hope that she didn't see—didn't feel—the two faint threads still clinging to her. Now I just had to remain alive long enough to make use of them. I wove a second spell around my fingertips, this time a repelling one.

The demon had disappeared once more. I scanned the skies, knowing she wouldn't have gone far, knowing she'd be back, and soon, if only because I was alone in the middle of nowhere. She'd never get a better opportunity to attack.

Vita came closer, and anger stirred through me. It very much felt like she was using me as bait—especially given her energy was similar in feel to the faint wisps that had lingered on the melted bit of the tire.

Had she set me up?

Possibly. More than possibly.

And yet, why would she do that if she wanted Belle's help? Didn't she realize the connection between us?

Probably not, came Belle's thought. *She's a very old witch, remember, and as far as we're aware, there's been no other cases of one witch becoming the familiar of another.*

True, though I had a bad feeling Vita's actions wouldn't have changed even if she *had* known. Our White Lady was very intent on gaining her vengeance no matter what it cost anyone else.

Which was just one more reason for Belle not to give her access.

Once again, something cracked deep in the forest, this time behind me. I jumped and turned, my heart pounding in the vicinity of my throat. Nothing. There was nothing.

And yet she was there.

What the hell was she waiting for?

What sort of game was she playing?

Perhaps she simply wants you to suffer. Belle's mental tones were grim. *Maybe you should just jump into the SUV and drive as fast as you can away from the area, flat tire or not.*

If I'm in the SUV, I can't see her coming at me. I don't want to end up like Byron.

Byron was stationary. You wouldn't be.

I'm not sure it'll make any difference. I scanned the area again, uncertain what to do, one part of me seeing the sense of Belle's suggestion while another warned it would be the worst possible step.

The decision was taken out of my hands.

Power surged, sparking across the night, its feel so fierce it sprayed across my skin like liquid fire. Light appeared—it was a churning mass of heat that shot through the trees and left a trail of flaming destruction behind it. It wasn't Empusae in origin. It was witch.

Vita.

The bitch was definitely using me as bait.

And her mass of burning destruction was headed straight for the SUV.

I swore and ran like hell.

I wasn't fast enough. I was never going to be fast enough.

The fiery ball hit and the vehicle exploded. Heat,

flames, bits of plastic and metal and God only knows what else cannoned into the air. The force of it was so strong it sent me flying. I threw out my hands, skinning them along the stony road as I tried to break my fall and protect my face. If it hurt, I didn't feel it. I stopped sliding and twisted around; saw the remnants of the SUV on fire. Saw the naked, furious form coming straight at me.

Terror surged. I clamped down on it, scrambled to my feet, and threw the spell still entangled around my fingers. She saw it and dodged, but I flicked a hand and the spell arced around and came at her again. Magic surged, this time to my left. A twisting mass of fiery, angry-looking threads shot out of the trees—and once again, its source was Vita.

The Empusae leaped skyward, her form once again shifting from human to owl. Vita's energy didn't follow; instead, it collided with my repel spell and a second explosion occurred, one that sprayed energy and spell remnants across the nearby ground.

A scream rent the air. My gaze jumped up. All I saw was talons. Sharp, gleaming talons, coming straight at my face. I flung a hand up instinctively and the firefly energy that had been dancing across my fingertips formed a thick lance that arrowed directly at the demon. She screamed, dropped away sharply, and then came in under the lance for another attack. More energy surged across my fingertips, its force fainter. I flung it anyway, even as I began another spell that was a combination of a repelling spell and an energy whip. Then I turned and ran into the trees.

Remaining on the road, in plain sight, with multiple directions from which she could attack me, was stupid. I might in reality be no safer in the trees, but they did at least restrict the speed with which she could attack.

An incoming sense of doom hit. I slid to a stop, spun

around, and cracked my whip toward her. She squawked and tipped to one side, but her descent barely altered in speed. I swore and dropped. Felt air rake my back, an indication of just how close her claws had come.

I thrust to my feet and lunged to the left, into the deeper undergrowth. Heard her scream, felt the wind of another approach. Lashed my whip around my head even as I ran on, crashing through the scrub, tearing clothes and skin in my desperation to escape.

A third swoop. I swore and dropped low. Felt her claws snag my hair and rip a chunk free. I bellowed and flicked the whip after her. Its end caught her tail and she squawked as feather remnants rained down.

It didn't stop her. Even as I watched, she curved around and arrowed toward me, low and fast.

I once again pushed to my feet and ran on. Felt the surge of Vita's magic to my right; saw, out of the corner of my eye, the flare of an incoming sphere. It didn't hold the fierceness of her original bolt, and I could only hope that it would be strong enough to kill.

If it hit, that was. She didn't appear to have the ability to alter the trajectory of her spell after it had been launched

Which meant I had to hold the Empusae's attention, and the only hope of ensuring *that* was for me to allow her to get closer.

My skin crawled at the thought. I gripped my whip fiercely, but fought the need to use it, fought the desire to spin around and slash the thing across her face, to scar her as she'd scarred me. But the whip wasn't designed to kill, and that was what mattered most right now. The bait had no choice but to run on.

At the very last minute, the Empusae must have sensed Vita's sphere, because she flung herself skyward. This time, she wasn't fast enough. The sphere hit and exploded, and the feathered fury was sent tumbling back into the darkness.

I skidded to a halt, my breath a harsh rasp that echoed across the night, and my heart a rapid-fire gun pulsing high in my throat. For several minutes, I simply stood there, scanning the nearby trees, every sense—human and psychic—searching for some sign of the demon. Vita stirred to my left, her force faint and filled with uncertainty. If *she* wasn't sure if she'd killed her quarry, then it was doubtful we had.

I bit my lip and continued to scan the area, hoping against hope that I was wrong, that the elder *was* dead and that we didn't have to worry about her anymore.

The soft breeze stirred, teasing my nostrils with the scent of blood and ash combined.

Then there was movement.

It was little more than a flicker—a flash of gold against the shadows of the night—but it was enough. The Empusae was injured but not dead.

I took a deep breath, gathering courage, the whip still gleaming brightly in one hand, then followed the scent of blood into the scrub.

But I'd barely taken three steps when the ground underneath me gave way and I tumbled forward into deep, dank darkness.

FOURTEEN

A mine.

Another fucking mine.

Horror and fear surged, but I ruthlessly thrust them aside and threw out my hands, trying to find something, anything, to latch on to before I fell too far and too deep. My left dug into the soft sides of the shaft but didn't catch. My right scraped against wood that crumbled away at my touch.

Below me, there was nothing but darkness. Then, out of that ink, loomed a deeper shadow. An old support beam, sticking out at an angle from the wall; it was right in the path of my fall.

I hit it just above my belly, and with such force it knocked the air from my lungs and cracked something inside. A tide of pain washed through me, and oblivion threatened. But if I gave in to the siren call of unconscious, I'd fall and die.

I've just contacted Aiden; he's ordering search and rescue out as we speak. Belle's mental tone was filled with tension and fear. *How secure is that beam you're wrapped around?*

I have no idea. And no immediate desire to move and find out. Not when it felt like someone had lit a fire inside my chest.

That could be the pressure of your weight against your ribs. You probably cracked one or two of them when you hit.

If that was all I'd done, I'd be damned lucky. I wriggled fingers and toes just to be sure, and they all responded. Relief swept through me, though I was a long way from safe.

My breathing was fast and shallow—the absolute wrong thing to do if I *had* cracked ribs—but with the pressure of the old beam digging in I had little other choice. I carefully turned my head and inspected the length of it. From the little I could see in the darkness, it appeared to be securely stuck into the shaft's wall, though whether it would remain that way with my weight dangling close to the end of it was another matter entirely. I needed to adjust my position and move back toward the wall.

It was going to hurt. A *lot*.

I could do it. I *had* to do it.

I carefully pictured exactly what I needed to do, and then, before the fear of what it would physically cost could stop me, swung my right leg toward the beam. Heat and pain and darkness surged, tearing a scream from my throat. It seemed to echo forever in the mineshaft, an indication just how deep this thing was.

Then, from darkness far above me, came an answering howl.

Imagination? Wishful thinking?

Possibly.

The heel of my boot caught the far edge of the beam. I shifted position, forced my entire leg over, and then shifted again, this time pulling myself around until I was lying along the length of wood rather than hanging limply over it.

It hurt. Lord, how it hurt. But I wasn't finished yet. Wasn't safe yet.

Slowly, carefully, I hooked my feet together under the beam and began to inch backwards. Sweat stung my eyes, making it difficult to see, and all I could smell on the dank air was my own fear.

It was a slow and painful process; by the time my butt hit the wall, I was soaked and shaking. But I was still conscious and still on the beam, and that was a miracle in itself.

I remained in that position for several minutes, but Belle was right. My weight was putting too much pressure on whatever I cracked. I closed my eyes, once again gathering courage for the pain that was about to hit, and then carefully pushed upright. For one intensely scary moment, I tipped sideways, but I gripped the beam fiercely and managed to stop the fall.

Then, and only then, did I look up. The stars twinkled brightly, looking far closer than I thought they'd be. Despite what I'd thought, I hadn't actually fallen that far—maybe only twenty feet or so.

People can be killed falling ten feet, Belle said. *Once again, lady luck has been with you.*

She does seem to have a soft spot for me.

Or perhaps you were a cat in a previous incarnation and you're just using up whatever spare lives you carried forward. It could also explain why Eamon dislikes you.

I snorted and instantly regretted it. I hissed and clamped a hand to my left side in a vague effort to contain the hurt, even though I knew it wouldn't help. *How far away is the rescue party?*

Aiden called me about five minutes ago—they'd just found the remnants of our SUV.

Meaning they should be close. *The council is going to be pissed.*

The damn council needs to be bitch slapped. If they hadn't been so damn recalcitrant about getting another witch when Gabe disappeared, none of this would be happening.

Something they'd at least admitted and rectified. It had just happened a little too late to prevent word of an unchecked wellspring spreading through the darker places of this world.

"Lizzie? Are you out there?"

The question rose out of the silence, making me jump even as relief shot through me.

Aiden. I briefly closed my eyes against the sting of tears. "Yes. I'm down a mine shaft."

Dirt fell from the rim of the hole, and then he appeared above me. Never in my life had I been so glad to see anyone. "Are you hurt?"

"Cracked a rib or two, I think."

"And that beam? How secure is it?"

"It hasn't moved."

"Paramedics and rescue are two minutes behind me. Once we get some painkillers into you, we'll get you out of there. In the meantime, if I lower a harness down to you, do you think you can put it on?"

"Yes."

He immediately did so. Putting it on was harder than it looked, but I eventually had everything strapped in. Securing it across my chest hurt like blazes, but falling would be ten times worse.

I swiped at the sweat dribbling down my face and then

looked up. Aiden's face was shadowed, but his eyes were as blue as sapphires. "Okay, secure this end."

"As we are here. You won't fall any farther, Liz."

Which didn't make me feel any safer. Nothing would until I got out of this goddamn shaft. I rested my head back against the wall and tried to curb my impatience. "Is Ashworth with you? Because the Empusae might still be—"

"She's long gone." Ashworth appeared on the other side of the mine's shaft. "You two had one hell of a battle, if the magic lingering on the air is anything to go by."

"There were three of us—the White Lady was also here."

"I take it she missed her quarry yet again."

"Sort of." I gave them a quick rundown and then added, "My tracker will probably last twenty-four hours, but the sooner you get me out of here, the sooner we can hunt this bitch."

"You're not chasing after the goddamn demon until you're fully checked out and cleared by the hospital," Aiden growled. "If I have to physically restrain you, I will."

"How about we get her out of the goddamn mine before we start any arguments," Ashworth said. "The rescue team has just arrived, lass. We should have you out of there in no time."

His idea of no time and mine turned out to be vastly different, but I was eventually dragged up and carefully extracted. Once at the hospital, they ran me through a series of checks and scans, but aside from two cracked ribs and a blooming array of bruises across my stomach, there was no major damage.

Aiden did make good with his promise, however, sitting by my side all night to ensure I didn't check myself out early. Which was only a little bit frustrating; truth was, between the ribs and the bruises, I could barely move without it hurting like hell. Painkillers helped, but it was pretty obvious I'd be next to useless in the café for the next week or so.

The following morning, after the doctors had given me the all-clear to go home and supplied me with painkillers and prescriptions, Aiden help me dress—replacing the hospital gown they'd stuck me in after they'd cut off my clothes with a spare pair of track pants and a sweater he kept in his truck—then grabbed my pack and took me home.

Belle was waiting by the front door. "Do you want a shower or breakfast first?"

"Shower," Aiden said. "Definitely a shower."

I gave him a deadpan look. "Are you suggesting I stink?"

"Of sweat, antiseptic, and dank mine. Yes."

"Charming."

"That's one word for it, though not one I'd personally use. Do you want help up the stairs?"

I hesitated and then nodded. While I could probably lean on the banister just as easily as him, I rather liked his closeness. The way his scent wrapped around me, warm and comforting. "But after I shower, we need to have a council of war—"

"Already on it," Belle said. "Monty, Ashworth, and Eli should be here for breakfast in fifteen minutes."

"We open in fifteen minutes." I looked around. "Where is everyone?"

"I explained what happened and gave them the day off. Figured it was easier than trying to juggle plans and customers."

"Good thinking."

"Go," she said. "I'll start breakfast."

Aiden carefully helped me up the stairs and into the

bathroom. "I can see why you enjoy my shower—there's barely enough room to swing a flannel in this thing."

"Which basically sums up our whole upper floor accommodation."

"Then why not move into my place on a more permanent basis?"

I touched his stubbly cheek and stared into his beautiful eyes. "I think we both know why that wouldn't be a good idea."

"Actually, no, we don't. You're all I want, Liz—"

"At this point in time—"

"Which is all I care about." He brushed limp hair away from my face, his fingers warm on my skin. "You spend far too much of *your* time worrying about the future. You need to live for now."

"I am. But I also can't afford to deepen a relationship that realistically has no future. We both eventually want marriage and kids, Aiden, and that's not something we can achieve together."

No matter how much I might wish otherwise.

He didn't immediately answer, but I could feel conflict in him. Could see it in his aura and smell it in his scent. His fingers tracked slowly down my cheek and caught my chin. Then he kissed me like it meant something. Like *I* meant something. Something far more than just another woman whose company he enjoyed.

And while I had no doubt he cared for me as much as he would ever care for anyone who wasn't a werewolf, to believe the depth of emotion I could feel in this kiss was the short path to madness.

He eventually released me, but if the shadows and uncertainty I could feel in him were anything to go by, the kiss had comforted him no more than it did me. We were stepping into dangerous territory and we both knew it—even if he didn't appear willing to acknowledge it.

"Do you need help stripping down?"

"I'll need help with your sweater, at least."

He gently tugged the sweater off, then kissed me again and left. I finished getting undressed, then got into the shower and let the hot water run over my body in an attempt to ease all the aches and bruising. I just had to hope that we caught the Empusae today, because I doubted I was going to be in a fit state to be chasing demons across the countryside tomorrow.

Once I'd dressed in my own track pants and a loose-fitting zip-up sweater I could undo easily, I shoved my feet into some shoes and headed downstairs. All three witches had arrived and were busily tucking into an assortment of bacon, eggs, and freshly made bread.

"I've put yours in the warmer," Belle said. "The horde's appetite is a bit voracious this morning."

"Midnight rescues will do that to you," Ashworth said. "Though I will point out that the young laddie here does not have that excuse."

"No. He just has a naturally healthy appetite." Monty's gaze was on Belle when he said that, and there was a wicked gleam in his eyes.

She gave him 'the look', which was met with an even wider grin. She shook her head and looked at me. "Do you need help with that plate?"

"No, I should be fine. Thanks." I grabbed a tea towel to counter the hot plate and then joined them at the table.

"So," Monty said. "How did you manage to pin a tracker spell onto the Empusae? And is it still active? Given she's magic capable, it's possible she's already countered it."

"Whether it's still active or not is a question I can't answer until I create a secondary spell to track it—"

"Meaning it was another of your freeform spells?" he asked.

"Yes—a demon net spell combined with a couple of tracker threads. I'm hoping they're not powerful enough for her to have sensed them. She didn't seem to."

"That might have been because she was too busy trying to kill you," Ashworth commented. "But she's had plenty of time since to feel and deal with your spell."

If she *had*, we'd either have to wait for her next attack or hope that, in the next couple of days, she went into that mine we'd found and triggered Ashworth's trap.

"Maybe not," Belle said. "It's possible the blows she took from Vita wiped her out."

"Given how little we know about White Ladies who were once also witches," Eli said, "anything is possible."

"Presuming Liz is able to track her," Aiden said. "What's the plan?"

"First priority has to be containment—we can't afford to have her escaping us again," Monty said. "Once we've done that, we can probably do to her what we did to the other one."

"There's two problems with that," Ashworth said. "Firstly, we're dealing with a demon who's far older and stronger than that other one—"

"And two," Belle cut in. "If we kill her without first giving Vita her chance, there'll be hell to pay."

I grabbed a fresh bit of bread to mop up the egg remnants with. "I'm still not liking the idea of you letting her into your body."

"Neither do I, but if we have to do this, then today is the

perfect time. She'll be wiped out after her efforts last night, and won't have the same sort of power or control."

"Her recovery skills—or lack thereof—are something I'd rather not rely on," Monty said. "It'd be better if we take other precautions."

"You thinking of a restrictor spell?" Eli asked. "Because they have their dangers."

"Which could be countered easily enough by placing the spell on Liz rather than Belle. The two will be connected, so it mutes the risks to Belle while still restricting what the demon can and can't do."

Eli nodded. "Worth a shot, certainly."

"Um, before you actually get set on that course of action, care to explain what this spell does and what the possible dangers are?" Belle asked.

"It basically wraps around your mind and stops the entity from invading. The problem is that sometimes the spell can wrap so tightly that it can tear the mind apart. There have been cases—very few cases—of witches being sent mad," Monty said. "That's very unlikely to happen here, thanks to the fact that you two are so deeply connected. Basically, you'll keep each other sane."

"Or so you hope," I said.

He waved a hand. "Hope is such a fragile thing that it's better not to trust in it. Trust in me and my knowledge instead."

"Oh boy," Belle muttered, "*That* really calms the nerves."

"It isn't like we really have many other options," he replied. "In the end, it'll come down to the strength of your connection with Liz. And that is the one thing you *can* trust and believe in."

A truth neither of us could deny. And yet, however

much we believed that our connection would repel all comers, the truth was it had never truly been tested.

"How are you going to contact Vita?" Aiden asked. "Or is she hanging about here somewhere?"

Belle smiled. "She can't get in here unless she's invited. I'll call her once we know whether the tracker is working or not. She said she'd respond if we use her name."

Ashworth glanced at his watch. "Midday is probably the best time to tackle finding the demon. Shall we reassemble here just before then?"

I nodded. "In the meantime, I'll work on a receiver and see if I can get anything."

Ashworth raised his eyebrows. "Were you ever taught how to do a receiver?"

"No, but that's never stopped her," Monty said before I could. "I keep telling her it's dangerous to make it up as you go along, but she won't listen."

"Because my very avoidance of the rules of magic might yet be the one thing that saves me."

Monty's gaze met mine, and all amusement fell from his expression. After a moment, he nodded and then rose. "Thank you for breakfast, Belle. I'll go grab my gear, then come back and talk you both through that restrictor spell. That way, you can just activate it when and if necessary."

I nodded and hoped like hell that it wouldn't be necessary. That Vita would do the right thing and leave once she'd gained her revenge.

But I wasn't about to risk Belle's life on it.

Ashworth and Eli followed Monty out the door. Aiden caught my hand and, as Belle gathered the plates and took them into the kitchen, dropped a kiss onto my palm. "I hope you realize I'll not be leaving your side during this whole tracking expedition. If this bitch wants a piece of you, she'll have to go through me first."

"While I appreciate the sentiment, don't forget what she is. I doubt she's afraid of me; she's certainly not going to be afraid of a werewolf, however fierce and determined he might be."

"Ah, but you're forgetting I'm a werewolf who's wearing a multilayered protection charm. Even if it only keeps her off me for a minute or so, teeth can do a whole lot of damage in that time. And while she's distracted by me, you can pin her, and Belle can help Vita stab her."

"Something Belle would rather not think about." She came out of the kitchen. "I'm generally not the squeamish type, but Vita wants to see her suffer—wants to feel her blood as it washes across my skin—and the thought of that is giving me the jeebies."

Aiden raised an eyebrow. "Jeebies?"

"As in, heebie-jeebies."

He snorted softly, then squeezed my fingers and released them. "I'd better go to work for a few hours."

"You're welcome to use our shower if you've another change of clothes in your truck," I said.

"We've one at the station, and it's werewolf sized. I'll see you soon." He rose, kissed the top of my head, and then left.

"I take it he just cast shade on our shower," Belle said. "Does he not realize that what it lacks in size it makes up for in pressure?"

"No, and I doubt he'd care. You've seen the showers at his place."

"The word palatial does come to mind. For a down-to-earth, straightforward man, he sure doesn't mind a bit of over-the-top comfort in his bathrooms."

"Which makes me wonder if a former girlfriend had some say in the fit out."

"I could go mind fishing, if you want."

"No, leave the man alone."

She simply grinned at me.

"Seriously, don't."

Her grin just got wider. I shook my head and gripped the end of the table to push upright. Pain swirled, and a hiss escaped.

Belle's amusement quickly fell away. "Have you taken your tablets?"

"I'm not due for another lot until eleven. But I will have a cup of coffee, if you don't mind making it."

She nodded and, once she was sure I was steady on my feet, headed over to make my coffee. I slowly made my way into the reading room, but didn't bother moving any of the furniture. I just propped on the table and began working on the tracker spell. Monty was right in that I'd never been taught the spell, but I'd seen him create one, and it hadn't looked too difficult. Thankfully, I not only had a good memory when it came to spell wording, but I could also picture the needed result in my mind and work from that.

Belle came in with my drink halfway through and watched through narrowed eyes as I tied it off and then briefly activated it. For several seconds, nothing happened. The gently glowing sphere of golden threads sat on my palm, seemingly dead. Then, faintly, came a pulse.

The two tracker threads were active. The Empusae hadn't yet sensed them.

Relief stirred. I deactivated the spell, placed it carefully on the table, and then accepted the mug Belle gave me. Despite the strong coffee smell, I could tell it had been laced with ginseng and basil, both of which had anti-inflammatory properties as well as being able to boost strength and lower stress.

The latter was certainly needed.

"Do you want to contact Vita now? Or later, when we're out in the field and have some idea where she is?"

Belle hesitated. "It's probably better to do it now. That way, I can rest up before we head out."

It also meant there was less chance of the Empusae sensing what was happening outside her lair, as we'd have to set up a protective circle to prevent Vita trying to take over too soon. Hosting a spirit was physically draining, and the longer the possession went on, the more dangerous it became. There had been cases of witches dying thanks to the stress it had put on their bodies.

I drained my coffee, then carefully eased down onto the floor and crossed my legs. Belle sat opposite and clasped my hands. "Ready?"

I took a deep breath that hurt like blazes and then nodded. Belle deepened the connection between us and said, her mental tone one of command, *Vita, appear before us. We need to talk to you. You may enter this building as long as you wish us no harm.*

There was no response.

Vita, appear before us, Belle said again, the demand in her voice stronger. The force of it echoed through the air, a call that would be heard well beyond the boundaries of Castle Rock.

Again, there was no response. Not for several minutes. But just as the echoes of her demand began to fade, the magic protecting this place pulsed as Vita arrived and passed through it.

Then she was in front of us. She was far paler than the

last time—far more indistinct. Belle was right—she hadn't yet recovered from her efforts last night.

What is it you wish of me? Her voice, like her form, was faint.

Liz placed a tracking spell on the Empusae last night. We're going after her in an hour. If you wish to be a part of the kill, you need to follow us.

Let me in—

No, Belle said forcibly. *When we have this demon cornered and leashed, I will give you your revenge. Until then, you bide your time.*

Annoyance shimmered across Vita's form, and it had my distrust rising.

I have no choice but to do this your way. But rob me—

If we're going to throw threats around, then let me give you one—any attempt to overstay will be met by force.

Her amusement stirred the air. My distrust sharpened.

Do not fear, little witch. I have no desire to stay where I am not welcome.

One more thing before you go, Belle said. *Is this demon capable of moving around in daylight?*

That I cannot tell you, but she's certainly powerful enough to do so if she wished.

Great, I thought. Just what we needed to hear.

I'll call again once we have caught this demon, Belle said. *Until then, depart this place.*

Vita obeyed. Belle took a deep breath, then squeezed my hands and released me. Wisps of weariness clung to her, but they were nowhere near as bad as the first time.

"Go upstairs and rest," I said. "I'll give you a call when Monty arrives."

She nodded and climbed to her feet. "Do you need a hand up?"

I shook my head. "I'll manage. Go rest."

She did. I grabbed the table for balance, then slowly got up. I didn't bother going up the stairs—I just made myself a big pot of tea, grabbed yesterday's *Herald-Sun*, and plonked myself down on the table to catch up on the news.

Monty came in about an hour later without his crutches and walked us through the restrictor spell.

"Seems simple enough," I said.

He nodded. "Just don't do any variations, because it can be a dangerous spell."

"I won't." I shifted position in the chair, trying to get comfortable. "How likely is it this Empusae will sense our presence when we approach?"

"Highly likely, but given demons generally can't move around in the daylight, we shouldn't be in any danger until we step inside her lair."

"Except," Belle said, "Vita says this one probably can move about."

"Even if she can, the cost of shielding herself from the sun would drain her of strength extremely fast."

"Given how old this demon is and just how fast she can move, she might not need much time to wipe us all out," I commented.

"We've got the power and the knowledge to counter her," Monty said. "We'll be fine."

I hoped he was right, but I couldn't help thinking he was seriously underestimating this demon.

The rest of the men arrived just before twelve. We left in two trucks—Belle, Monty, and me with Aiden, and Ashworth and Eli following. Once seated, I reactivated my tracker sphere. Its faint pulse rippled across my fingers, and relief stirred. She still hadn't sensed it.

"Head toward Maldoon," I said after a moment.

"That's a distance from where she's been hunting," Monty commented.

"She's winged. Distance doesn't really matter to her. And after what has happened to her two offspring, maybe she's decided to try somewhere safer."

"Somewhere safer would be off this reservation entirely."

"She won't leave until she gets her revenge or she's dead."

Aiden glanced at me. "Is that your psi senses speaking?"

"Yes."

"Then let's hope this hunting expedition is a success." His voice was grim.

The closer we got to Maldoon, the stronger the pulse in the tracker became. Eventually, we went off road, following a series of dusty tracks as we wound our way through the scrublands that surrounded the old town.

"Here," I said eventually. "Turn right here."

"Surprise, surprise," Monty said. "It's the ruins of another mine."

One that had toilet facilities, BBQs, and a picnic area, from the look of things. Aiden stopped in the vacant parking area and we all climbed out. Dust swirled as Ashworth stopped beside us.

I scanned the area but couldn't see the mine. Nor was there an immediately obvious place for the Empusae to hide. But she was out there somewhere, and it wasn't just the strong pulse coming from the tracker that told me that.

It was the growing sense that the shit was about to hit the fan.

"Which way, lass?" Ashworth said as he jumped out of his SUV.

I pointed to the trees beyond the picnic area.

"Makes sense," Aiden said. "That's where the mine ruins are."

"It's the 'where' in those ruins we need to pin down." Monty slung his pack over his shoulder. "And that means you've still got the lead, Liz."

I walked through the picnic area and into the scrub beyond. It didn't take long for remnants of old buildings to appear; at first, they were little more than piles of bricks and stone rubble, but gradually, as we neared the industrial heart of the mine, they became more defined.

The tracker tugged me left, past a couple of water tanks and toward what looked to be three old kilns. The ceilings of two of them had obviously collapsed, because slivers of sunshine were evident beyond their small semi-circular entrances. But in the middle kiln there was only darkness.

Darkness and evil.

The latter was extremely faint, though, which was odd given the strengthening pulse within my tracker sphere. Maybe the kilns were deeper than they looked. Or maybe there was something stranger going on.

I tried to ignore the gathering cloud of uneasiness and stopped well short of the kilns. "The signal is coming from the middle kiln."

Ashworth stopped beside me. "It's not an ideal area to be placing a circle around."

"I don't think we need to," Eli said. "I think it'll be better if we simply raise a snare around the entire kiln."

"It'll take some power to cover an area *that* large," Monty said.

"Yes, but better safe than sorry," Eli said. "I'll head to the top of the hill behind the kiln and spell from there. That leaves you two to go inside and deal with this bitch."

"Watch where you're stepping," Aiden said. "The ground doesn't look that stable."

Eli nodded and followed the fence line around to the back of the kiln. Monty and Ashworth pulled off their backpacks and began readying their spells.

"Once the snares are set," Belle said. "I'll need to call in Vita."

Monty glanced at her. "Are you sure that's really necessary?"

"You don't play games with White Ladies," Ashworth said. "Not unless you're willing to pay a very heavy price."

Monty raised his eyebrows. "Experience speaking?"

"Yes. Get a move on, lad."

As the two of them continued their preparations, Belle retrieved our spell stones from our backpack and began laying them on the ground, creating a circle large enough to hold Aiden and us. He might be determined to be our protector, but he could do so from within the safety of our circle.

We just had to hope that the combination of both Belle's magic and my own was enough to hold off the Empusae if she did somehow escape the net and attack. Otherwise, the three of us would be in serious trouble.

I glanced down at the sphere in my hand. The pulse coming from it remained steady and it was definitely originating from that middle kiln.

So why was I uneasy?

Why was I becoming more and more certain that we were all being played?

I didn't know, and if my psychic senses had any clue, they weren't forthcoming.

With our spell stones set out, there was nothing more we could do but watch and wait. Until both the snares were set, we dared not raise our magic. The Empusae had felt the sting of my magic twice now and would probably be sensitive to its presence.

Eli reached the top of the hill overlooking the kilns. Ashworth motioned him to proceed, then he and Monty climbed the fence surrounding the kilns and walked toward the middle one. There was no stirring of magic, no sense that the demon hiding in the deeper shadows had moved, and yet... and yet, a sense of expectation and anticipation bled into the air. It wasn't coming from the three men ahead. It was simply staining the air, its direction difficult to pin thanks to the softly stirring breeze.

I flexed my fingers and resisted the urge to raise the circle or even call to the wild magic that stirred within. I had to be patient. To do anything now, before the others were ready, could just bring disaster down on us all.

And yet that was going to hit, no matter what we did now.

Eli began to spell, his magic rolling swiftly down the broken hillside and flooding the brick and stone mass that was the kiln. At the same time, Ashworth and Monty placed a net across the kiln's entrance; its threads were as thick as my fingers and pulsed with power. If it couldn't contain the demon within, then we really would be in serious trouble.

There was no response from within the cave. No indication that the Empusae was either alert or aware.

Had Vita's attacks drained her?

Or was this, as my psi senses were now all but screaming, nothing more than a trap? One that was about to be sprung?

"Right, laddie," Ashworth said. "Let's force this bitch's bones into the net and wrap her up tight so our White Lady can claim her vengeance and leave us in peace."

As the sting of their magic surged, Belle said, "Shouldn't we raise our circle now?"

I hesitated. "Let's see if she's in there first."

Aiden glanced at me sharply. "Isn't your sphere telling us that she is?"

"Yes, but something feels off."

"What?"

"I don't know."

"Which is the perfect reason why we should raise the circle," Belle said. "If it all goes to hell in a handbasket, then this may be our only—"

The rest of her words were drowned out by Eli's sharp bellow.

My gaze jumped up the hill. Saw him fall—tumble—down the broken slope toward the kilns, his back a bleeding mass of sliced flesh.

Saw the shimmer in the air.

Caught a brief glimpse of bloody claws before they winked out of existence again.

The Empusae wasn't in the kiln.

She was out in the sunshine, using magic to protect and hide her body.

And she was coming straight at the three of us.

FIFTEEN

There was no time to get the circle up. No time, even, to raise a repelling spell or demon net. Energy surged to my fingertips and it was wild mix of magic that had no defined purpose other than destruction. That was not what we wanted right now, but I threw it anyway.

The tumbling mass of threads and power spun toward the concealed Empusae. She swerved sharply, dipping underneath it, her form briefly appearing before whatever spell she was using reasserted itself.

"Ashworth," I yelled, even as Belle began raising a protective circle. "She's outside and concealed."

Aiden growled, the sound low and dangerous, then his form shifted from human to wolf and he was running, leaping high into air. His teeth snapped and feathers fell even as claws appeared, raking his back, sending fur flying.

And still she came at us.

I swore and flung out a hand, directing the tumbling of threads and power around, sending it chasing after the Empusae. But it wouldn't hit her soon enough to deflect her trajectory. She was too damn close.

I swore again and knocked Belle sideways. We hit the ground in a tangled mess of arms and legs, and for a second, a red mist rose across my vision, and I couldn't breathe. Sucking in air did little to ease the wash of pain, but I pushed away from Belle and got up. "Get Vita here, stat."

"On it. What are you going to do?"

"Keep the bitch away from you."

I activated the restriction spell and then turned and ran in the opposite direction. Saw the Empusae scream and swoop around for a second attack. I recalled my ball of power, felt it skim over my head, and flicked it up to meet the Empusae. Magic—her magic—rose to meet it. There was a brief, blinding flash as the two hit, and then a surge of energy that knocked me back several feet. I looked up, saw the remnants of both my magic and hers falling like dull snow to the ground. Saw her, no longer hidden, coming straight at me.

A deep and dangerous growl rose from behind me, and I automatically dropped. Aiden leaped high above me and then somehow twisted in the air so that he was no longer coming straight at the Empusae but rather from the side. She tipped a wing and dropped away but not fast enough. His teeth snapped down on one foot and he hung on tight, his weight forcing the demon to drop several feet. The Empusae screamed, a sound that was fury and pain combined, and magic surged again, this time flowing over Aiden, attacking him so fiercely that his whole body glowed with the force of it. For one horrible second, I thought I'd failed him. That he was about to die defending me because my magic simply wasn't strong enough.

Then the charm I'd made him came to life and a fierce, bright light speared out, swiftly countering the Empusae's magic. A heartbeat later, the force of his bite and the sheer weight of him took its toll and he tumbled to the ground, half her leg in his mouth and her blood staining his fur.

More power surged, this time Monty's and Ashworth's. A net appeared, the threads of its magic widening as it swept toward the Empusae. She swerved upward and her wings pumped hard, her desperation to escape obvious. The net followed her trajectory, its thick tendrils reaching for her.

Another surge of magic, and a second net appeared, this time above her. Eli. He was alive.

She flicked a wing, cutting sharply sideways, but this time, there was no escape. The two nets hit and wrapped tightly around her, allowing no room for movement. She tumbled to the ground, hitting hard enough for feathers and dust to fly. But she wasn't beaten yet. A darker energy rose, and Ashworth yelped as the ground underneath him crumbled away. Monty grabbed him and pulled him to safety. The Empusae screamed and raged, and another wave of energy attacked the two men. This time they were ready for it, meeting like for like, but I had to wonder how long they could withstand her force. The bitch was *strong*.

Vita appeared. Belle reached out to me, forcing a deeper connection, linking us so closely that I was her and she was me. There was no separation; there was just us.

Vita's energy hit like a wave; we tasted her hunger, her need for revenge, her determination and near madness.

As her spirit flooded through us and took over, the restriction spell came alive. It felt like claws in our brain, claws that somehow anchored the spell as its force surrounded Vita's spirit, corralling her, restricting her, even as a soft timer began to count down.

"If you're going to do something," Ashworth barked, "do it now. We can't hold her much longer."

Our gaze jumped toward the penned Empusae. She was twisting, fighting against the nets that held her. Magic flowed from her body in waves, threads of foulness that attacked the three men and their magic. The latter was already weakening—several threads were beginning to unravel. Soon they would snap and the demon would be free.

No.

The denial echoed through us, fierce and furious. We grabbed the backpack, pulled out the silver knife, and then pushed upright. The Empusae paid us no heed. She continued to battle the three men.

But that would change and soon. Soon she would feel the silver in her body and she would stare into our eyes and see the death that had been chasing her for so long...

We gripped the knife so tightly our fingers ached. The Empusae caught the wind of our approach and her magic spun toward us. It battered us, shredded us, but it did not stop us.

"This," we said, as we stopped before her, "is for Aldred, whose life you stole and whose future you destroyed. May your dark master shred your being for all eternity, and may you never know peace or life again."

We raised the knife and plunged it down. Straight through the netting and into the Empusae's dark heart.

There was no blood to stain our skin, but we did feel her life ebb away as her flesh became dust and her spirit fled to whatever hell awaited.

It was done.

But this body was a good one...

This body is not yours. Leave.

I think not, little witch. You should have listened to your friend.

That friend is here. Leave or we will force you.

You have not the strength.

She started to twist, to fight, even as she locked meta-physical claws deep into flesh. Every movement tore at our strength, and yet we were not one but two, and she would not defeat us.

You underestimate us.

The claws dug deeper. Reached for our souls. Attempting to destroy and claim what would never be hers. *I underestimate nothing. If you think I cannot counter a restriction spell, then you are indeed—* She cut the sentence off and then added, with a hint of fear, *What are you?*

I didn't answer. I simply flooded her with the magic that was mine and mine alone—a force that had melded to my very DNA and changed me in ways I couldn't yet fully understand. It swirled around Belle's spirit, protecting her even as it caught the restriction spell and changed it, empowered it.

Then it tore the tendrils of the witch's spirit from Belle's body and cast her away—far, far away—and forbade her to ever enter this place again.

One became two again. I collapsed onto the ground and dropped my head into my hands. My lungs burned, and my brain felt as if it was on fire. Every single bit of my body hurt, but it didn't matter. Vita and the Empusae had been banished, and somehow we'd all survived, even if somewhat broken and bloody.

Sometimes life didn't really get much better than that.

It took six weeks for my ribs to heal and for some sense of normality to return to our lives. While Aiden's natural healing ability meant he bore no lasting reminder of the Empusae's attack, the same could not be said of Eli, who had an impressive array of thick scars down his back despite the fact we'd used holy water on them. My own were nowhere near as bad, and I was left with little more than three faint white lines down my forearm as a reminder of just how close death had come.

I pulled on a sweater as I clattered down the stairs to begin the day's jobs.

Belle handed me a coffee and then said, "I broke it off with Kash last night."

"Are we celebrating or commiserating?"

She shrugged. "Bit of both. He was fun to be with, but I was just getting some bad vibes."

I nodded. It had become apparent that when I'd flushed her body with my native wild magic to force Vita away, a few odd remnants had been left behind and had visibly strengthened her magic.

"I'm not full-on dreaming, like you do," she continued, "but it seems I *have* gained a little insight precognition. And it's damn annoying, let me tell you."

"Yeah, sorry, but let's be honest—it's better than that bitch ruining your life and running your body."

"Oh, totally." She wrinkled her nose. "Anyway, said bad vibes said Kash was going to be big trouble if I didn't watch it, so I broke it off. Better safe than sorry when it comes to a relationship that was only ever casual."

I clicked my coffee mug against hers. "Shall we head on over to the club tonight and have a celebratory drink or two?"

Her eyebrows rose. "You're not going out with Aiden tonight?"

"Nope. He's got a family run on. It's the full moon tonight, remember."

"Ah." She took a drink, her expression contemplative. "It must stick in his mother's jaws something chronic that he's showing no signs of getting tired of your relationship and moving on."

"Oh, it really does." I'd met her briefly in the supermarket a few days ago, and though outwardly it was sweetness and light, the underflow was fierce. Deadly, even. "I dare say she'll be breaking open the champers when we finally do split."

"Which hopefully won't happen for a little while yet. Let the bitch suffer a bit more."

We clicked mugs to that sentiment. Someone knocked at the rear door and then came in without either of us saying anything.

"Only me," Ashworth said as his steps echoed in the small hall.

"It's too early for cake and coffee," Belle said, amused. "Unless you want instant like us."

"Instant's fine, and I'll grab two if you don't mind. Eli's waiting for me outside."

"So why come here for coffee when you've a perfectly good machine at home?"

"Because I thought you'd want to hear the news."

"You two are already married, so it can't be that," I said. "Have you perhaps decided to extend the family and adopt?"

"No, idiot. It would hardly be fair on the child to have me as a father."

I smiled. "But he'd also have Eli, and his sweetness would counter your gruffness."

"Thanks, but no. I've enough trouble coping with the young witches currently in this reservation."

"Then why, pray tell, are you here?"

He hesitated, and the sudden seriousness in his expression had my gut clenching. "Because I have some news."

"What?" It came out breathy. Filled with fear.

"I heard from my sister." He hesitated, and took a deep breath. "Clayton Marlowe left Canberra yesterday, and no one knows where he went."

I didn't say anything. I didn't need to.

We all knew what it meant. The tracer's report had finally hit his desk, and the one thing I'd been running from for twelve years was about to happen.

My husband was on his way here to reclaim his wife.

ALSO BY KERI ARTHUR

The Witch King's Crown

Blackbird Rising (Feb 2020)

Blackbird Broken (Oct 2020)

Blackbird Crowned (June 2021)

Kingdoms of Earth & Air

Unlit (May 2018)

Cursed (Nov 2018)

Burn (June 2019)

Lizzie Grace series

Blood Kissed (May 2017)

Hell's Bell (Feb 2018)

Hunter Hunted (Aug 2018)

Demon's Dance (Feb 2019)

Wicked Wings (Oct 2019)

Deadly Vows (Jun 2020)

The Outcast series

City of Light (Jan 2016)

Winter Halo (Nov 2016)

The Black Tide (Dec 2017)

Souls of Fire series

Fireborn (July 2014)

Wicked Embers (July 2015)

Flameout (July 2016)

Ashes Reborn (Sept 2017)

<u>**Dark Angels series**</u>

Darkness Unbound (Sept 27th 2011)

Darkness Rising (Oct 26th 2011)

Darkness Devours (July 5th 2012)

Darkness Hunts (Nov 6th 2012)

Darkness Unmasked (June 4 2013)

Darkness Splintered (Nov 2013)

Darkness Falls (Dec 2014)

<u>**Riley Jenson Guardian Series**</u>

Full Moon Rising (Dec 2006)

Kissing Sin (Jan 2007)

Tempting Evil (Feb 2007)

Dangerous Games (March 2007)

Embraced by Darkness (July 2007)

The Darkest Kiss (April 2008)

Deadly Desire (March 2009)

Bound to Shadows (Oct 2009)

Moon Sworn (May 2010)

<u>**Myth and Magic series**</u>

Destiny Kills (Oct 2008)

Mercy Burns (March 2011)

Nikki & Micheal series

Dancing with the Devil (March 2001 / Aug 2013)

Hearts in Darkness Dec (2001/ Sept 2013)

Chasing the Shadows Nov (2002/Oct 2013)

Kiss the Night Goodbye (March 2004/Nov 2013)

Damask Circle series

Circle of Fire (Aug 2010 / Feb 2014)

Circle of Death (July 2002/March 2014)

Circle of Desire (July 2003/April 2014)

Ripple Creek series

Beneath a Rising Moon (June 2003/July 2012)

Beneath a Darkening Moon (Dec 2004/Oct 2012)

Spook Squad series

Memory Zero (June 2004/26 Aug 2014)

Generation 18 (Sept 2004/30 Sept 2014)

Penumbra (Nov 2005/29 Oct 2014)

Stand Alone Novels

Who Needs Enemies (E-book only, Sept 1 2013)

Novella

Lifemate Connections (March 2007)

Anthology Short Stories

The Mammoth Book of Vampire Romance (2008)

Wolfbane and Mistletoe--2008

Hotter than Hell--2008